ERIN LISBETH

The Dating Debacle

Copyright © 2024 by Erin Lisbeth

All rights reserved. No part of this publication may be reproduced, stored or transmitted in any form or by any means, electronic, mechanical, photocopying, recording, scanning, or otherwise without written permission from the publisher. It is illegal to copy this book, post it to a website, or distribute it by any other means without permission.

This novel is entirely a work of fiction. The names, characters and incidents portrayed in it are the work of the author's imagination. Any resemblance to actual persons, living or dead, events or localities is entirely coincidental.

Erin Lisbeth has no responsibility for the persistence or accuracy of URLs for external or third-party Internet Websites referred to in this publication and does not guarantee that any content on such Websites is, or will remain, accurate or appropriate.

Designations used by companies to distinguish their products are often claimed as trademarks. All brand names and product names used in this book and on its cover are trade names, service marks, trademarks and registered trademarks of their respective owners. The publishers and the book are not associated with any product or vendor mentioned in this book. None of the companies referenced within the book have endorsed the book.

First edition

This book was professionally typeset on Reedsy. Find out more at reedsy.com

*Never give up on dreams
and happily ever afters*

CHAPTER ONE

I look to my right as I hear Jake sigh over the sound of a hockey stick hitting a puck. He's wiping a layer of sweat off his brow with the sleeve of his blue jersey. The sight of the darkened material turns my stomach. I don't know when it started, but all those traits of his that I used to think were adorable now make me cringe. Those kissy noises he used to make from across the room, as he called me, or the red ball cap he used to wear, which smelled like feet. Why does it even smell like feet?

I take a sip of my drink and turn back to the game. The scoreboard reads 2-1. Last month, I bought Jake these tickets for his birthday. Hockey is more his thing, but I don't mind going to a game or two. I look around, hearing people shout out the names of their favorite players. Crossing my arms, I tug my sweater tighter around me to block out the cool air from the ice below.

Two players body check the guy with the puck into the boards, and I hear Jake sigh again, raising his arm and checking his watch. I ignore him and turn back to the game.

Jake and I have been together for two years. We met at a little diner one night after a few too many drinks and a lot of karaoke. My friends and I had been out celebrating a friend's birthday.

Lucy, Briar, and I have been friends since college. Lucy and I had shared a tiny dorm room that barely fit more than our two single beds and a desk each. You can say we had no choice but to be up in each other's business.

I studied English literature while Lucy focused on communications and media. We met our friend, Briar, during our second year when we teamed up one night at the on-campus pub, where a heated game of trivia was taking place. The theme of the night was TV sitcoms and movies. You can say we had it in the bag, and after that, the three of us became inseparable.

After our night of karaoke, we walked out into the brisk, frigid air and followed the crowd of people on the street, all in desperate need of some greasy food. We saw a diner across the street with its glowing sign advertising that it was open 24 hours, and we knew they had a reputation for making amazing pulled pork poutine. We made our way through the crowded diner until we found a large booth occupied by two guys with room to spare.

The moment our eyes met, I felt a spark with Jake. He had crystal blue eyes and thick blond hair. The kind you want to run your hands through. Lucy slid right into the booth and motioned for the guys to move over and make room for us. We ordered lots of food and water and laughed until the sun rose.

When we left the diner that morning, Jake and I exchanged

CHAPTER ONE

numbers, and by that afternoon, I had a text from Jake asking me out on a date. It didn't take long before I was spending all my time at his apartment.

He lived in a much larger place than mine, and although he had two roommates who were a bit on the messy side, I was head over heels for Jake. I wanted to be around him as much as possible. He was an obvious sports fan, who not only loved to watch hockey but also played a few times a week. I was in awe of his amicable but loud personality and the confidence he exuded, something I sometimes lacked.

As time went on, that loud personality became obnoxious, and the confidence seemed a bit more egotistical than I was comfortable being around. Things just changed. The rose-colored glasses were off, and I was having second thoughts. We had gone from spending most of our weeknights together to once or twice a week in the last few months.

Jake glances at me as I sip my drink a little too loudly, trying to get the last few drops of it through the paper straw that is now starting to deteriorate. I place my cup under the empty seat next to me.

The crowd is cheering as the scoreboard changes to 3-1. The noise level is rising, and people are getting up from their seats and singing along to the music. I can feel the bass vibrate through the bottoms of my feet. Jake, who usually loves this sort of thing, is still sitting, looking nervous. I turn to him, crossing my arms to stay warm, wishing now that I had not left my oversized puffer coat in the car, but it would hardly fit in the chair with me.

"What's going on? Are you not feeling well tonight?" I ask, seeing sweat appear on his forehead once again.

He wipes it with the back of his hand, turning to me with a

The Dating Debacle

nervous grin. How is he sweating, and I am here shivering? My toes feel like ice cubes as I look down towards my feet, wiggling them in my gray faux-suede ankle boots.

"I'm good, Sof. I kind of wanted to talk to you."

I lean into him, not sure if I heard him right. The crowd is clapping and singing to the music, drowning out the sounds of the skates gliding across the ice.

Jake turns in his seat to face me directly. As though he is trying to find his keys, he places his hands inside his pockets. Jake's gotten a little OCD about his keys since last winter when we got locked out of his car after a movie one night. It had been -15, and we had to wait outside for a cab to come and help us break into his car. The keys had fallen on his seat. It had kind of turned into a romantic night. Jake embraced me under the light post, shielding me from the cold. Snow was falling from the sky, and I nestled into his neck, breathing in his musky scent. Those moments were few and far between now. Maybe Jake was starting to feel the distance between us as I have. I know I should have spoken to him about this sooner. Life just kind of got busy, and we were familiar.

I spend most of my days at this cute shop where I work. Plants, Pottery & Books is sort of like my second home. I work in the back, in the tiny used bookstore. We have a lot of regular customers who I have grown to love, and of course, there's Ben.

Ben's uncle owns the shop. His uncle took him in when his parents passed away, so the shop is sort of his second home too, I guess. I like to call him my work BFF, but he usually just grins and ignores that statement. Work is always more fun with a friend.

I've been working at Plants, Pottery & Books for just over

CHAPTER ONE

two years. I found the job in the last few months before graduation, when I was running out of my student loan and needed some extra money. Working at the shop allows me time to freelance. I guess I sort of put work and my friends ahead of Jake these days. We just have little in common anymore, and I can't see him being the one.

I guess this is it. We're probably breaking up. The thought isn't making me feel overly sad. I feel myself frowning while I think about this. Shouldn't I feel sad? I guess that is probably a good sign that this is the right thing to do.

"What's going on?" I raise my voice so he can hear me, leaning in closer. I can smell the face cream I bought him. It took me forever to get him to use a cleanser instead of washing his face with shower gel.

"Score!" someone yells behind us. I turn to see a group of guys with their arms raised above their heads, laughing and cheering.

"This isn't the best place or time to talk, Jake. Maybe we can talk after the game?" I ask, turning back to him.

Jake looks at me, shaking his head. "I can't wait any longer. I need to do this." He plays with the zipper on his coat, moving it up and down on its track, my eyes following the movement.

I get the whole pulling off the Band-Aid, but this is hardly the place to do it, I think to myself, wiggling my toes more, trying to build some heat in my boots.

"Why don't we take off early, then? I can barely hear you," I say loudly, pushing my hair aside as I lean towards him once again.

People are getting up from their seats as the intermission begins. I turn my legs to the right of me to let a few people pass by. Someone steps on my frozen toes as they squeeze

The Dating Debacle

past me. I squint, feeling it radiate up my foot. Ugh, I could use a warm bath right now, with a good book and a glass of wine.

Jake shakes his head again, grabbing one of my hands with his. I look him in the eyes and notice the look of happiness that has settled across his face.

Well, that's weird. I mean, yeah, it's for the best, but could he pretend to be sad just a bit?

We were together for two years. It's not like a casual dating situation. I have a whole drawer at his apartment, as well as many pairs of shoes and some of my best face creams. I'll have to go back to his place. I can't live without my eye cream and lip gloss. Plus, Jake has a few things at my place too. He could probably live without his sweats and a hoodie or two, but it makes little sense to keep his stuff, either.

Okay, maybe I shouldn't judge him for feeling some type of relief since I am now more worried about my abandoned beauty products than the breakup itself.

Jake is gazing at me. I am suddenly thinking about the cute little clutch I left there last week.

Oh. My. God, Sofia. Pay attention. This dude is about to break up with you, and all you can think about is your inventory at his place.

I try to focus on Jake, bringing my awareness back to him and placing my hand on top of his. If being dragged to yoga once a week by Briar has taught me anything, it is to be present. I'm a work in progress. Rome wasn't built in a day. I look up at Jake again as he lets go of my hand. I see him take something out of his pocket, and the next thing you know, he's on the ground.

"Geez, Jake, get up from there. Do you know how gross these

CHAPTER ONE

floors are?" I say, utterly disgusted. "What are you doing?" I feel my eyes roll before I can stop myself.

Jake looks like he has no intention of getting up. I see him get into a comfortable position that looks vaguely familiar.

Oh, hell no! What in the actual fuck is happening?

Jake grabs my hands once again and smiles shyly. I am going to throw up. Yes, I am going to throw up right here, right now, for everyone to see. With my luck, the Kiss Cam will come on, and everyone will see it. I will be known as that girl who threw up on her boyfriend as he proposed.

I try to pull back from his grasp, and I pull so hard that my hand whacks me in the forehead as it lets go of his grip. I rub the slightly sore spot above my right eye.

Perfect, this is going simply great. I look around to see if anyone has noticed Jake down on his knee. A few people are looking this way. I feel my cheeks flush.

I am so embarrassed. We have never, not once, spoken about getting married. We aren't even living together. There are steps you must take. Everyone knows it! First, you date, then you're a couple, then you move in with each other, then you get married. Plus, I thought he was about to break up with me! I stare at him in disbelief.

"Sofia, you mean so much to me," Jake starts.

Oh, God, he is going there. I feel so bad. I force myself to turn away, looking down at the floor.

"Sofia, please look at me."

I turn back to face Jake, feeling a lump in my throat, not quite sure if that is the vomit that is about to come up or if I am going to burst into tears. Either one would not be ideal right now. I'm a crier. Stressed, embarrassed, sad, or even hangry, yup, I cry. I would say that I'm quite stressed right now. I can feel my underarms sweating profusely, and I no longer notice my frozen toes as heat creeps up my body.

"Do you remember the night we met?" Jake is still staring, now waiting for a reply.

"Uh, yes, Jake, I do…" I start to reply, but Jake cuts me off mid-sentence.

"I felt an instant connection the moment our eyes met. You have become not only my best friend but my soul mate," Jake continues.

A small laugh escapes me. My hand flies up to my mouth to cover it as if I can take back the laugh or stop the words that are about to spill out.

"Jake, come on. You know I don't believe…"

"Yes, yes, Sofia, I know you don't believe in soul mates, and that's okay. I do. I know we are perfect for each other, and I want to spend the rest of my life showing you that we are." Jake lets go of the one hand that didn't manage to escape his grasp earlier.

Oh, here it comes. I swallow hard as the lump moves its way up my throat. I cringe at the sour taste in my mouth.

He looks down at the silver box in his hand. I hear a gasp and turn to see where it came from. I notice there are now quite a few people watching us and pointing. They don't appear to be turning away anytime soon.

Who proposes at a hockey game during intermission, anyway? I'm not even a hockey person! People are standing and squeezing by, making their way through the rows, coming back from the washroom, or filling up their nachos or drinks. The music is blaring. This is hardly a romantic setting in front of all these strangers.

"Jake, listen," I start to say. "Let's get out of here and go talk,"

CHAPTER ONE

I plead with a look in my eyes, willing him to catch that I'm not exactly feeling his vibe—this vibe.

Jake doesn't appear to notice. If we were soul mates, wouldn't he catch on?

Opening the box, I see a small princess-cut diamond sitting high on a simple gold band. It is pretty. *Wow, look at that thing sparkle.*

No, stop it, Sofia! Don't let the bling blind you! I blink a few times and gather myself.

He raises his voice slightly to be heard over the music. "Sofia..." Jake is taking the ring out of the box.

"Jake, I'm serious. Please stop," I say as my voice starts to quiver.

I grab the front of my sweater and start to pull it away from my skin as I suddenly feel hot and clammy. Jake doesn't appear to be taking in any of what I am putting out. He is pulling the ring out of the box and holding it up to my ring finger.

Jake has a huge smile on his face. "Sofia, will you marry me?"

How can he be so oblivious?

Do I look happy right now?

Do I look like someone excited about what is happening?

Jake starts to slip the ring on my finger before I can even open my mouth to reply. I hear clapping coming from behind me and someone shouting, "She said yes!"

"No." The word comes out harsher than I intended. Jake looks up at me as he finishes sliding the ring onto my finger. "I don't want to get married, Jake," I say a little softer. Jake's eyes meet mine. I see a flash of pain cross over his face. "I'm sorry, Jake." I start to pull off the ring.

A man is standing right behind Jake, carrying more than he

The Dating Debacle

seems capable of holding.

"Excuse me," he says.

Jake turns around, still with one knee on the ground. I see one of the two drinks the man is balancing with what appears to be three slices of pizza start to waver.

The man's eyes widen.

Before anyone can react, the drink falls from his grasp, landing on the floor right beside Jake and splashing him down his left side. Jake jumps up quickly from the shock of it.

He looks towards me, and I see anger setting in.

"I'm sorry, man, my bad." The man shrugs. "But you're not exactly in your seat now, are you?"

Jake slumps next to me to let the man pass, turning his legs away from me. He closes the ring box and puts it back into his pocket. The man walks past. I look down at the ring in my hand. He gets up and makes his way towards the aisle.

"Jake!" I yell after him, grabbing my purse that I had stuffed under my seat.

The bottom of the bag is damp from the drink that was just spilled. I get up and follow him out. He pushes his way through the people coming back from intermission.

"Jake!" I yell at him again, not knowing if he even heard me the first time.

He keeps walking. I break into a little jog, coming up behind him as he makes his way onto the escalator going down. I step on and start walking down the moving steps, ignoring the uncomfortable feeling of walking on a moving escalator.

"Sof, just stop," I hear him mutter.

"Look, Jake, I love you, but I just don't think we're working anymore, you know?" I say as I steady myself on the step beside him, grabbing onto the railing.

CHAPTER ONE

"No, Sofia, I don't know. I just asked you to be my wife. I thought we were working." Jake stares straight in front of him. I see his jaw clenched, his face hardened. We reach the ground floor and step off at the same time.

I grab his hand. "Jake, wait." He stops, not turning to face me. Making my way in front of him, I place the ring in the hand I'm holding. "I'm sorry, Jake. I thought you were going to break up with me tonight, and I started thinking that maybe that was a good idea." He winces, so I soften my voice. I feel my shoulders relax a little. "I just think we've grown apart. Can you really say you're happy?"

Jake looks down at the ring he's now holding, then back up to me. "Yeah, Sof, I was." He's walking again towards the exit. "Don't follow me."

I stop as the door closes behind him. My heart sinks as I wipe the tears that have started to fall with my sleeve. This was not how I thought today was going to go, although it's probably for the best. Jake and I were not meant for each other. It'll be okay. Jake will be okay when he realizes he is better off. We're both better off.

I pull out my phone from my bag and request an Uber.

I push open the door and step into the frosty night air, once again wishing I had on a coat. The parking lot isn't very busy since the game is still going on. I put my phone back into my bag and waited for my ride to show up.

CHAPTER TWO

I squint as I see the sun coming through the sides of my blinds.

I'm guessing it's only about 7:00 a.m. based on the amount of sun trying to shine through my blinds. I pull the duvet over my head and squeeze my eyes closed.

I can hear Bob throwing his food on the floor in the kitchen next to my room. He's a rescue that I adopted last year, and he still won't eat out of his cat bowl despite getting him the cutest little dishes with his name imprinted on them. I know he can't read, but still.

I hear more food being tossed on the floor.

I feel irritable.

I turn over in my bed, my legs getting tangled in the sheets, irritating me. Maybe I'm PMSing, or maybe there's a full moon coming.

I called Briar and Lucy after I got in last night after the game. We spent three hours on video chat dissecting the proposal and the last two years of my life while taking shots of Fireball.

CHAPTER TWO

I rub my forehead, regretting the latter. I don't even know how that bottle got into my apartment.

I hear a loud grumble come from my stomach as hunger sets in. Bob jumps onto my bed and starts walking across my stomach, not a care in the world for my organs. My stomach growls again. I lift the covers off my face and sit up.

"Bob, can you not?" I ask.

He jumps down.

I know I should feel sad or like there should be a hole in my heart where Jake used to be, but I just don't. I don't know why, but it's just not there.

I mean, I cared for Jake, and I still do, but I don't think I was in love with him. Yeah, I guess I'm officially one of those. I love you, but I'm not in love with you. How did this even happen?

I swing my legs over the side of the bed, my feet dangling. I'm 5'2", and it's not uncommon for me to not reach the floor sitting on most chairs. Just last week, I had to buy the more expensive orange juice at the grocery store because I couldn't reach up and grab the no-name brand. Usually, I would just climb up onto the bottom of the fridge to reach up, but there were too many people in the aisle for me to do that without embarrassing myself. And, of course, being Miss Independent, I'd rather spend the extra money than ask for help. Short-girl problems, I sigh. Ugh, I hate it when people sigh. Clearly, I'm PMSing.

I stand and walk to the window, pulling open the blind. I may live in a small one-bedroom, but I've got a great view of the river. The snow has melted, and you can tell spring is on its way, but it looks cold out. I feel a shiver run through me.

My phone buzzes, and I turn around to reach for it. Lucy

The Dating Debacle

and Briar's pictures pop up on my screen. We're supposed to make vision boards today, Briar's idea, *obviously*.

I've been collecting magazines since I was a pre-teen during the days of mail-order subscriptions. I flinch at the thought of cutting up the pictures and words in the magazines. Briar would insist that it's recycling.

I turn from the window and peer around at the clothes lying on the floor. I can see some magazines that have slid from their pile under my bed, slowly making their way out and into sight. Lucy's right; I am a bit of a hoarder. I look down at my phone in my hand as it buzzes again. I see the notification indicating my daily horoscope is in my email. My phone buzzes as I set it on the nightstand and plug it in, noticing the battery is at fourteen percent.

I get on my hands and knees and look under my bed to where I stash pretty much anything that is on my floor for longer than a week.

I start pulling shoes out, and some clothes. Last year's vision board comes into sight on a bright yellow bristle board. I pull it out and sit back on my heels, lifting the board to my face. Well, oh shit. There it is: a picture of a bride and a groom. I don't remember gluing that on there. I close my eyes, rubbing them with the tips of my fingers. What is wrong with me? Did I seriously manifest the proposal?

No, I couldn't have.

I thought you had to display your vision board where you would see it every day for the stuff to come true. I look at what else is on there and see palm trees and a vacation I never went on. I see a girl lifting weights—nope haven't done that either. Geesh, I'm not really sure why I make these when I have no intention of eyeing them every morning, wishing and

CHAPTER TWO

hoping.

This one will be different.

Will it, though?

Clearly, I don't have much faith in myself.

I fold it in half, then fold it again and again until it is small enough to fit in my kitchen garbage, and set it aside.

I peer back under my bed and see the stacks of magazines that have been sliding out. I reach and pull them out, standing and placing them on my bed. Bob jumps back onto the bed and steps onto the pile, circling, obviously about to make the pile his new throne.

I undress and toss my pajamas onto my bed beside the stack of magazines where Bob is now cleaning between his toes. I hate when he does that, especially on my bed. I make my way into the bathroom and turn on the shower, letting the hot water run down over me.

* * *

The intercom crackles loudly, and I walk over to the wall and buzz the girls in. I don't have to ask who it is. I can hear them laughing from in here. The walls are paper thin, and I can hear Lucy's cackle from miles away.

I smile to myself. I am so lucky to have such great friends. I open my door as they make their way up the two flights of stairs. I see Lucy with a large brown paper bag in her hands, and I know from the smell that Chinese is what we will be having for supper. My mouth waters at the thought of some Kung Pao chicken and egg rolls. Briar, a few steps behind Lucy, is slowly making her way up. I noticed that she pulled her long chestnut brown curls back and piled them high on her head in a bun, making her look like a ballerina.

Briar glances up and sees me. "Hey, Sof!"

A wide smile spreads across her face. Lucy looks up from the stairs as she reaches the last step. She has on hot pink lipstick, and I see that her nails are painted matte black. Her jeans are ripped in an artful way, and I know they are one-of-a-kind because she made them herself. Lucy always expresses herself in her clothes, jewelry, and hair. She may dress loudly, but she has one of the softest hearts.

"Hey," I say as I open the door a bit wider to let them in.

I step back and take the food from Lucy's arms, noticing the aroma quickly filling the space, and I head towards the kitchen, making room for them to take off their boots and coats.

I walk back and see Briar fixing a strand of hair that has come loose from her bun. She is all elegance and poise. Briar is a teacher at an elementary school. If anyone can handle a room full of loud kids, it's her. I don't think I have ever heard her raise her voice or get irritable in all the years I have known her. Maybe all this meditating and vision board stuff actually works for her, and I mentally urge myself to take this more seriously. I run my hand through my thick, short hair, which falls just above my shoulders, my fingers getting caught in a knot. I'm kind of in between the two, not quite as calm and collected as Briar, obviously, seeing that I get irritated at the bed sheets getting tangled around my ankles, but not quite as loud or outgoing as Lucy.

* * *

"I ate too much!" Groaning, I lean further back on the couch,

CHAPTER TWO

trying to stretch my stomach out to make room for the food I just consumed.

I prop my feet up on the coffee table and knock a glue stick onto the floor. Bob is there sniffing it almost instantly. Briar is lying on her stomach, hugging one of the couch pillows under her.

"I can't believe we ate it all." She closes her eyes and rests her chin down on top of the burnt orange fuzzy pillow.

Lucy is on the chair next to the couch with her feet also up on the table, turning to me with a satisfied smile. "You guys are amateurs."

She cracks her fortune cookie open and pulls out a thin white piece of paper, opening it to reveal her future.

"If you eat something and nobody sees you eat it, then it has no calories." Lucy squints at the small piece of paper. "Geesh, what kind of fortune is that?"

Briar lets out a muffled laugh, her face now smothered in the orange pillow.

"Read mine!" Briar says in words that are barely recognizable.

"No one can crack open your cookie for you, or your fortune won't come true," I say, rubbing my belly, trying to aid in the digestion of one too many chicken balls.

Briar props herself up onto her elbows and reaches toward one of the cookies on the table. She splits it open and pulls out the fortune. She rolls over onto her back, laughing hysterically. Lucy throws a pillow at her, and we both join in, laughing. We're not quite sure what is so funny, but Briar's laughter is contagious.

Briar sits up as she opens the fortune again. "I cannot help you, for I am just a cookie," she reads, her voice shaking as she

The Dating Debacle

starts laughing again. "I got ripped off!" she says, still laughing. "But that's okay. I make my own fortune."

She turns to the bright pink bristle board beside her, which is now jammed with photos and words written in colorful markers. She goes all out on her vision boards. The queen of manifestation.

"Pass me a cookie," I whine, making no effort to move from the reclined post-food binge position I have managed to slide into.

Briar tosses me the last cookie. I open the cookie with less grace than both of them as the cookie starts to crumble, spilling crumbs all over my boobs and belly. I pick up a few and pop them in my mouth.

"You miss one hundred percent of the shots you never take." I lay my head back. "Is this cookie trying to refer to the proposal I was so quick to decline last night?" I ask both of them but look directly towards Lucy, to my right.

"Sof! Come on, don't do that to yourself. I know you feel bad, but he wasn't right for you," Lucy says, leaning down to pick up her own vision board, running her hand over the magazine pictures, and playing with the edges that have already begun to lift.

I pick up a few more crumbs and pop them in my mouth with the rest of the cookie. My stomach groans, obviously thinking it's a bad idea for me to stuff more food inside my mouth when I am already at maximum capacity.

Briar gets up and walks over to the couch. "There are so many opportunities out there for you, you'll see." She winks at me in her comforting, schoolteacher way.

"I know of one opportunity that is right in front of your face." Lucy's eyebrows raise as she sits back, turning her attention

CHAPTER TWO

to me.

"And what opportunity is that?" I ask. "I'm already writing and gaining experience. I know I have yet to start my novel, but I just have so many ideas, and I need to figure them out in my head before I get started. I want it to be about love, like the real love stuff," I add, thinking of the dream I keep shoving to the back of my mind, too scared to put any effort in, worrying I will fail.

"I'm talking about Ben. That man is so into you," Lucy says, and my eyes widen as I sit up.

"What are you talking about?" I ask frowning, confused.

She smiles. "You know that guy is head over heels for you."

"Ben is just a friend, a work friend. He's a great guy, yeah, but just a friend," I say, now thinking about Ben.

He has an undergraduate degree in botany and plant science and moved back to help his uncle out at Plants, Pottery & Books. It's kind of cute he's always talking to his plants. In fact, he has even named a few.

Ben makes a point of coming to the bookstore during his lunch. I think he just likes the comfortable chairs we have that fill the small space. No one actually sits in them, other than him and me, but they give the bookstore a cozy vibe. Plus, our lunchroom is kind of small. There are no windows, and lately, it seems to always smell like hard-boiled eggs.

Ben's uncle Jeffrey is my boss. He's always following new fads and researching healthy lifestyles. He's currently on the three-day boiled egg diet, considering we are going on about two weeks of eau-de-egg in the staff room, he is clearly enjoying this one.

Anyway, Ben is a great sounding board for my ideas. Whenever I'm working on something, he's always so supportive and the first to read it. Even all my blogs on lawn care lately. Who would have thought I'd be writing about lawnmowers? I mean, I'd rather be writing about anything else, but hey, it pays well. He gets me. He doesn't push or ask why I haven't started my novel, and I appreciate that.

Yes, definitely just a friend.

"I am in no rush to jump into anything, anyway," I say. "I want to write more. I've thought about reaching out to some of the magazine editors that I have worked with."

I play with a thread that has come loose from the bottom of my sweater, twirling it around my finger till it looks like it will cut off my circulation, then I let it go and repeat.

"I'm just saying, he likes you, Sof, and you're single now," Lucy continues.

"He is kind of cute, too," Briar chimes in.

I roll my eyes. "I haven't even been single twenty-four hours, guys. Give it a break."

Lucy stands, picking up some of our takeout containers. "Just remember what the great fortune cookie said to you tonight. You miss one hundred percent of the shots you never take." She turns and makes her way toward the kitchen.

I pick up my vision board and press down on the magazine cutout that reads "write" with a pile of colorful books next to it.

I will, I think to myself, I will.

CHAPTER THREE

I see a man urinating on the side of a large garbage bin.

It's Monday morning, and I'm pulling into one of the empty parking spots facing the back entrance of Plants, Pottery & Books. The staff has to park in the back alleyway. It's kind of sketchy back here, especially at night.

Last summer, Ben and I twirled a bunch of fairy lights around the railings and columns of the back deck, sprucing it up a bit. It actually looks kind of magical at night until you catch some strange man peeing on the side of a random dumpster.

Monday mornings are usually busy in the plant shop. Ben likes to hold mini-events, and on Mondays this month, they're focusing on growing your own vegetables.

I take my keys out of the ignition and open the car door. I pretend I don't see the man and walk up the steps. As I make my way into the back of the building, I hear a group of women laughing. They spend most of the time flirting with Ben, who seems oblivious to the mischievous grins and winks

The Dating Debacle

they throw his way. He has his regulars who attend every week. The retired crew, they like to call themselves.

I walk into the bookstore. It's the smallest room in the building, but I'd say the coziest. I make my way behind the counter and pull out my laptop from the soft bag I got for Christmas that reads "Bookworm." This was a gift from Lucy. I mean, she's not wrong. I spend most of my free time caught up in a novel. It is one of the best parts about working here. I get the freedom to write, read, and chat with customers or friends who enjoy the same pastime as I do: reading about love. I mean, who doesn't love to be swept away into a world full of love and grand gestures?

I shove my purse and bag under the counter and set myself up on the high stool. Another roar of laughter echoes through the small building. I don't even think Ben is all that funny, well, not in a comedic way. I mean, he is kind of cute-funny. He doesn't try to win people over. He's not fake, or arrogant. He's just himself.

The calendar pops up on my screen. We have a book signing later this week with a local author. I log on to our social media page and create a sponsored ad with the author's name, book title, and the details for Thursday's event.

The next hour is spent checking emails and responding to comments and posts. Two customers come in and make purchases, and now I'm just about to refresh the main display table. I load my arms with more books than I can carry, the hardcover edges digging into my arms. Before I can turn to set them down, I'm stopped by something blocking my way. I can't see over the tower of books in my arms.

"Oh, my God!" I blurt out as the books begin to fall out of my arms, and my face comes into contact with something

CHAPTER THREE

hard.

I step back, look up, and realize that I just collided with Ben's chest. Damn, he must be ripped under that soft blue sweater. I shake my head and look down at the books all sprawled on the floor.

I look back up at Ben. "I am so sorry. I didn't hear you come in behind me." I fumble, still a little shaken by the surprise contact between my face and his chest.

"No worries," Ben says. "Let me help you."

He starts to bend down just as I lean forward to pick up last week's collection from the display table. Pain shoots through the front of my forehead. My hand flings in response to where the pain is radiating, just above my eyebrows.

"Oh, shit," Ben interjects as I realize we just collided once again, this time with our foreheads.

I straighten and start to laugh, rubbing the sore spot. Ben is doing the same, a smirk appearing across his face.

I stop laughing just long enough to say I'm sorry. Ben is laughing now, his voice deep.

"Are you okay?" I ask.

"You've got a hard head," he says, snickering.

"Lots of info up in here," I say as I tap the side of my temple with my index finger. "Stay right where you are. I'm going in," I remark before once again bending down to pick up the mess I've made.

As someone who is mostly impatient, I should have known better. I have a bad habit of trying to do everything all at once. I can't count how many times I've dropped my groceries or hurt myself trying to hike up the two flights of stairs to my apartment after hanging every single bag on both arms. I refuse to do two trips.

The Dating Debacle

I place the books onto the counter, and Ben bends down when I'm safely out of reach and gets the rest.

I smile at him. "Thanks," I say.

"No problem." He hands me the rest of the books. "How was the hockey game the other night?" he asks.

Oh, crap. I forgot I told him Jake and I were going to one.

"Well, the game was good, but we left early. We sort of broke up," I say, looking down, avoiding his eyes, feeling awkward.

It feels like forever ago already. I texted Jake once to see if he was okay, and I never got a reply. I'll give him some space before asking for my stuff back.

"You broke up?" Ben asks, looking confused. The lines on his forehead crinkle as he raises his eyebrows quizzically.

"Jake proposed to me at the game," I say, licking my lips, my mouth feeling suddenly dry. I grab my water bottle from under the cash drawer, taking a long sip.

"Wait, what? He proposed to you?" Ben asks, his back straightening. I put the cap back on the water bottle. "You said no?" he asks before I've had time to answer his first two questions.

"I said no. I don't know. He was acting so strange, and I legit thought he was going to break up with me. Next thing you know, he's on his knee with a ring in his hand," I say, replaying the scene in my head.

"Wow, that's quite the turnaround. You were with him awhile." Ben blinks a few times and starts playing with the leaf of one of the plants sitting on the counter between us. "He was kind of a *moutard*, though, to be honest," Ben says, smiling at me.

I laugh at our inside joke.

About a month ago, we were making sandwiches in the staff

CHAPTER THREE

room, and we couldn't find any mayo, so we used an old bottle of mustard that we found in the fridge. I don't know if it was just the long week, but Ben started talking in a French accent while building his ham and cheese, and he kept going on about the *moutard.* The next day, I had a pretty rude customer, and as he walked by Ben to leave the shop, he muttered, 'What a *moutard'* (said like moo-tard). It kind of just stuck and has been our inside insult since.

"He was not a *moutard*," I say, smiling back at Ben. I hop up onto my stool, digging my thick heels into the footrest to adjust my position.

I prop my elbows on top of the counter and rest my chin in my hands. Ben leans onto the counter, towering over me slightly. I may have short-girl problems, but Ben has his fair share of tall-boy troubles. He refuses to let me drive him home in my small hatchback. His legs bend right up into his chest. The one time I picked him up when his car wouldn't start, I laughed for hours after remembering the sight of him squeezed into the seat.

Ben winks at me. "He was definitely a *moutard.*"

What was that? Did Ben just wink at me? Never in this lifetime has Ben winked at me. My stomach flinches.

I hop off the stool and come around the counter. "Okay, Ben, I've got work to do." I walk towards the display table, picking up the last few books that are still standing.

"Sure, I'll talk to you after, Sof." Ben pulls awkwardly at the bottom of his slightly frayed Thor t-shirt as he turns and walks back towards the plant shop.

* * *

The Dating Debacle

I pull out my lunchbox, and I'm just biting into a bold BBQ Dorito when Ben walks in.

"Can you chew any louder?" he teases, sitting down across from me.

"Hey!" is all I can say since my mouth is still full.

Ben looks over my shoulder. "Your display turned out great."

"Thanks," I say as I bite into another chip. I take out my cut-up apples and almond butter. I have to counteract the Doritos for lunch. I lean back in my chair and let myself relax against the soft white backrest. When I first started working here, the bookstore looked kind of tired and dusty. The major business, where most of the income comes from, was the plant shop. When Jeffrey offered me the job, I suggested that the place needed a makeover.

He gave me a budget, and I had so much fun revamping the place. I went with a Boho vibe to fit in with the plant shop. We have plants everywhere. Some are hanging from the ceiling in earth-tone macrame plant holders, while the others have been placed strategically throughout the small store.

I only have two small windows in here with limited natural light, so Ben keeps an eye out on the plants for me. I definitely don't have a green thumb. The bookcases that line the four walls were all made of oak, so it was easy to bring them to life by decorating the rest of the space. I found these cute little unique tables where the legs are a pedestal-like, star-shaped base with a distressed white top with matching chairs. I look around the room. This place feels like a little haven.

"Was it busy this morning?" I ask.

"Yeah, actually," Ben says. "A guy came in from a new shop opening up this week. It's down the street from here. His wife sells clothes and stuff, I guess."

CHAPTER THREE

He puts the lid back on his container and grabs two granola bars from his bag. I notice they're covered in chocolate and suddenly wish I could steal a bite when he's not looking.

"Nice, I'll have to go check it out," I say, making a mental note to take a walk down the street sometime.

With parking in the back alleyway, I haven't really paid any attention to the shops that have come and gone in the last two years. I am so used to the same drive every day that I kind of zone out and then wonder how the hell I made it here alive.

We hear someone come into the store, and I notice Ben's shoulders stiffen. I turn around to see Jake standing there, holding a box with one of my sweaters draped over the side.

"Jake," I say his name, looking at him.

"Hey." He nods towards Ben. "I just thought I would come and bring you the stuff you left at my place," he says, looking back and forth between Ben and me.

I stand and take the box from his hands. "Thanks. I'll bring your stuff by later this week."

I frown, noticing his unshaven face, his weekend joggers, and the sad look in his brown eyes. I suddenly feel awful that I haven't even really thought much about him.

"No need. I used my key and stopped there this morning. I grabbed my stuff already," he says, pulling out the key to my apartment and handing it to me. "I went back home and got this stuff for you and thought I'd just drop it off. It's closer than going back to your place."

"Oh." I'm not sure what to reply. I walk towards the counter and set the box down, grabbing my purse and taking out the key to his apartment. "I guess I should give this back to you, then."

He takes the key, quickly looking away when our fingers

The Dating Debacle

touch. The spark that was once there is now just a memory.

"Alright, well, I'm off." He's already turning to leave.

"Wait!" I inhale abruptly. "I'm sorry for how things turned out, Jake."

I lean on the counter, not sure what to do with my hands. How is it you can spend two years with someone and then, just like that, in a matter of seconds, you suddenly don't know how to behave around them?

"Me too," he says, nodding at Ben again before disappearing through the door.

Ben stands, grabbing his lunch box and crumpling the granola bar wrappers in his right hand before reaching around the counter and dropping them in the garbage beside me.

"Well, that was awkward," I blurt, and I avoid his gaze not wanting to notice any looks of pity.

He places a hand on mine. "You'll be fine, Sofia. Maybe now you will have time to start your novel," Ben offers, a gleam of excitement can be seen behind those green eyes of his.

I look down at his hand on mine.

"Yeah, maybe," I reply.

* * *

The afternoon flies by, and I finish cleaning up after the weekend. Customers tend to pick up books, read the back cover, and then put them back down in random places. It was a lot of work placing them in alphabetical order by author name and genre, and I try to keep it that way.

I also managed to finish my latest blog for "Lawn Maintenance Weekly." I've been writing for them for two months. I had no idea there was so much information one needed to

CHAPTER THREE

consider before buying a weed wacker or a lawn mower. I receive a small stipend for each blog I write. They tell me which product they want me to write about, and I do the research. Easy money, however, it's not at all satisfying.

I close my laptop. Emily will be here shortly to take over for the evening.

I look down at the box my feet are resting on. It really is baffling to think that just last Monday, I had a boyfriend, this job, and great friends. I was just living day to day in my routine, content with just being content.

I rest my chin on my hands and close my eyes. Is that what I want? Do I want to just be content with my life? Jake and I had a pretty passionless relationship. The butterflies had long since flown away.

I think I need to find my purpose again. I need to break my regular habits and start trying new things. Emily walks into the store carrying an iced coffee and a book. I hop off the stool, grab my purse and box of stuff, and move out of the way so she can squeeze behind the counter. I smile at her.

"Have a great night, Emily!" I say.

"Thanks!" she says, already making herself comfy on the stool and setting down the novel she had been holding under her arm.

I smile and wave to Ben before I head out. "See you tomorrow!" I call, not waiting for his reply.

Yes, maybe it's a good time to re-invent myself. I press my back into the door to open it since my hands are full. I hear it shut behind me with a loud bang.

I look up at the clouds in the sky. They're covering the sun. Maybe I will start this whole re-inventing myself tomorrow.

CHAPTER FOUR

I push my glasses back up onto my nose as I glance around the optometrist's waiting room.

I've been wearing contacts for years, and a few days ago, after chipping my middle fingernail, I made a tiny slice while taking out my contacts. Of course, I tried wearing them anyway, but they felt like they were trying to murder my eyeballs, so here I am.

I had been meaning to stop in and order some, but the last five weeks have been a blur of work and takeout. Mostly pizza and donuts, if I'm being honest.

I think I'm in a slump since the breakup.

I've been waiting about five minutes for my eye appointment.

From the moment I walked in, I noticed him. Of course, I would notice the one guy my age in the room. I can spot a dude from across the room. It's like I have tunnel vision lately, but that's not the reason I'm here. I laugh to myself. On the inside, of course, a bad joke. From the moment I walked in,

CHAPTER FOUR

I've caught him glancing my way several times.

I think when you're single, you just know when others are single too. It's a vibe—like I can feel their single energy. It's been a long time since I've dated, and although I have been in the same old routine for the last month, I have definitely been awakened by the sight of men. I'm not boy-crazy or anything. I haven't spoken to any of them, but I feel it. I rub my hands together, warming them up.

Anyway, this guy has been looking at me on and off for the last five minutes. Of course, I wouldn't come out and say anything. I am the worst at flirting, as awkward as they come.

The receptionist stops in front of me with her giant clipboard. "Sofia?"

Man, she looks amazing in those cat eye eyeglasses. I wish I could pull them off. I see the guy glance my way again.

"Yeah, that's me. I have an appointment with Dr. Scott," I say, and then, against my better judgment, take a not-so-casual glance at the cute guy.

He has gorgeous, thick, dark hair. Mm, it has been a long time since I ran my hands through someone's hair. Okay, so maybe this trip to the eye doctor is exactly what I need to get me out of my funk. I feel butterflies, or maybe it's gas from all the cheese I ate at lunch.

"Okay, Dr. Scott will be ready shortly. Can I just confirm your address?" She peers at me through those chic red frames.

"Yup," I reply and push my cute purple glasses back up my nose.

I really hate wearing glasses in the summer. The heat makes them all sweaty on my face, and they slide down my nose. Just another thing to make me irritable. I won't forget to stock up on my contacts again. I should probably get these tightened

The Dating Debacle

while I'm here, too.

After confirming the address, she confirms the phone number, reading it out loud.

"Okay, it won't be long." The receptionist turns and starts back for her desk.

The guy with the dark hair looks my way. "So, when is a good time to call?" he asks, his lips opening up to a wide smile, showing a dimple on his left cheek.

Of course, he has a dimple. His eyes are gleaming. I see his large hands grasping the arms of the rigid plastic chair under him.

An awkward laugh escapes my mouth. I'm caught off guard. Is he really talking to me? He laughs nervously. There really is only one other person in the waiting room, and he must be about eighty, so yeah, Sofia, he is talking to you. This is like in the books I read or the movies I watch where people meet someone at the grocery store or in line for their morning coffee.

Say something, Sofia.

I look at him. He is looking at me, waiting for a response. His smile is slowly fading the longer I take to reply. I can feel my cheeks turning pink. I smile back with a smile I can only assume makes me look as weird as I feel.

Can he hear my heart beating? I can feel it pounding in my chest, anxiety rolling in.

Think of something, come on, anything!

It just has to be words Sof, any word. One word!

Why can't I think of a single thing to say? He starts to look away. I uncross my legs and sit up straighter.

What the hell, Sofia?

I feel like all these little butterflies are fluttering around in

CHAPTER FOUR

my stomach and not the good kind. The kind that also makes you sweat and gives you a dry mouth. To be honest, I don't know how I have managed to date at all before Jake. I am one of those people who says "Thanks!" when someone says "Hi."

Great, now I'm getting nervous gas. My stomach grumbles.

A teenage boy walks into the reception room, and I turn to him. The guy, who could have been the man of my dreams but now I will never know, stands up and walks over to him. Okay, he is obviously his brother. He walks up to the reception counter and says something I can't hear. I can't believe I could not think of a single word to say. Smooth, Sofia, smooth.

For someone whose friends constantly laugh at her for being such a romantic and loving love, I sure have no game. The guy turns and glances at me once more before opening the door and walking out.

Fuck.

It's not like I get asked out every day by a tall, dark, and handsome man with a dimple.

"Sofia Daria?" I look up from playing with a hangnail on my thumb. Dr. Scott waves to me from across the room. Geez, do all the women who work here look like sexy librarians? I'm feeling slightly jealous.

* * *

The next morning, I pulled up to work and see Ben getting out of his car. He stops and waits for me.

"Good morning," I say, handing him a coffee.

I don't drink coffee very often, but sometimes, a morning just calls for it, and I know Ben likes his morning coffee black.

He takes the coffee. "Hey, thanks."

The Dating Debacle

We start up the back stairs and make our way into the building.

"You finally bought some contacts, I see," he says, eyeing me.

"Yeah, thank God. Those glasses were getting on my nerves," I say, turning into the bookstore. He touches his own glasses as if suddenly aware of them.

"I don't know. I think you looked kind of hot in them," he remarks, winking at me and shrugging his shoulders as he makes his way around me.

I freeze, startled by his comment, and say nothing as he continues to walk toward the plant shop. I shake it off. I don't know what's with him lately and his winking. Maybe he's got a new tic, a stress tic.

I feel a little more alive today than I have in weeks. I have my coffee, the new novel I'm reading that I just can't seem to put down, and Briar and Lucy are going to stop in and see me today at the store. As I'm setting my stuff up, I catch a glimpse of myself in the mirror behind the counter.

After my eye appointment yesterday afternoon, I stopped at that new boutique that Ben had told me about. I bought this amazing dress that cost a small fortune, but it's perfect. It fits like a glove from the top to my waist, sort of like a '60s housewife vibe, before flowing into a big skirt. The best part about it is the print. The material feels thick but soft to the touch, and the print is covered in books and cats. Two of my favorite things in this world.

Bob, for sure, is one of my faves. He seemed to like my dress this morning since I caught him trying to make his bed on it when I came out of the shower. That'll teach me to lay out my clothes in the morning.

The morning passes by quickly. I restocked my display

CHAPTER FOUR

table. Beach reads - one of the most popular genres we sell, especially at this time of year, when everyone's tired of the cold and looking forward to spring, summer heat, beaches, and ice cream.

Mm... ice cream.

I'm just taking out my laptop to check my personal email when I see Lucy and Briar come in. Ben follows them and smiles when our eyes meet.

"Hey, lady!" Lucy calls out, making herself at home at one of the tables.

"Hey guys," I greet them with a smile and come around the counter to show off my new dress. Lucy loves fashion, so I twirl.

"Sof, wow, you look amazing in that! Where did you get that dress?" Lucy asks.

I can see Ben looking me up and down. I suddenly feel shy. Why is he looking at me that way? I turn back to Lucy and Briar. Maybe it's all part of his new tic. I should probably tell him about it, in case he's unaware he is doing it. I would want to know if I was randomly winking at people, unaware.

"Thanks, I got it at this new shop down the street. You guys have to check it out!" I exclaim, thinking it probably is my new favorite store.

Briar and Lucy both sit. Ben stays for a bit, catching up with both of them while I place a few more books on the display table and help a few customers who come in.

I'm behind the counter when I see a new email pop up on my screen. It's from Miriam, the editor I worked for at Lace & Dots Magazine, mostly doing freelance stuff. I open it excitedly, wondering if she has something for me. Briar sees me and bounces up to the counter, her curls bouncing with her.

"What are you looking at, Sof?" she asks curiously.

"No porn on work hours." Ben laughs at his own joke.

I roll my eyes at him.

"Don't you have plants to tend to?" I ask, making a face at him.

He leans back in his chair, obviously not in a hurry to get back to the plants. They have enough staff out there, maybe too many, because it gives Ben a lot of free time to come and bother me. If I am being honest, I love it when he does.

I turn to Briar and Lucy, who have now joined us at the counter.

"I got an email from Miriam," I say. "Maybe I can stop writing about lawnmowers."

I click on the email, and a feeling of excitement rushes through me.

"Or you can start your book," Ben declares.

I shush him. We're not going there today. I keep telling everyone that I just don't know where to begin, and although that is partly true, I also don't know if I am ready to put myself out there yet. I want to write a romance novel, but I just haven't felt the type of love I want to write about yet, and I want to feel fully inspired to do so.

I began reading the email. I can feel three sets of eyes on me.

"Read it out loud!" Lucy exclaims.

To: *Sofia Daria*
   From: *Miriam Cassidy*
   Subject: *Dating Article*

CHAPTER FOUR

Sofia, I have some freelance work for you. I recently ran into Jake, who tells me you are no longer together. I was sorry to hear this news, but this works out perfectly for me. I am looking for someone to write a series on dating online. A weekly article detailing the App, the dates, and your respective feelings on both. I am looking to start publishing this in two weeks, so I will need your answer by this weekend.

Talk soon,
  Miriam.

"Well, that's a flat-out no," I say, closing my laptop with a thud and picking at one of the random stickers that have started to peel on the top.

"What do you mean it's a no, Sofia? This is absolutely perfect for you!" Lucy's voice has taken a pitch higher than usual.

"I have never been on an online dating site in my life, and I've heard stories. Mostly from you, Luce." I turn to her, eyebrows raised accusingly. "This isn't for me. I don't want to see any dicpics. Definitely a no-go," I say, tucking my hair behind my ear. It falls right back out. I ignore it.

Briar is quiet, as usual, but she has a smile on her face. She's looking right at me, her eyes are twinkling with mischievousness.

"What, Briar? I know you must be on the same page as me here. There is no way I can meet total strangers online, date them, and then write about them," I say as I imagine the whole awkwardness of what online dating must feel like.

Briar leans in. "Sofia, I think you should do it," she says, catching me off guard.

"What?" I ask, shocked. My body stills.

The Dating Debacle

"You should do it. Look, we have all seen you in a funk the last month. It's time to get back out there. You look amazing today, and I feel a bit of spark vibrating off you. It's time. You need to meet new people. You can't just hang out with Bob every night."

Ben laughs. I turn to him and glare.

"There's nothing wrong with hanging out with Bob," I say. Man, am I actually talking about Bob as if he were a person and not my four-legged organ-squishing feline?

Ben is starting to look uncomfortable.

"What is it?" I ask him.

"I don't think you should do it," he says firmly, crossing his arms.

"See, Ben doesn't think I should do it either," I reply, feeling happy to have someone who has my back on this.

I see Lucy and Briar exchange glances.

"Okay, you need to do it," Lucy says. She pulls out her phone and opens an App and turns it to me. "Look at all these guys, Sof! You just have to swipe right on the ones that interest you and left on the um, not-so-interesting ones."

I peer at her phone.

"Come on, don't push her into doing something she doesn't want to do," Ben advocates for me. "She said no. I think we should respect her feelings." I look towards him. "You don't know who you will meet on there; you have to be careful, and you're not exactly a serial dater. You might be a bit too naive for online dating," he finishes, looking proud of his lecture.

"You don't think I can tell a bad guy from a good one?" I ask him, getting a little annoyed at his lack of trust in me.

He's probably right, although I won't admit that to him. I've never been on a date with someone I met online. I would have

CHAPTER FOUR

no idea what I'm doing, but his lack of faith in me is kind of irritating.

Lucy looks at me. "It's only going to be a month or two. What do you have to lose?"

Briar is smiling and nodding her head.

"I will think about it," I say. "It's Tuesday. I have a few days before I need to respond to Miriam." I turn and smile saying hi to a customer who has just walked in.

"Sleep on it tonight, but I mean it, Sofia. You need to get back out there. Remember that fortune, 'You miss out on one hundred percent of the opportunities you don't take.'"

I tuck my hair behind my ear once again. She's right.

***

I get home around 6:00 p.m., and Bob is waiting for me at the door. He's waiting for his soft food.

"Hi, Bob, look at you, you're so cute."

Bob makes his way to the kitchen, sits in front of the fridge, lifts his right paw, and looks up at me. My God, this cat knows how to pull off *Puss in Boots*. What a cutie. I look over at his food bowls.

"Bob, how many times do I have to tell you to stop throwing your food on the floor?" I exclaim a little too loudly.

The look on his face shows that he couldn't care less what my thoughts were on him throwing his food on the floor. I feed Bob his chicken pate and hold back my gag reflex as I spoon it into a small bowl. I take out the leftover sub from last night and make my way to the living room. I peel out some of the lettuce that's turned soggy, and I prop my feet up on the table. I turn on last night's episode of *The Bachelorette*. I spend the next two hours watching TV. Bob is now cuddled up next to me.

Maybe Lucy and Briar are right. I mean, I know there is absolutely nothing wrong with some self-care or alone time, but maybe there is such a thing as too much alone time.

Bob rolls off my hip as I get up from the couch, clearly annoyed with my sudden movement. I take my vision board out from the hall closet and sit back down with it in my hands. I see all the things I want to do this year. I really do want to travel, take dance lessons, and try new things. I want to go to a football game, write at a coffee shop as they do in the movies for hours sipping coffee, and spend more time outdoors.

I think I have made my decision. I'm going to do it. What's the worst that could happen… I fall in love?

CHAPTER FIVE

It's Friday, and I feel nerves enter my body before I've even opened my eyes.

Bob stirs at my feet as I roll over to shake the blankets off my legs. I'm meeting with Miriam this morning since it's my day off, and I'm working weekends at the bookstore this week. I pick up my phone and see that my daily horoscope for Pisces has been emailed to me.

Today, you will be focused on professional endeavors. The day looks remarkably good for you in all aspects of your life. You may find yourself wanting time alone or daydreaming throughout the day.

My horoscope is usually pretty dead-on. I stretch my arms over my head and point my toes, annoying Bob. He sits up and stares at me. I've clearly woken him before he is ready to get up. He crawls on top of my legs and settles on my stomach. I pick him up to cuddle, and he takes off running out of my room.

Blah, Bob obviously wears the pants in this relationship.

The Dating Debacle

Everything is on his terms.

I swing the rest of the blankets off me, and they fall onto the floor. I make myself an almond milk smoothie with spinach and bananas and toast with cheese whiz. I finish up, feed Bob his soft food, and hop in the shower.

I spend a little extra time on my makeup, getting my eyebrows exactly right with my pomade. If someone had told me five years ago that my eyebrows would be this important to me at some point in time, I would have laughed in their face.

I had a chiro appointment last week, and I felt my face sweating into the paper that lined the face hole, and when I got up, my eyebrows were left behind. Let's just say I wasted no time buying a new waterproof pomade after that.

I wing my eyeliner, plop on some gloss, and grab my bag.

When I arrive to meet Miriam, I park underground and make my way to the fifth floor of Lace & Dots magazine. I look around and notice the modern decor with glass side tables filled with magazines to browse. I choose to sit on the black leather couch facing the reception desk. As I sit, my skirt slides up, and the backs of my thighs instantly prickle at the cold fabric beneath them. I pick up the latest magazine to flip through when I'm offered something to drink.

I'm about to take a sip of my mocha bubble tea when I'm told that Miriam is ready to meet with me. This is crazy. I still can't believe I'm about to do this. I emailed Miriam right away after making my decision, so I couldn't change my mind. This probably won't be the worst thing I'll ever do in my life.

I place my bag over my shoulder and straighten my skirt as I walk towards her office. I smile. It's a nervous smile, but still a smile. Fake it till you make it, right?

CHAPTER FIVE

I find myself actually a little excited about this. To be honest, I think I'm more excited about writing articles. These articles should generate more readers than the grass clippings blogs.

Speaking of... I also made an appointment for a Brazilian wax this afternoon. Lucy says I need a wax and some new undies to spice up my life.

One thing at a time.

Miriam waves me into her office from her desk. I can see she's on a call. Sitting down in the dark gray bucket chair in front of her desk, I glance around. I met Miriam at an event last year that Lucy and Briar dragged Jake and me to, and we hit it off right away. I've done quite a few reviews for Lace & Dots. I've reviewed little shops, cafes, and even a yoga studio. I enjoy writing about new things and going out of my comfort zone because it isn't something I normally would do without a push.

I'm a predictable girl. I stick to the tried and true. Why eat spiral Kraft dinner when the original is already good enough?

"Sofia, I'm so happy you decided to come on board," Miriam says as she puts her phone down.

I look from her to the photograph of her husband and two children facing me from her desk. She smiles widely, showing me her dazzling white teeth, and I notice her lips painted in this incredible red shade. I don't think I've ever seen her without it on, to be honest. I watch her tap her long nails, which are all glam in their stiletto shape with black tips.

"Thank you for thinking of me, Miriam. I'm excited about this opportunity," I say, trying not to fidget and holding my nervous smile.

She smiles at me and starts clicking on her laptop.

"So, have you ever dated online before, Sofia?" Miriam asks,

The Dating Debacle

looking up at me.

"Actually, no, I haven't, Miriam," I say a little shyly, pressing the palms of my hands on my thighs so I don't start pulling at random threads or biting my nails.

"That's fine, it's great, actually. You can write about your quest to find your other half from scratch. Have you downloaded an App yet? It really doesn't matter which one you join." She continues clicking.

"No, I haven't. I plan to create my profile later today with the help of some friends who have a bit more knowledge about the whole online dating thing." I reply. Lucy, a regular App user, is coming over tonight. She says I need some new selfies for my profile.

"Sounds good," Miriam says.

We spend the rest of the meeting going over all the details. Miriam explains her expectations, and we reach a mutual agreement on the deadlines for each article. We talk about date ideas and the number of dates - it is all up to me as long as I keep an open mind and write all the raw nitty-gritty. She wants readers to feel they are living through me and that they can relate to me on some level.

This will be for all of those who have already gone through this, the ones who want to date but don't know where to begin, and the ones who have sworn off dating but still enjoy hearing about love all the same.

Miriam is leaving it up to me whether I tell the guys, but she strongly suggests I don't tell them unless it goes beyond a date or two. I agree. The last thing I want to happen is a whole *How to Lose a Guy in 10 Days* sort of thing. I mean, I doubt that the guys I choose will be working on their own agenda or pushed to do some kind of bet, but hey, you just never know!

CHAPTER FIVE

If it happened to *Andie Anderson*, it could happen to anyone!

* * *

I make my way to the spa on 43rd Street.

I'm greeted by a middle-aged woman dressed in all black with a high bleached-blonde ponytail and equally high heels as I push open the heavy barn-style door. She smiles at me as she says my name. I look around and notice the waiting room is empty. I'm five minutes early. I did not want to start this appointment by pissing off the woman who would play with hot wax and my nether regions.

I notice the calming music playing from the speakers overhead. I feel my underarms sweat and the wetness pooling, mentally thanking myself for choosing a dark sweater today. So much for that $15.00 all-natural deodorant I picked up at the market last week. It clearly wasn't made for the stress of a Brazilian wax appointment.

I remove my boots where she shows me to, and I hang up my coat on the rack next to the door, sliding on a pair of baby-pink slippers. I follow her down a long hallway to the room on the left. She lets me enter in front of her as she moves to the side, gliding effortlessly in those high heels of hers. I look towards what appears to be a massage bed with that noisy white doctor's paper on it. This now feels more like a gyno appointment than being at the spa. Maybe they will have room for a manicure after this. Seeing Miriam's nails got me a bit jelly.

"Now, Sofia, my name is Lexi." She closes the door behind her. "Have you ever had this wax service before?" she asks.

I tell her no and why I'm here. She raises her eyebrows at me

The Dating Debacle

as she hears me tell her that I have never met anyone online before. She goes on to tell me that I should refrain from doing the dirty for 24 hours to let my will-be sensitive skin calm down.

I remove everything from the waist down after she leaves me standing there in a bundle of nerves. I crawl onto the papered bed.

"You all set in there?" I hear Lexi's voice through the door.

"Yup," I reply, my voice crackling slightly.

I'm nervous as hell. I think about aborting this mission, but she is opening up the door before I can hop off the bed and get dressed.

I lay there, staring at the ceiling tiles, noticing the tiny little patterns above me as she moved around the room, pulling a tray towards the bed. I see the wax sitting in the small pot, a soft purple color. Lexi explains that she will be applying the wax, and it will feel rather warm. She then goes on to warn me that I will feel a slight pinch.

I can feel my butt sweating underneath me, causing the paper to stick to my ass. Just awesome, I think sarcastically.

Knowing this won't be the most embarrassing part of this appointment. I see her putting gloves on, snapping them as if she were a surgeon about to prep me for surgery.

The waxing starts off not too badly. I'm lying here, and I'm suddenly wondering why Andy made such a big deal in the movie *The 40-Year-Old Virgin*. It's only been about five minutes when Lexi tells me I need to hold my leg up. I grab at the back of my thigh and pull my leg towards me, realizing I could use a good yoga class.

I was not aware that I needed to stretch prior to being waxed. I'm shockingly not flexible in any sort of way. I haven't been

CHAPTER FIVE

able to touch my toes since middle school. People think it should be easy for me since I am already so close to the ground. Ha-ha, yes, people actually think that's funny, but I've got long legs and a short torso.

"Oh, Kelly Clarkson!"

I secretly scream in my head, quoting Steve Carell who played Andy in the movie, and I suddenly feel bad for ever judging his wax sesh.

I hear ya, karma. Well played, well played.

I try to count the little patterns on the ceiling, which are now blurring.

Lexi tells me I can switch legs and that she's almost done. I can feel the so-called pinch she said I would feel and silently call her a liar. This is a full-on burn. I mentally make a note to stop for some Epsom salts on my way home. I clearly will need a bath after this torture.

Within five minutes, Lexi left me to get dressed. I spend a few minutes at the table rehashing what I'm about to do and meet a bunch of strangers online. Yikes!

I get off the table and spend another few minutes' eyeing this fresh new look in front of the full-length mirror from all angles. Huh, this has me feeling kind of sexy. I'm also wildly aware that perhaps I was being a bit of a dramatic. The pain has now died down, and I'm left with a slight sensitivity. I slip on my skirt and stuff my undies in my bag, not wanting to feel the friction of the material against my fresh, raw skin.

* * *

I spend the rest of my day getting a manicure and doing some shopping. The nail tech had an opening just as I was paying

The Dating Debacle

for my wax. I look down at my newly shaped nails, colored in a soft pink. I'm feeling slightly sensitive, but overall, I'm very happy Lucy talked me into this appointment.

When I leave the spa, I visit the outlets and the brand-new lingerie store. Out with the old, in with the new! I try on about a dozen bras, and I find a few I like and decide to buy the matching panties to go with them. As I make my way to the cashier, I spot some cute little PJs and think it's time I get rid of the ratty old t-shirts I wear to bed. I buy some little shorts with matching tanks and a few lacy cropped pieces. Not really sure if they're supposed to be worn as a bra or to bed, but they're cute and girly, and I wanted them. Plus, they match my new nails.

I step into the parking lot with the bags in my hands, not quite ready to end my day of spending. I don't really have the money to be doing this, but whatever, a girl has to treat herself once in a while, and I never did anything like this when I was with Jake. My credit card will understand.

I decide I need a few go-to date clothes and make my way to a couple of other shops before heading home.

I pull up to my apartment and see Lucy sitting in her car. She's early. I can hear the bass from her music as I park in my designated spot. Sounds like angry teen music. Lucy looks up and waves at me.

Alright, time to get myself on an App so I can start swiping.

We spend the next thirty minutes catching up, and I show Lucy all my new purchases. She wholeheartedly agrees with every purchase. Lucy helps herself to my closet to choose a few other random items.

The next hour is spent laughing and trying on potential date outfits. If we were in a movie right now, this is the part

CHAPTER FIVE

where some cool music would come on, and we'd be in a movie montage. We laugh and collapse on my bed.

Lucy turns to her side and faces me, seriousness glazing over her glassy green eyes.

I look at her. "What's up?" Lucy is pretty carefree and doesn't take things too seriously, so when this look appears, it's time to listen.

I roll onto my side to face her.

"I'm so proud of you, Sof," she starts. "You've come a long way from the girl I met in college."

"Awe, thanks, Luce. I don't really feel like I've changed much." I reply to her statement and roll onto my back, staring at my ceiling.

"Sure you have. You were so shy and sort of a pushover. You let people take advantage of your kindness, and now, since that proposal, I see you standing up for yourself, owning your truth, and not afraid to just be you."

I laugh. "Oh, I am definitely afraid."

"You know what I mean," she continues. "I'm proud of you for getting out there and taking this job. I think it will be so good for you."

I smile. Lucy is so supportive. I've got the best friends a girl could ask for.

"Okay, well, let's get on with it then," I say as I pull out my phone.

Lucy recommended I download Swipe & Meet. As we wait for it to download, we take a few pictures and go through my photo gallery to choose which are the best and most wholesome and natural for my profile.

We start googling usernames and try to come up with one close to who I am. We settled on Booklover. Simple and to the point. We click off the basics.

Booklover (Sofia) 25 years old, writer & retail worker, Pisces, doesn't smoke, drinks socially, wants kids. 5'2", brown hair, brown eyes, medium build. Hobbies include reading, writing, game nights, spending time with friends, and watching movies.

Now for the hard part. Writing about yourself and your achievements, goals, or wants in life, knowing they will be judged, is a bit tough. We come up with a few different versions but ultimately settle on one.

Just your girl next door who loves cats & books. I love to laugh and spend time with friends. I am a writer who aspires to be a novelist. Looking for someone down-to-earth with a kind heart. I've yet to travel the world, but I hope to one day. I am looking to date and see if I can find my special someone.

I click the *Publish Now* button and see my profile come to life as hearts flutter across my screen. Lucy says we should start swiping, but I turn off my phone and tell her I'll start tomorrow. It's been quite the day.

We order a chicken pesto pizza, which Briar picks up on her way over. We pick out an old rom-com and settle into our usual spots.

When I finish my third slice, I lay back and glance at Lucy and Briar.

I feel grateful at this moment.

CHAPTER SIX

I pick out my new pink floral cheeky underwear and matching bra and pull my dress over my head, smoothing it down over my hips. I slide my feet into my gray suede ankle boots to match. I glance in the mirror, happy with my choice.

A feeling of excitement comes over me.

I'm pumped!

I walk into work and see that Ben's been in to water the plants. There are random spots of dirt on the floor, and my OCD kicks into gear. I take out the broom and sweep it up. When I'm done, I lift my fingers up to grab hold of one of the new small tips that are spiraling from the small trunk of the *ponytail palm*.

"Hey," Ben says, strolling in nonchalantly.

Speak of the devil. Or think of the devil? I climb on my stool behind the counter and slurp my smoothie through the reusable straw that tastes like rubber.

"Hey," I reply, watching him.

The Dating Debacle

Ben is pushing up the sleeves of his long-sleeved shirt, revealing his dark, muscular forearms, a glimpse of a dark line from the tattoo hidden beneath showing itself. He leans onto the counter and comes face to face with me. Hmm, he smells like he's in a rainforest.

Something flickers inside of me. I frown at the thought, confused. Why am I thinking about how good Ben smells, and why can't I take my eyes off his arms?

I turn to look away and break his stare.

What is going on here?

Maybe it's this new lingerie and the feelings of spicy that a good wax has recently restored. Maybe I have opened up the sexy, single side of Sofia that's been closed off. It must be that. Having opened my mind up to the world of dating, I suddenly have super senses and can detect men's cologne and muscular attributes.

I don't know, so with that thought, I reach for my phone and turn it on.

As my phone comes to life, it starts beeping like the garbage truck backing up in the back alleyway.

"Someone's popular," Ben says in a playful way, raising his eyebrows and looking at me questionably.

"I must have some new emails, or Lucy is going on a rant," I say, looking down.

I see pink hearts flooding my screen, suddenly aware that these are all notifications from the dating App. I swipe to open my phone because, yes, even in this day and age, I do not have a passcode. I always forget my passwords, and I just can't chance being locked out of my phone despite the constant warnings from Ben, Lucy, and Briar that my phone will be stolen and my identity taken.

CHAPTER SIX

I click on the hot pink heart to open the App.

"Looks like I have some likes," I say to Ben. I turn my phone to him, and he glances down to look.

"So, you're going ahead with this dating article, then?" he asks, his deep voice steady.

"Yeah, why not? I'm actually kind of excited to write about something other than weeds," I say, yawning at the thought of writing one more article about lawnmowers, which reminds me, I have to hand in my last piece this week.

I bring up the notifications tab, and I see that I have thirteen new likes. I click on the first pic. Ben makes his way around the counter and peers over my shoulder casting a shadow over my phone.

"Let me see, I don't trust the guys on these Apps," he says. I can feel his breath on the back of my neck, sending shivers through me. I shoot him an annoyed look.

Gamerboy (Marc) 25 years old. Accountant, Pisces, loves sunrises and sunsets, fishing, drinks socially, smokes often, does not want kids.

I look at the giant fish he is holding in his first picture, with a cigarette hanging out of his mouth, and wince. "Um, thank you, next. I want kids someday," I say and swipe left. Ben sighs behind me. I continue on, ignoring him.

Looking4U (Jeffery) 23 years old, starving artist, Capricorn, loves dogs, has kids, and wants more, 420 friendly.

"Um, I don't think I am ready to date someone with children," I say and swipe left again, although taking a mental screenshot of his dreamy blue eyes and naked torso, showing off a tight stomach with that V-thing guys have just below his waistline.

Globetrottie (James) 27 years old, real estate agent, Leo, nature lover, wants kids, drinks socially, doesn't smoke.

The Dating Debacle

"Oh, he sounds great," I say and go through the rest of his profile. His pictures vary from being on a mountaintop to drinks on a patio with him smiling, showing off an impressive set of teeth.

6'2", brown hair, brown eyes, medium build. Hobbies include volleyball, trivia, movies, and hiking.

I swipe right, and a heart suddenly appears over both our profile pictures. Ben sighs again behind me.

"Can you stop?" I say as I continue to scroll through James' profile.

"I don't think you should do this," he says, peering down at the pictures I am scrolling through.

James is... let's just say James is hot!

"So what happens now?" I ask.

"You can send him a message, or he can send you one," Ben says as he makes his way back around the counter.

"Have you ever met anyone online?" I ask him, looking up from my phone.

"No, but I have friends who do," he says.

I don't remember Ben ever talking about any girls except for Mel. He doesn't talk about Mel. I guess she broke his heart in college about a year after his parents passed away. I think he's closed himself off to love. It's just Ben and his plants.

My phone pings.

You have one new message.

"Oh! I have a message already!" I yelp and jump up off my stool just as two women walk into the bookstore. I put my phone down and greet them, smiling.

"Be careful, Sof," Ben says before walking out of the store.

I help the ladies who seem to have an obsession with Stephen King as I hear them bicker about which was better: the movie

CHAPTER SIX

Rose Red or the book. The book, *obviously*.

* * *

I spend the rest of the morning messaging James between customers and work. He sounds pretty down to earth. We talk about our pet peeves, mine being people who can't park straight between the yellow lines at the grocery store, and he tells me that he can't stand people who don't signal before changing lanes. He talks about his love for traveling and basketball. He tells me that his parents are still together and that he wants to find a girlfriend. Our conversation gets serious about our life goals and dreams.

On paper, he pretty much sounds fantastic.

Ben walks in just after noon, his lunch in his hands. The store is empty right now, so I grab mine from under the counter. I can see Ben has his usual sandwich. I pull out my salad and pour on some lemon and garlic dressing. I stab at the lettuce, my fork picking up way more than I know can fit into my mouth, but I choose to ignore this fact. A large piece of lettuce, which obviously should have been chopped a bit smaller, smacks the sides of my mouth with its oily dressing before making its way in for me to chew. I cover my mouth as this happens, trying to shield Ben from my clumsy eating. He doesn't seem to care.

"So, how's that App going?" he asks after swallowing his own large bite of what appears to be an egg salad.

"It's good. I think I found someone for my first date," I say, taking another bite. I think about my conversation with James this morning.

Ben leans back in his chair, his expression showing concern.

The Dating Debacle

"You know a lot of guys on there are only looking for hook-ups."

"James isn't like that," I say, leaning back in my chair and pulling a chocolate bar from my lunch bag.

Ben's look of concern grows. "You've only been talking to him for a few hours. You can't possibly know someone in that amount of time."

I process this for a second. "Look, Ben, I know you don't agree with me doing this, but I can take care of myself. I get to write about something fun and exciting. Why can't you just be happy for me?"

"What about your novel?" he asks.

"What about my novel?" I push my chair back, standing. I suddenly feel pressured, overwhelmed maybe.

"You want to write a novel, isn't that your goal? Why don't you start that?" Ben asks.

Ben is the only one who knows why I haven't started my novel.

"It's complicated. You know that," I say, feeling a warm sensation creeping through my body.

From the time I was a little girl, I loved everything about books. I loved their smell. I loved the feeling of the pages between my fingers. I loved the covers, especially when they had the characters displayed on them. After finishing the entire book, I would study the characters and see if they matched up with who I had created in my head.

After my mom tucked me in each night, I would pull out my book, pull my blankets over my head, and turn on the small flashlight I got for Christmas one year. I loved diving into the make-believe worlds. My mom once took me to a rummage sale, where we found a ton of books, and after that, we spent

CHAPTER SIX

many Sundays going to flea markets and yard sales. It became a thing we did together. My book collection grew, and so did my love for stories.

As time went on, I loved anything to do with love and romance. I was infatuated, following stories of love blossoming, of two teenagers meeting and choosing each other. And then, as I grew up, more complicated and passionate love stories. Something I longed to have one day, myself. That ultimate love-consumes-you type of love.

The love I saw my parents have as a child before my mom passed away.

I remember my dad grabbing hold of my mom's hips as she was doing the dishes after supper, pulling her back towards him, and spinning her around on the kitchen floor. I would run to the stereo, put on some music, and dance around them, laughing and smiling. Some of my best memories were moments like that when I felt the love between my parents, and I could see it in the expressions on their faces.

I wanted my first novel to be about that raw, all-consuming love.

After my mother passed away, the love in my dad's eyes faded.

He was a great dad, even while hurting. We would cry, lying on my bed while he tucked me in at night, remembering her. As time went on, we healed together. He helped me with my homework. He took me shopping for my prom dress. But the dancing in the kitchen stopped. A part of him was gone, and I felt that.

I dived deeper into romance novels, the ones that were written so well you felt your heart ache for the characters. I would speed through the book just to get to the ending,

The Dating Debacle

where I could feel some type of relief in my chest. By the time I went to college, I had decided that I wanted to write a love like the one my parents had. I wanted to live a love like that.

But…how does one write about something they have never felt? Maybe that is why I am doing this. I will be writing about love or the possibility of love. This is enough for now.

I snap out of the memories that have flooded my thoughts and put the rest of my lunch away, meeting Ben's gaze. It feels intense. I feel a spark deep down in my belly.

He leans towards me, across the table, grazing my hand with his fingertips gently. He's looking at me with intent. Ben has had his own share of loss and understands this, so why is he pushing me to do something I'm not ready for?

I pull my hand away from his soft touch and the butterflies that are starting to build deep inside of me. I will the butterflies to stop fluttering, and my emotions take on a life of their own.

"What about you, Ben? Maybe you should put yourself out there and meet someone. It's been a long time since Mel," I blurt out.

Ben turns his head. I can tell I hit a nerve.

He starts busying his hands, packing up his own lunch bag. "I don't want to waste my time."

"What does that even mean?"

Ben pushes his chair away from the table and stands. I am about to continue when I hear voices nearing the bookstore. I put my lunch bag away and when I turn around, Ben is gone.

I feel a sadness within me, not sure if it is from reliving the memories of my parents or the fact that Ben just left without saying anything.

* * *

CHAPTER SIX

The rest of the day went by quickly. I had an author come in, wanting to drop off some books she had just self-published. I took her contact information and added it to the front display table. We talked about possibly doing a book signing next month.

I unlock the door to my apartment and slide in, kicking off my boots and throwing my coat over my living room chair.

I'm just finishing eating when my phone pings, and a small pink heart appears on the screen.

My heart flutters in a combination of nerves and excitement. I feel like a giddy teenager getting her first good morning text from a boy she likes.

I put my phone down. I don't want to seem too desperate and answer right away. Although, is it really desperate if you just happen to have your phone next to you? I mean, doesn't everybody have their phones either in their hands, next to them on the couch, and even, um, while in the bathroom?

I busy myself for about a half hour before I reach for my phone again and open the App.

Damn, he sure is gorgeous.

Globetrottie (James): Hey! How was the rest of your day? :)

Booklover (Sofia): Hi James, my day was good actually. Went by super fast.

Globetrottie (James): That's good!

I've never done this before, and I don't quite know how to go about this. What do I even say? Before I can think of anything, there is another message from James.

Globetrottie (James): What's your cat's name?

Seriously, did he just ask me about Bob? Hmm, points to him on actually reading my profile. Lucy said I'd get a lot of messages based on my pictures and not on my actual profile. She even went on to say I would probably get some racy messages. I laughed when she told me and waved her off, not taking her too seriously.

Booklover (Sofia): His name is Bob. Do you have any pets?

Globetrottie (James): No, I don't, but I love animals.

This is going well so far. I'm feeling hopeful about James.

Globetrottie (James): What's your favorite season?

Booklover (Sofia): I think I would have to say spring. I love it when all the snow has melted, and you can see everything coming back to life. The green grass, the flowers blooming, and the days start to get a bit longer. :)

Globetrottie (James): Yeah, I get that. I love the summer, beaches, road trips, and campfires.

Booklover (Sofia): Do you camp often?

Globetrottie (James): I get together with the boys, we camp a few times every summer. We go off-grid. It's awesome! We have to park and canoe to the sites, no plumbing, no noise - well, we are the noise. Hahaha.

Okay, so I am definitely not an off-grid girl, but that's okay. Boys need their boy's time, right?

Booklover (Sofia): Lol, that's cool.

We spend the next hour chatting; the excitement is growing in my belly. I'm taking a few notes here and there for the article. I have to remember this is work. I mean, so far it's fun work, but Miriam will be expecting me to report in and write about this.

I learned James has two older brothers. I tell him I'm an only child. We agree we are probably both spoiled, him being the youngest and me being an only child. I don't tell him that

CHAPTER SIX

my mother is gone and that my dad is the one who raised me alone. It's too soon for that. We talk about the trips we have both taken. He has me beat there for sure. I like that he seems to be more outgoing than I am. This could be good for me. I'm not anti-social, but you could say I tend to follow the crowd instead of taking the lead.

Globetrottie (James): Well, I've got to log off for now. How do you feel about meeting up Sofia?

Oh, wow. I wasn't expecting things to move this fast. I mean, I guess it makes sense to meet him. I'm suddenly warm with nerves. Keep it cool, Sof, I tell myself.

Booklover (Sofia): That sounds great!

Globetrottie (James): I'm free on Thursday. How about dinner at The View? You know of it, right?

The View is a restaurant on the water. It's fairly pricey but worth every penny.

I start to feel anxious. I have to actually go out and meet this random stranger…from the internet. What was I thinking? Now I'm excessively sweating.

Booklover (Sofia): Sure, I know it.

We write back and forth for a few more minutes, confirming the details. Once I've signed out of the App, I immediately call Lucy and Briar.

"Guys, I have a date! *What do I do?*"

CHAPTER SEVEN

I get a lot of random messages leading up to Thursday. I don't know if I'm repelled by the dating App or in shock at how some guys really put themselves out there and how many are incredibly perverted.

I roll over. I'm just waking up, and I can see the sun is already shining. I reach for my phone, which is about two feet further than I can reach, and I am suddenly doing what feels like an acrobatic move off the side of my plush double bed. I grab hold of the end of my phone and pull, unplugging the charging cable during the act.

I turn it on and see that I have four new messages. Although I already have my first date tonight, Miriam wants me to have multiple dates - the whole reason for the article. I spent the last few nights with Lucy and Briar, swiping left and right.

I bend my knees to release my lower back to the mattress and, in doing so, unintentionally knock Bob off my legs. I can see him trotting into the kitchen. Within seconds, I can hear him throwing his food on the floor again. I sigh at the thought

CHAPTER SEVEN

of the mess I will have to clean up later. His new thing is also scooping water from his water bowl and dumping that on the floor. Hard food, plus water, equals soft, mushy grossness on my kitchen floor.

I turn my attention back to my phone.

You have 4 new messages.

I am instantly excited, although combating anxiety on the inside.

I have to say, although some of the attention is rather unwanted, it does sort of boost the ego, having all these guys message me. I make a mental note to write about this in my first article. I click on the first message.

Talldrinkofhotness (Roch): Looks like you could use a tall drink of me ;)

Really? I delete the message, not interested in even glancing at his profile. I open the next message.

Freehugs (Paul): What up?

Delete. I'm starting to feel a little picky, but come on - where's the effort? I responded a few days ago to someone who wrote the exact same line, and it went nowhere. I asked how his day was going, and his reply was, "Okay." Just okay. Nothing followed it. I am not going to waste my time being the sole conversationalist. I click on the next message.

MakeMeMelt (Mike): Send me a nude xoxo

Oh, My God. Seriously? Each message is worse than the one before. I'm so happy that I have a decent guy to go on a date with tonight. Although I'm starting to be a bit more than just a little annoyed, this will make for great writing material. I can't be the only online dater who gets messages like this! I open the last message.

SoulSeaker (Jonah): My girlfriend and I were scrolling

The Dating Debacle

through your profile, and we would love to meet you. She thinks you are very pretty. We're looking for a down-to-earth girl to hook up with. So what do you say? You interested?

Okay, enough for this morning. I delete the last message, a little taken aback. Isn't there a different App for stuff like that? Maybe threesnotacrowd.com?

Hmm, I wonder if that exists.

I shake my head and go back to my messages with James.

We haven't spoken since we made the date, but I'm not worried. I start scrolling through the messages, trying to decode any other hints about him. I decide to try to find him on social media and see if I can dig up any other pictures or facts about him. I write James in my search bar, and I see a bunch of random dudes—and some girls—pop up. I scroll through slowly, trying to spot someone with some resemblance to the pictures I have already seen. I click on one of the pictures, and it takes me to a James Wilcox. I shuffle through his pictures. I guess it could be him. I finally come across a picture of the James I have been messaging at a wedding.

Oh, shit!

It's his wedding. I zoom in on one of the pictures of him with the bride, suddenly expanding my creeper status from zero to one hundred. My stomach is starting to form knots. I sit up so I can focus, crossing my legs and letting out the breath I've been holding. This guy has a dimple on his left cheek. I'm suddenly seeing more differences: thicker eyebrows and thinner lips. I open the dating App and pull up his profile picture. Nope, he is smiling wide, and he has no dimples.

Phew..not him.

CHAPTER SEVEN

I continue my social media search. I prop up my pillows behind me, and I lean back, thinking. He's a realtor, he has to have some sort of a business page. I squint, trying to look for clues. Maybe a realtor logo.... and then boom! *Found him.*

A wicked smile spreads across my face. He is so cute, and his profile is public. So, is it really creeping if someone willingly puts all that information out into the world? I'm trying to downplay any stalker vibes that I'm giving off and think about how I'm just being careful, being curious one might say.

Proactive, even.

I click on his A*bout Me,* and right at the top - Single. Yes! Well, that's a good start. At least he is being honest about that. I start to wonder if I'm doing myself more harm than good and decide to take one last look at that smile of his and close my phone.

* * *

I'm just pulling into the parking lot of The View. The place is already packed, and I can hear the laughter and conversations coming from the patio that overlooks the river. I hope James reserved us a table overlooking the water. How romantic is that for a first date? I swoon a little at the thought. I park in a spot and turn off the car, pulling my purse onto my lap. I'm trembling on the inside. The nerves set in about two hours ago when I got in the shower.

I spent a little extra time getting ready today. After shaving my legs, I opened up the lime and bergamot scented body lotion that's been sitting in my cupboard for probably longer than its shelf life and moisturized from neck to toe. I even pulled out some of the beauty samples I'd hoarded and did a face scrub.

I pause, wondering why I did all this for a date, for some rando? I should be doing this for myself regularly. I make a mental note to up my self-care game.

I tilt the mirror on the sun visor down and wipe a spot of lip gloss that has smeared. Once I've checked that everything is good, I get out of the car and make my way to the front entrance. I'm five minutes early. I hate being late and rushing. I always strive to be at least a few minutes early, however striving for and actually being early are two very different things. I wanted to get to our table before James arrived so that I could familiarize myself with the space and take some deep breaths to calm my nerves and the flare-up of my generalized anxiety.

The hostess greets me with a smile.

"Hi," I say. "Reservation under James." I smile as she looks at her reservation book and nods.

"Follow me."

She grabs two menus and turns towards the back of the restaurant, leading me out onto the patio. The sun is shining, and the spring air is warm without any breeze. The patio is packed, and I speed up to stay close to the hostess as she veers in and around the already full tables. She stops when she arrives at the last table, in the far corner, overlooking the water.

My heart jumps. This is so romantic.

She places the two menus on the table and tells me my server will be by shortly to take my drink order.

I slide onto the chair facing the restaurant so I can see when James arrives. Another reason I like to arrive first, I get to pick the seat I actually want to sit in instead of pretending that I'm

CHAPTER SEVEN

okay with my back facing the crowd. I take out my phone and check the time. I still have a few minutes. I place my phone on vibrate and drop it back in my purse. I look over the ledge and notice a cardinal perched on a nearby dock. That has got to be a good sign.

I glance around at the nearby tables to check out what other people have ordered when I see him.

It's him.

James is walking right towards me, teeth showing through his smile, hair blowing slightly in the breeze - wait, there's no breeze. How is his hair doing that? I feel as if the rose-colored glasses have just planted themselves onto the bridge of my nose, where this man of significant hotness is striding towards me in slow motion. I lift my hand and wave, feeling awkward.

He comes right over to my chair, so I stand, and he embraces me in a big bear hug as if we've known each other for years. He says my name, although the sound comes out muffled with his mouth smothered against my hair. I take in a deep woods scent, not quite as attractive as Ben's rainforest, but he smells good nonetheless. I pull back as we seem to be tiptoeing into an overly long hug meant for condolences and long absences.

I sit back down, and he pulls out the chair across from me and sits.

"It's so great to meet you, Sofia," he says.

"It's nice to meet you too, James. This is a great spot, isn't it?" I ask, looking over the water. His gaze doesn't leave me as he smiles and nods.

A server makes his way to our table wearing crisp black pants and a white polo shirt with The View logo embroidered on the pocket.

"What can I start you off with for drinks?" he asks, turning

The Dating Debacle

towards me.

I look at James and glance quickly at the menu in front of me.

"I'll take a glass of white wine, please."

"I'll have a glass of whatever you have on tap. Surprise me."

I could never just leave my drink order in the hands of a random stranger. What if I don't like it? James really is much more outgoing than me. I could learn a few things from him, I guess. Maybe I could open up and try new things and be a little more adventurous. I'm a girl of routine. I like what I like, and I don't tend to veer off from that mental list of my likes.

James reaches over and grabs my hands abruptly. I'm gasping in surprise, not used to the forwardness.

"I'm so happy we're doing this," he says. I smile back at him, unsure of what to say. "Tell me about yourself. I want to know everything." His voice is filled with the confidence of a superhero.

"Um, I don't know where to begin. What do you want to know?" I ask shyly, feeling my shoulders raise, not quite feeling relaxed yet.

"Anything, your favorite color, the way you take your coffee, what style of eggs do you eat?" he persists.

I squint as the sun hits my eyes. I move over slightly, allowing the sun umbrella to cast a small amount of shade just over my eyes.

"My favorite color is yellow. I don't drink coffee often, but when I do, I prefer one milk, well oat milk, and one sugar, and I prefer my eggs scrambled," I say, meeting his gaze. "What about you?"

He ignores my question and asks if I'm serious that I like my eggs scrambled. I frown at his question. What's wrong

CHAPTER SEVEN

with scrambled eggs?

"How do you prefer your eggs?" I ask again.

"Poached. There's no way else to eat them," he says, picking up the menu.

Um, OK, if you say so.

"I see," I respond, unsure what else to say to that.

He looks up at me again, smiling. No dimple. I'm thankful my first online date is mostly a normal guy. He isn't giving creepy stalker or murder vibes, so that's good. Geesh Sofia, where have your standards gone? As long as he doesn't look like a murderer, you're good? I think of a few more messages I received earlier today. They just kept getting worse as the day went on, but I did match with a guy slightly younger than me. He wrote me a message, but I didn't respond. I thought I would wait until after my date with James. I don't know how one could manage to talk to more than one person at a time. It seems so confusing. I don't want complicated.

I shrug off James' odd response and continue on. "So, have you been here before? What do you usually order?"

The menu is on the small side, but I see the smashed chicken I ordered last time I was here. It was so good. I will definitely be ordering that.

He's looking at the menu when he responds. "Yeah, I come here every few weeks. I'm not a fan of cooking, so I eat out quite a bit."

I nod, understanding completely. I dislike cooking very much. I tend to set off the smoke detector. I think I just get busy or forget what I'm doing, so I leave my food to cook longer than they're supposed to.

"I think I will get the mushroom caps for starters," he continues. "What do you think?"

The Dating Debacle

Inside, my stomach is turning at the thought of mushroom caps. "I think I'm good for a starter, but thank you."

"Your loss," he declares as he ponders the menu further.

I'm not quite sure if he is being playful and joking or if he is starting to come across as a little less desirable than he was on the App. "I'm going to order the ten-ounce prime rib," he says, closing his menu.

I wait for him to continue. The spark in his eyes seems to be gone. We've been here less than fifteen minutes, and his demeanor seems to have shifted.

I shrug it off. It must just be nerves.

The server arrives with our drinks and takes our order. The mushroom caps arrive shortly after, and James devours them in minutes. I'm slightly turned off, if I'm being completely honest. He doesn't even close his mouth to chew his food. He seems to have gotten a second wind and has been talking about himself and the real estate he has recently sold, all while popping in one appetizer after another, barely swallowing. I drink the last of my wine as the server arrives with our entrees. I ask for a glass of water.

"Another beer, my man," James says to the server as he waves him off.

He's kind of a douche through the rest of the meal—or actually a *moutard*. I smile as I laugh to myself inwardly, thinking of Ben. Ben would definitely call out James as a *moutard*. I spend the rest of the date listening more than talking since James clearly likes the sound of his own voice. I'm mentally already ruling him out for a second date when he tells me he is having such a good time.

Really, James, *really*?

I'm about to respond as I finish a bite of my chicken when

CHAPTER SEVEN

he cuts me off again to go on about a fish he caught last week. This dude is all about his stories. I finish off my chicken, and I am slowly tuning him out as the thought of Ben and his hands reaching out towards mine the other day causes a tingle to appear out of nowhere back in the depth of my abdomen. I brush the thoughts of Ben out of my head and look across the table at James. He just laughed really loud, loud enough to make heads turn, and he was staring at me, waiting for my reaction. I have no idea what he just said.

"Sofia, did you hear me?" he asks. "My buddy, Boe, fell off the boat when he was reaching down to take off something that had caught on his rod. It was a bra! Can you believe that, Sofia? A bra." He laughs again, just as loudly as the first time. I let out a tiny laugh, more out of embarrassment than anything else.

I place my napkin on my plate. That chicken was the bomb, as usual.

James follows and downs the rest of his beer. He makes eye contact with the server and orders another one loudly across the room, pointing to his empty glass.

I pull out my phone and glance at the time.

"James, this was really great, but I actually have to get going," I say shyly.

"It's still early. How about we go back to my place? We can get to know each other a bit more there?" he asks. "Maybe a little Netflix and chill?"

Do people actually still say that? I shouldn't be surprised. James turned out to be very different from his profile and the guy I was speaking to.

"Sorry, I can't. Maybe another time?" I reply, knowing full well that I will be deleting James from the App as soon as I get

The Dating Debacle

into my car.

"Your loss, Sofia." He turns to see our server still at another table. "Man, where's my beer?" He shouts.

I go to stand up. I've had enough of James.

"It was nice to meet you, but I do have to rush out," I say, glancing down at my blank phone, willing some sort of emergency call to come through to make this less awkward. Of course, it doesn't vibrate. I pause for a moment before turning wondering if I'm supposed to offer to pay for half, hands clasped on my bag as I ponder this. Jake paid for most of our dates while we were together since he made more money. I never asked Lucy about this, and I make a note to bring this up.

"If you change your mind, hit me up," he says, leaning back in his chair.

I give James a smile and thank him for the meal before I go.

I apologize to the server for James' behavior as I pass by him. He smiles in acceptance, and I make my way out of the restaurant as fast as I can.

CHAPTER EIGHT

I'm pushing my hair back with a headband to wash my face when my phone pings from the bathroom counter beside me. Seeing a little heart on my screen, I reach for it, a new message from James. I sigh and feel my shoulders stiffen. I haven't taken the time to delete him yet. When I got home last night, I fell right into bed. Now's as good a time as any. I close the lid on the toilet and sit, but I'm not prepared for what is about to imprint on my mind forever, FOREVER!

I'm at a loss for words. I can't seem to look away. I'm blinded by a screen filled with flesh-colored, taut skin.

Yup, there it is.

It's happened.

One very up-close, dicpic.

Not believing this has actually happened, I rub my forehead, feeling the lines between my eyebrows appear. Right above the very graphic Rated R photo is the caption, "Your loss." I will myself to close my mouth as the shock starts to subside, and I am just coming back to my senses when my phone rings

The Dating Debacle

in my hand. It's Lucy.

I swipe the screen to answer, or actually, I swipe the X-rated picture, pushing it off my display screen and back into the dating App. I answer the call, still feeling baffled, and my eyes a little violated.

"You'll never guess what James just sent me!" I exclaim before Lucy has a chance to say anything.

"Awe, you've got your first dicpic!" Lucy laughs a loud cackle. I let last night's events slide off me as I join in on the laughter with my best friend.

* * *

It's odd for me to have two days off in a row, but I'm working all weekend, so I decide to use today to write my first article for Lace & Dots magazine.

I've spent the better half of the morning replaying last night's date in my mind. Lucy assured me that this probably won't be my only bad date. I don't see how things could possibly get any worse. I'm hopeful, but last night's event opened my eyes and has given me quite a few ideas for how to go about my article.

My phone sounds from across the room.

I spend a minute contemplating getting up from the cozy position I've settled into on my couch. Bob is by my side, but ultimately, I can't seem to leave an unread text unanswered.

I think I have boundary issues.

When I get to my phone, I turn it over and see one unread message from Ben. We don't text all that much, Ben and I. We're like really close work friends. We love hanging out together at work but just don't seem to get together after

CHAPTER EIGHT

hours more than once every few months, randomly.

Ben: Mornin'. How'd the date go?

I make my way back to the couch and plop down.

Me: I won't be going back out with James again.

It's mid-morning. Work must be going a bit slow for him today as he replies immediately.

Ben: What happened?
Me: It's no big deal.

I reply quickly, not wanting to let him know that maybe he was right about online dating. But things could turn around. James was only the first. My phone sounds again, notifying me of another incoming text.

Ben: Any other dates lined up?
Me: Not yet I'm writing my article today. You working tomorrow?
Ben: Yup.
Me: I'll see you then. Have a good day! :)
Ben: Can't wait.

I put my phone down and grab my laptop from the coffee table. I take one of my couch pillows and place it on my lap, with the laptop on top. Okay, so I'm not set up the best to be a writer. Hmm, maybe I should make more of an effort and create a writing space in here.

Yup, it's settled. I'm hitting IKEA.

I turn off my laptop and put it back on the coffee table. I lean down to pat Bob on the head.

"I'll be back Bob. Mamma's going shopping!"

Bob looks at me with a blank expression. I grab my coat and keys and head out.

I arrive thirty minutes later. I'm grinning so hard that my face kind of hurts.

The Dating Debacle

There's something about walking through here and seeing all the designs that gets me excited. I think it's my love for home renovation shows. I like it when the designer does the final staging, decorating every last corner of the place right up until they karate chop the last couch cushion. I've really only decorated my bedroom. I once read that your bedroom should feel like an oasis, a place of serene vibes.

I stand in the short lineup of people going in for carts and wait patiently. I take a cart and follow the line of people heading in. Thank God for the carefully mapped-out walking path. I pass by a stand with tiny pencils and paper and take one of each.

My eyes light up as I pass the first of the bedrooms. There's a large white wardrobe with glass doors. This would take up one full wall in my bedroom. They paired it with a hanging chandelier, a fuzzy white throw rug, and an ottoman. I think this was meant for a walk-in. A girl can dream.

I continue on, making mental notes along the way of decor goals until I reach the 'office' section. I veer off the main walking path and make my way to the desks, my hand gliding across the top of each one as I pass. I don't know why I do this. These aren't cashmere sweaters. I move my cart and stop in front of a smaller-sized desk. I don't have a ton of room in my apartment, but I have a little nook in my living room, which I have been meaning to turn into a writing space. I even have the measurements saved on my phone.

I open my notepad and scroll down until I see the one titled *space.*

I look back at the desk, and I reach for the little tag with the dimensions. This one will be too big. I push my cart through the desks until I spot one that looks just right. The top is

CHAPTER EIGHT

made of bamboo, and the legs are white. I reach for the tag, the dimensions are perfect.

This is it.

I pull out the tiny pencil from the pocket of my jeans and write down the aisle and bin number for later.

I make my way back onto the walking path and to the chairs.

I see a chair with a wicker back and white legs and fall in love with it immediately, making a note of the aisle and bin number. I sit back and look around at the shoppers. I push my foot off the floor and allow the chair to twirl in circles. When it stops, I feel my ears buzz, and dizziness sets in. When it settles, I notice a clerk watching me, so I stand and walk on as if I didn't just spin around in a random desk chair like a five-year-old kid.

I continue on, picking up a small cushion for the back and a circular mirror that hangs by a rope.

I walk through the rest of the store, eyeing everything as I walk by. I find an abstract piece of art that will look good in my writing area and also match my living room.

Once I get the desk and chair from the warehouse section, I continue to the self-checkout.

About forty-five minutes later, I'm struggling to lift the box for my desk up my stairs while my purse slides off my shoulder and bounces off my knee.

I curse under my breath.

I plop down on the bottom step and drop my bag. This isn't going to work.

I check the time and wonder if Ben's at lunch.

Me: Hey, are you busy?

I ask, not sure if he will see the message right away. I'm contemplating putting the desk together in the parking lot, so it will be lighter to carry up - if need be. Why are the boxes always so heavy? My phone buzzes.

Ben: No, why, what's up?

Me: Any chance you can come over and help me bring some furniture up the stairs to my apartment?

Ben: Sure, omw.

I stay seated on the bottom step until he arrives ten minutes later. I stand when he enters the building.

"Thanks so much for coming like this," I say before he has a chance to greet me.

"Not a problem. Do a little shopping?" he asks, eyeing the box that has slid half off the step.

I turn to the desk. "Yeah, I bought a few things to make myself a writing space."

"That's great, Sof," he continues. "If you build it, it will come."

I roll my eyes. "Did you really just quote *Field of Dreams?*" I ask, laughing, knowing that Ben and his uncle are both movie fanatics.

"Sure did, best movie," he says, leaning down to pick up the box. He lifts it in one swoop. Huh, maybe I need to get to a gym.

I make my way up the stairs in front of him, unlocking the door.

"Out of the way, Bob," I call. He meows in annoyance and hops up onto the couch, eyeing Ben with judgment.

I motion to Ben to the little nook, and he leans the box against the wall.

"Thanks again, you're a lifesaver."

"Got anything else that you need to be brought up?" he asks, making his way back to the door.

CHAPTER EIGHT

"No, I just have random things, and the chair I bought came in pieces. It's fine."

We walk out the door, and he follows me to my car. I open the trunk and start taking things out. Ben comes right up behind me and grabs the wicker bucket for the chair and the legs. I take the art and cushion.

"Thanks," I say, closing the trunk.

We're back upstairs, and I realize this is the first time Ben's been inside my place. "Do you want something to drink?" I ask, seeing that he's made friends with Bob.

He's leaning down to give the purring cat belly rubs.

"Sure. I'll have water."

I get two bottles, one for each of us. He twists his arm to look at his watch.

"How's the store today?" I ask.

"It's pretty quiet for a Friday."

"I'm sure it will be busy this weekend. People are starting to plant their spring flowers."

"So, what happened on your date last night?"

Oh, we're back to this.

I play with the sleeves of my shirt, suddenly feeling shy. "He just wasn't exactly as perceived to be by text."

"He didn't hurt you, did he?" Ben says, his tone suddenly becoming protective, his body stiffening.

"No, nothing like that!"

He takes a sip from his bottle. "I better get back. Have fun putting together your furniture." He looks towards the small space. "It's going to look good with what you've picked out."

I grin and walk to the door. "Thanks!"

He leans down and gives me a quick, one-sided hug. I feel jitters pass through my body, warming my insides. I move back, unsure how to take this physical connection with him that's appeared out of nowhere.

"I'll see you tomorrow," I say.

"Tomorrow," he says, smiling at me before he turns and heads back down the stairs.

I close the door and turn on some music.

Music fills the room, and I start unpacking my desk, singing along in rhythm.

CHAPTER NINE

My head's a billow of thoughts as I press my back into the small cushion between me and my new wicker chair. I look to the right, where my smoothie sits, flexing my wrists up and down, stretching out the slight kink. I watch the condensation slide down my glass, pooling at the base, thankful for the matching bamboo coasters I sprang for. My drink has gone from a bright shade of purple to a questionable brown color.

I've been writing all morning, neglecting my breakfast, in a writing whirlwind.

I feel a pit in my stomach. Nerves. I'm writing about my real life, about the people I'm going on dates with. Obviously, I won't use their real names or anything - just my experiences. Still, my stomach feels like it is twisting inside.

I spoke with Miriam yesterday. She is expecting my draft by the end of the week.

Bob jumps up onto my desk and walks across to my glass, sniffing it. I pick him up and put him back on the floor.

The Dating Debacle

I unplug my laptop and take it to the couch. I lift my legs up and tuck them underneath me. I karate chop the pillow beside me, getting comfortable so I can read through my draft.

Excitement takes over the nerves - for now.

Two hours later, I attached my draft, a recap of the past few days, and hit send.

I take a sip of my brown-colored smoothie and make a face. I walk to the kitchen to pour it out, trying to force the tiny bits of banana down the drain with my straw.

I go to my room and let my body fall onto my bed, face first. Thankfully, I have an obscene amount of pillows to break my fall and not my face. My eyes feel heavy. I feel Bob jump onto my bed, walking over me, stepping his heavy little toes across the backs of my thighs to plop down next to me.

I feel myself drifting. I have about two hours before I need to be at work. I have time for a nap.

I call out right before falling into dreamland, "Alexa, set an alarm for thirty minutes."

* * *

Ben is looking at me, his eyes twinkling, our fingers intertwined as we walk down the beach. Sand tickles in between my toes as my feet pad through the thick, warm, golden beach.

He stops unexpectedly, which pulls me back to him. I bump into his side. He lets go of my hand, turning me to face him.

There's quite a difference in height between him and me. The top of my head is inches from the bottom of his chin. I tilt my head upwards. Gazing over me, a smirk is displayed across his lips.

His touch sends a chill down my body despite the warm air.

CHAPTER NINE

Goosebumps rise on my forearms. He lifts his hand, grazing the side of my face with a gentle caress until his hand comes around the back of my neck, scooping up my disheveled, wind-blown hair in the palm of his hand as he presses firmly against the back of my head.

I hear a dog bark in the distance.

The sound of waves crashing, seagulls calling out.

I hear these sounds, but it feels like we are the only ones on this beach.

He leans towards me, his breath so close to mine that I can feel the warmth and smell the peppermint off his breath.

My heart is racing. He's looking at me, meeting my eyes with a longing I can't ignore. I feel it inside my body. I lift up onto my tiptoes, which only makes me sink further into the sand. I can't quite reach him.

Our lips hover millimeters away from each other.

A truck is backing up somewhere.. beep, beep, beep. My thoughts become distracted. Beep, beep, beep. Why is there a garbage truck on the beach? The sound is blaring louder now. Beep, beep, beep.

I startle awake, my skin damp. Beep, beep, beep. I hear the sound of my alarm going off.

"Alexa, turn off the alarm."

I roll over, sticking to the sheets on my bed.

What in the actual cheese and crackers was that!?

CHAPTER TEN

Down the block from Plants, Pottery & Books is the best little donut shop. I decide to stop on my way to work to grab a few for Ben, a thank-you for helping me yesterday.

I push open the heavy door, setting off the bells above my head. I see Garrett look up from the customer he is serving, and I wave as I make my way to the display counter. My mouth is watering as I look over the impressive assortment of irresistible donuts.

I lean closer to the cabinet when I feel my forehead hit the glass.

Oops!

That's embarrassing.

I bring my hand up to my forehead and rub the spot that just collided with the glass. I see Garrett looking at me, amused. I can't say this is the first time this has happened, or that Garrett has not witnessed it. I have eaten my fair share of these delicious donuts.

CHAPTER TEN

"Hi, Sofia, how are you today?" he says as he makes his way to me.

"I'm good," I say sheepishly. I'll pretend that it did not just happen, I think. I look back towards the selection I was just admiring but from a safer distance.

"Do you want two of your regular raspberry lemon?" he asks casually.

Um, okay, so I might have a favorite, and I might be a regular.

"Sure, and I would like to get a s'more and an Oreo, please." I smile brightly, knowing Ben loves chocolate and sweets even more than I do.

Ben turns to me as I enter the shop. I can see he notices the familiar box in hand, his clenched jaw softening, a look of desire as I approach. For the donuts, not for me, *obviously*.

"Look what I brought!" I exclaim happily, thinking back to the dream that's still fresh in my mind.

Ben makes his way to me, setting his watering jug on the nearby table.

"What's this for?" he asks.

"You know, just for helping me bring up my desk and stuff." My thoughts take over as I think back to the kiss we shared in my dream.

"That was no big deal," he says, "but I won't say no to a donut."

I hand over the small yellow box, our fingers colliding. A jolt of electricity runs through me.

I step back, startled not sure what to make of this. His eyes meet mine, darkening slightly.

I cough, an awkward feeling coming over me. Okay, so maybe I need to lock that dream up—way back into the deep, dark crevices of my brain.

The Dating Debacle

"Let's see what you got me," he says, opening up the box and smirking. "I think it is me who now owes you a thank-you."

I wave him off as I start backing up and turning to the hallway that leads to the bookstore.

"No worries, enjoy!" I say, willing my feet to move faster than they're used to.

I say hi to Emily, who's behind the counter, reading a book.

"Hey, girl," she says as I approach.

I place my bag on the counter and take off my coat, throwing it onto one of the stools behind the cash. It's not often we work together. Weekends tend to get busier, so our hours overlap sometimes. Emily is pretty quiet. She spends most of her time reading when not helping out customers.

I'm browsing through some of the boxes we just received as donations. I bend over to pick up one of the boxes and place it on a nearby table. I spend the next few hours shuffling through, reading covers, and pricing them.

The store picks up from time to time, and Emily and I are both helping customers when I see Lucy and Briar come in. They make themselves at home at one of the tables. I catch their attention, greeting them with a smile.

Once I finish with my customer, I head over to them.

"Hey, Sofia." Briar smiles warmly.

"Hi," I say.

"I hear your date didn't go so well," she says, glancing towards Lucy.

I shrug my shoulders and look from Lucy to Briar. "Not quite what I was expecting," I say, trying not to think of the picture imprinted in my brain.

Lucy has a devilish smile, and I know she's thinking about the X-rated pic.

CHAPTER TEN

Emily's just saying bye to her customer when she heads over. "What's this? Sofia is dating?" she asks, looking at me quizzically.

Oh, I don't think I told her that Jake and I broke up. We get along great. We just don't chat too much, seeing that, for the most part, when one of our shifts ends, the other one begins.

Lucy's eyebrows raise.

Lucy and Briar spend the next five minutes updating Emily on my dating status.

"You're writing for Lace & Dots magazine?" she asks. "That's awesome, congrats!"

"Thank you. It's def out of my comfort zone," I reply.

"So, who is the next big date, and when?" Briar asks.

"I haven't actually been on the App much the last few days. I just sent in my first article yesterday," I add casually.

"Sof, you have to keep on it!" Lucy exclaims wide-eyed. "How are you going to meet Mr. Right if you just sit back and wait for him to come to you?"

"I think I'm just focusing on what to write in the articles more than anything. It's a little daunting right now. But you're right. I need guys to date if I am going to have any articles to write."

"Why don't you just think of it as finding Mr. Right Now," Briar chips in.

I ponder this. She may be on to something.

"Well, I did match with someone a bit younger than me. He sent me a message a few days ago, but I haven't replied yet." I make my way to my coat, pulling my phone out of its pocket.

"Sof! A few days in online dating time is like weeks! Let's see who he is." She goes to grab my phone out of my hand, but I manage to pull it away just in time. I press it to my chest.

The Dating Debacle

"Hold on, will you?" I ask, laughing.

"I want to see too," Emily demands, seeming fully invested in my dating life now.

I open the App and start scrolling until I reach the message.

Funnyguy (Tarak): Hey beautiful. I like your profile. Wanna chat?

I click on his profile. He seems perfect, but he doesn't really match his message tone. I turn my phone to the girls so they can see. Lucy grabs it out of my hand, Emily peering over her shoulder, and Briar leaning in toward her.

"Normally, I would say to stay away from guys who start off by calling you beautiful. Kind of a yellow flag - he probably says that to all the girls he messages. It's not very personal, *but* his profile is pretty amazing."

She returns the phone.

"I think you should talk to him. Why not?" Emily says as she makes her way to help a customer.

"Emily's right." Briar claps her hands. "What's the worst that could happen? Take a chance!"

Booklover(Sofia): Hey, I like your profile too. What do you do for work?

I'm not the best at messaging, so when I get his reply a few hours later, I let the grammar and spelling errors slide and try to get to know him as a person. He works at a shop downtown, although he doesn't tell me exactly where, but we seem to hit it off. He's funny and is making me laugh. We make a plan to meet up for pizza tomorrow night.

Emily and I close up the shop for the night, and I head home, anxious to start a new book I found in one of the donation boxes. I am a sucker for a good friends-to-lovers storyline. I pick up some takeout on the way home and grab my box

CHAPTER TEN

of donuts from the passenger seat. I'm glad I kept these for dessert. I can't wait, I think as I head inside.

* * *

I'm heading into the pizza parlor. The sign is in a vibrant red and hard to miss. I'm feeling rather nervous, but not as bad as I was on my first date. I think because Tarak seemed so funny; I felt some of the edge taken off.

The place is pretty full, but I see a spot at the counter facing the sidewalk outside. I'm squeezing through the small spaces when I hear something.

"Sup, Sofia."

I turn to find where the voice came from, but I don't see anyone matching the picture of Tarak. A young teenager is seated really low in his chair, looking at me, grinning. I must be hearing things. I keep walking and set my things down on the counter as I prop myself onto the tall stool. My coat takes up the empty one beside me. I spin around slowly, eyeing the room again to make sure I didn't miss him, when I see the same teenager approaching me. I notice his jeans are slung low on his hips, giving off skater-boy vibe.

I turn to face the window.

The teenager leans his elbow onto the counter beside me, closer than I'd like him to be. "Wassup, Sof."

I sit up a bit straighter, adding a few more inches between us. "I'm sorry, but do I know you?

"It's me, Tarak," he says nonchalantly.

"Tarak?"

"Yeah, babe, it's me," he says casually.

I am so confused right now. I frown. What is happening?

The Dating Debacle

"Whoa, Tarak, your profile looks nothing like you. What are you, fifteen?" I'm rubbing at my temples, trying to understand this.

"Sixteen, actually. And aren't these just numbers?" He slides a little closer to me. I can smell garlic radiating from his breath.

I lean further back, trying to keep my distance, when I feel my stool teetering.

I manage to slide off the stool and grab my coat.

"You created a fake profile?" I say unblinkingly. "That was you I was talking to?" I am trying to wrap my head around this as the room starts to spin a little.

"Babe, I don't see the big deal. You're hot, I'm hot, let's make magic happen."

"I can't believe this," I say. I'm making my way to the entrance when I hear him come after me.

"Babe, come on." His arms are raised, and he's shaking his head at me as if my reaction is uncalled for.

I'm on the street now, standing in front of the pizza place. I can feel the anxiety forming, and my head starts to feel cloudy.

"Don't!" I turn to say to him. "I can't believe you did that. Do. Not. Follow me," I say, astonished at what just happened. I turn on my heels towards the parking lot.

"Age is just a number!" I can hear him yell from behind me.

I lock the doors as soon as I get in my car. I don't understand. I pull out my aromatherapy roll-on from the glove box and spread it thickly on my wrists, sniffing the essential oils to help calm my racing mind.

I pull out my phone.

I text Lucy: **I'm on my way**

CHAPTER ELEVEN

Lucy opens the door before I even bring my hand up to knock. She owns a cute little cottage-type home just a few minutes from the city.

"Girl, what is going on?" she asks, pulling the door wide as I make my way inside.

Every spot is sparkling clean, but the scent of garlic and tomato sauce fills the air, tingling my nose. My mouth salivates as I breathe it in while trying to take a calming breath.

"My date, he was sixteen!" I holler, still feeling shaken up from the shock of it all.

"*You were catfished?*"

"Oh. My. God. I was catfished!" Realization setting in.

Lucy closes the front door. I take off my shoes and go to the island in the middle of her kitchen. I lean my elbows on the cool marble top and rest my chin in my hands.

Lucy is cooking pasta.

"Want some?" she says, taking the pot off and pouring the noodles in a strainer.

The Dating Debacle

"Yes, please." I pause then ask, "Have you ever been catfished? Why would someone even do this?"

Lucy takes out two bowls and divides up the pasta.

"Nope, can't say I have, sorry. I'm guessing your teenager thought he might have a chance at getting laid," she says flatly.

My eyes grow wide at her response. I grab some silverware from her drawer and two placemats and set the table to the left of the kitchen. She follows with our pasta and some Parmesan. She comes over to my chair before sitting down and quickly hugs me.

"They won't all be like this," she assures me.

Lucy returns to the oven, letting out steam as she opens the door. My nose immediately recognizes the scent of garlic bread as it fills the air. *Oh, thank God*, what is pasta without the bread to dunk it in?

We eat the pasta, and then she helps me review more profiles. I clearly need help with this.

I ended up matching with a few different people, and she urged me to send messages to each of them. I tell her I'm worried I won't be able to keep them straight, what if I say the wrong name on a date? She tells me I don't have to meet every single guy I talk to. She's right. I'm just chatting, just getting to know the guys.

Lucy has had her own fair share of bad dates but loves going out. I respect her determination and her ability to be so carefree about it all.

I leave just before midnight, yawning. I hear my phone ping. That will have to wait till morning.

* * *

CHAPTER ELEVEN

I spend the next few days talking to multiple guys and questioning my dating skills. It's a lot, but I'm having fun. One guy is a chef at a local restaurant I've visited a few times with my dad. I'm sure we've crossed paths at some point in time. It's not a huge city. He's the same age as me, and we seem to have a lot in common, but I'm taking this one a bit slower, so I'm not caught off guard quite as horrifically as I allowed myself to be with the first two dates.

The other guy I'm chatting with is a bit older than me. He enjoys ballroom dancing, mostly salsa, and theater. I like that he is more creative, and I like him so far, except for his love for all types of dance. His personality isn't wildly exciting. He suggested we go salsa dancing for our first date. I've sort of been avoiding the subject, not quite ready to commit to the date yet.

And then there are a few other guys I've been messaging about random stuff, but it's clear nothing will come of it.

Lucy's been urging me to go dancing. Apparently, Salsa is a sexy, sensual dance, and I could use some heat in my life. She's not wrong, but I don't want a one-night stand. Or do I?

It'd be nice to have some attention, maybe some flirtatious vibes, a boost to my ego after the disastrous first two dates.

I'm unpacking a box of new books just brought in from a new self-published author and adding them to our indie display beside the cash register when I see Ben walk in. We haven't spoken since the electrifying donut moment. He's popped in to say hi, but I've busied myself every time so as not to make things more awkward than they already are.

"Hey," I say, not looking directly at him.

He makes his way to my plants and feels the soil. "I'll come back later to water these."

The Dating Debacle

I nod. I really don't have a green thumb.

He picks up one of the books and turns it over, though I know he's not interested in romance books. Ben is more of a sci-fi or superhero type of guy. I mean, I am assuming, based on the number of comic-type t-shirts he wears to work.

"Everything okay?" he asks me.

I face him. "Yeah, why do you ask?"

"I just thought maybe you were ignoring me. You've been quiet," he says, and I can feel my cheeks turning pink.

Can he read my mind? I stop myself before I have any other thoughts that he can read.

"Not at all, just busy in the store and the dating stuff," I say casually, knowing full well I sound anything but.

"How's that going?" he asks.

I reach for another box of books. As I bend to pick it up, Ben appears at my side, resting a hand on my shoulder.

"Let me get that for you."

I step back, and he picks up the box as if it weighs nothing more than a decorative pillow.

"Thanks."

"You're welcome, so any good dates?" he asks again.

"I was catfished earlier this week," I say, looking down, still feeling slightly embarrassed.

His eyebrows raise in curiosity. "What do you mean you were catfished? What happened?"

"I showed up for my pizza date, and the dude was sixteen," I say, turning my back to him and continuing on as if meeting a sixteen-year-old on a date isn't a big deal.

I start breaking up the empty boxes for recycling. I hear a loud fit of laughter from behind me. I turn to see Ben grasping his stomach in a fit.

CHAPTER ELEVEN

"It's not funny!" I exclaim, staring at him in disbelief.

His laughter continues. I see the corner of his eyes crinkling and his glasses slide down his nose. I smile at his scrunched-up face. He's got a friendly face.

I grab a pillow off the chair and playfully smack him on the arm with it.

"Seriously," I say, trying to hide my smile.

"So you showed up, and a sixteen-year-old approached you and declared his love for you, or what?" He's gasping for air between words.

Okay, seriously, it isn't *that* funny.

I sigh but let myself feel some of the humor in the situation.

"It was more of a 'you're hot, I'm hot, so let's make some magic' type of love declaration," I say, mimicking the teenage boy.

I feel the tension ease from my shoulders. I allow myself to fully laugh at the sad attempt of a date and my impression.

"I can't believe that. I'm sorry that happened, Sof. But he wasn't wrong."

"What do you mean?"

I can see his eyes twinkling. He looks mischievous. "You're hot." He grins and heads towards the door. "I'm going to go grab my water jug. I'll be right back."

I stand there, unsure of what to think or what to say. This thing between us - what is this? I mean, I guess I have been noticing that Ben is kind of hot too. But I don't think I would ever tell him that to his face. We're friends! I get back to the books in my hands and add these new feelings to that little locked box deep inside my mind.

* * *

The Dating Debacle

I sucked up my pride and wrote about the whole humiliating encounter in technicolor for Lace & Dots magazine. Miriam loved it. I can't believe my luck so far. She's thrilled with the feedback she's received and is enjoying reading my articles. Who knows, maybe this will lead to more jobs with Lace & Dots, I can't help but silently wish.

My confidence in the online dating process hasn't been boosted yet, but I'm not giving up. After all, if at first you don't succeed, swipe, swipe again!

Bring on the Salsa dancing!

CHAPTER TWELVE

My brakes screech when I come to a stop at the gas station. I sit back and watch the attendant fill the car in front of me as a young guy washes my back window.

I wouldn't say I'm overly high maintenance, but I found this little gas station close to home that is full-serve, and I haven't gotten out to pump my gas since. Okay, so a little close to home is a slight exaggeration. Let's just say it's worth the drive. I no longer have to freeze my hands in the middle of winter, standing in -15 degrees and blowing snow.

I roll down my window.

"Hi, can I get forty, regular, please?" I ask the attendant.

He nods and doesn't respond.

I can see him in my side mirror, watching me more than the pump.

I look down, playing with the little beads on my key chain to avoid his gaze in the mirror.

When the gas is done filling up, he walks up to my window.

The Dating Debacle

"Debit?" The guy is wearing a bright yellow safety vest, a goatee, and a smirk.

I drop the key chain I was playing with into my cup holder and reach for my purse in the passenger seat.

"You look familiar," he says.

I turn to him as I take out my wallet.

"I've been coming here a few months now," I say, unsure how else I would appear familiar to him. I take out my debit card as he hands me the machine to tap.

The line between his eyebrows crease. "No, that's not it."

I glance up at him, wishing I could roll up my window without appearing rude. "I'm sorry. I don't think I know you."

He extends the receipt. "Wait a sec, it will come to me."

I put my wallet away, mentally willing him to move on to the next car. I sigh. I feel bad. I should be attempting to converse with this guy. Isn't this whole online dating thing supposed to be teaching me to be more open or something?

I laugh awkwardly.

He raises his hand to his chin as if deep in thought as he leans into his right hip. It's really bugging him. I see him glance at the mountain of TBR on my passenger seat and then back to me with a look of recollection in his eyes.

"Booklover or something like that, right!?" he asks a little too enthusiastically for my current anxious state.

"I'm sorry?"

"I've seen you on the App," he says, leaning one arm on the top of my car, allowing him to peer closer to me in an attempt to be flirtatious. I assume it's to be flirtatious.

"Whoa," I whisper to myself. I can feel my cheeks starting to blush in embarrassment. Here it comes, the sweat pooling

CHAPTER TWELVE

under my arms. Geez, why do I sweat so much? I can't believe someone on the street is recognizing me from the App. I'm not one for attention from random strangers.

I notice his smile as he looks down at me. He doesn't look familiar to me at all.

I see him pulling out his phone and swiping. I watch him silently.

Isn't it illegal to use your phone at the gas station? I pick up my crucial chain again and let the beads fall through my fingers in an attempt to self-soothe.

He turns his phone to face me. I see a picture of a group of guys. I remember looking at the photo and swiping because I didn't know which guy I'd be dating.

I don't know how to respond. I see a few cars lining up behind me, waiting their turn.

I start my car.

"Hey, yeah. I think I remember seeing that picture now."

He is grinning from ear to ear. "So, what do you say, wanna go out sometime?"

I shield my eyes from the sun, stalling. "Yeah, maybe. I'll message you online," I say, putting the car into drive.

"Sounds good." He straightens and smiles widely, showing a few more wrinkles on his forehead. "Talk soon, Booklover!"

I drive off. He waves as I'm pulling away, his brightly colored vest blinding me in my rearview mirror.

I feel bad.

I have no intention of finding him online.

* * *

I'm pulling in as Ben is getting out of his car.

The Dating Debacle

He sees me drive in and leans back against his car. He's wearing beige khakis and an olive green shirt with his sleeves pushed up, showing his tanned forearms. His legs are crossed at his ankles, and I have to will myself to look away.

"Mornin'." He straightens and nods towards me the way guys do.

I tried this once, but I'm not sure the female population can pull that move off, or maybe it's just me, and I don't have the swagger.

"Hey," I say, grabbing my stuff and heading to the back door, Ben following close behind.

Ben grabs my hand from behind, and I stop abruptly, turning towards him. I look up and notice a sparkle in his eyes, though a serious expression has taken over his face. His hair is slightly tousled.

I gulp. I feel my stomach go into overdrive. The butterflies are being set free. His hand is still holding onto mine.

I blink a few times, meeting his gaze, waiting for the words to come out of him.

I've never had these feelings with Ben before. I don't know if I quite understand where they're coming from, but they have been slowly creeping up. I've only been in a relationship the entire time I've known him, so it's not like he was ever an option. But I don't think he ever thought of me that way. I thought we were friends but how was I so oblivious to his feelings?

I feel responsible for the serious energy radiating off of him. I think I'm starting to care a bit more about Ben than I initially did. Maybe I haven't been such a good friend to him afterall.

I adjust my bag, which is slowly falling off my shoulder.

"What's up, Ben?" I ask, trying to move along the conversa-

CHAPTER TWELVE

tion before the butterflies take control over my entire body, and I'm no longer able to act human.

I'm highly aware that he still hasn't let go of my hand, but I don't pull away either.

"Wanna get some supper tonight after work?" he asks. "Kind of congratulations on this new writing gig with Lace & Dots," he finishes, and I can see him scanning me for a reaction to his question.

My stomach tightens. I mean, he is probably referring to a friend's type of dinner together. Nothing more. Maybe he just wasn't as touchy-feely before because I was with Jake.

"I thought you were against this entire online dating article?" I ask, curiosity taking over me.

He shifts his weight and lets go of my hand. I feel a certain type of disappointment I'm not familiar with.

"Look, I think you deserve to write your book. I know you are capable, and it would be great, but if this is what you want to do, I will support you. But I do think you deserve a guy who knows your worth." He starts walking up the back steps, leaving me to process what he just said.

I hurry to catch up to him as he unlocks the door. "Sure, let's do dinner. Where do you wanna eat?"

* * *

Booklover (Sofia): Hey, so how's your week going?

I decided to message Blake, the ballroom dancing guy. I mean I do have an article to write, so I do need dates to go on. Plus, what harm can be done with a little dancing? No pressure, one night of dancing. I think I'm becoming an expert at self-talk. I'm my own little cheerleader in my head. Some

The Dating Debacle

of the time, anyway.

My phone pings right away. I'm at work, and it's been pretty busy all morning. Ben and I decided on a restaurant, but I can't shake the feeling that is starting to grow inside of me. I know this is a friend's thing, but why can't I stop thinking about the dream I had the other day or how it felt when his fingers slid through mine as he let go of my hand?

I shake my head. Let it go, Sof, I tell myself, You've got guys to meet!

I pick up my phone and see that Blake has responded.

FollowMyLead (Blake): Sofia, nice to hear from you again. My week is starting out well, thank you for asking. Have you thought any more about trying a salsa class with me? There's one tomorrow night ;)

I smile. The attention feels good. I mean he does actually write full sentences and knows the differences between *their, there,* and *they're*. He isn't half-assing his responses like a lot of the guys who have messaged me.

Booklover (Sofia): I have, actually. I would love to meet up and try a class tomorrow night. What time does it start?

I can't believe I am going to be dancing with a stranger. Like, I know how to back it up, tootsie roll even, but Salsa - Yikes! I'm a little overwhelmed at the thought of dancing with someone who sounds so professional. I've seen *Dancing with the Stars*, and without a doubt, I may very well get vertigo from all the spinning.

FollowMyLead (Blake): That's great! The class begins at 8:00 p.m. It's at a local bar downtown.

Booklover (Sofia): Okay, that sounds great.

I shudder. That sounds terrifying, but I decided not to let

CHAPTER TWELVE

on.

Booklover (Sofia): I'll meet you there :)

Blake sends me the address, and we continue talking for a few more minutes. He tells me he works a desk job throughout the week, nothing he is overly passionate about but something to pay the bills. I get that.

I look at the time and hear a few customers making their way to the store from the plant shop. I told him that I would see him tomorrow, and I put my phone away.

"Hi," I greet two elderly ladies, each carrying a large plant. "Let me set those down for you while you look around."

"Thank you, dear," the one with the bright purple streak blending into a neat bob haircut replies with a toothy smile.

I return her smile. "I see Ben has sold you each a Lucky Bamboo."

The other woman, who has already made her way to the Nora Roberts section, nods. "That is one handsome gentleman," she says. I see the one with the purple in her hair nodding wildly, agreeing.

"If I was only fifty years younger," she chirps and lets out a cackle that makes me smile.

The two of them laugh together as if in on a secret. "He could sell me a lot more than a Lucky Bamboo."

She makes her way to her friend, and they spend the next hour bickering, laughing, and teasing one another. They may be sisters or even best friends. I think of Lucy and Briar and hope to have that same type of companionship as we age.

Ben appears, and the ladies straighten up as they see him, adjusting their cardigans. They're beaming.

"Ladies," He greets them with a sincere smile, maybe even a brief look of flirtation.

The Dating Debacle

He approaches as I type on my laptop. I've been Googling what to wear to a dance class. Apparently, I need to wear heels and a dress. I close the laptop.

"I'm heading out for the afternoon," he says. "I have some errands for the shop. I'll pick you up later?"

I light up at the thought of tonight. So much for downplaying my feelings. I'll work on that. I have lots of time. We see each other nearly every day. I notice that the women are eavesdropping on our conversation.

"Sounds great," I say, "I'll be ready."

"Can't wait." his dimple appears, a glint in his eyes. How easy it is to look at him. I can see a small portion of his tattoo peeking out from one of his sleeves that he pushes up nonchalantly. My eyes trail up his arms to his shoulder. I notice how they stretch the fabric ever so slightly.

Shit. I'm in trouble. This attraction is hitting me like a heat wave in the middle of July.

I sit back on my stool. "See you then." I manage to utter. My mouth dries up as if I have been walking in the desert all afternoon.

He turns to the ladies as he is about to leave. "Remember, they don't require a lot of water," he says, pointing at the bamboo I placed on the table.

They nod in comprehension but remain silent, grinning ear to ear

I wave to him as he leaves.

They both turn to me. "Is he your boyfriend?" The shorter one asks.

I laugh, God, I wish.

What? My subconscious seems to be taking over my thoughts. I am officially losing it.

CHAPTER TWELVE

"No, we're just good friends," I admit.

"Seems like a waste to me." She grins and says something about how she would let him 'boil her cabbage.'

I can guess what she means.

CHAPTER THIRTEEN

I'm adding a little bronzer when Ben arrives. I buzz him in and add a little mascara as he climbs up the stairs.

"You look great," he says.

I feel his eyes follow me down to my ankles and back up again, meeting my gaze, sending those damn butterflies into a cahoot.

"Thanks."

We arrive at the restaurant and decide to sit bar-side. A hockey game is playing on the large TV over the bar. It's quite busy here. Even the stools facing the bar are occupied.

Hockey nights draw such a crowd. I always thought it'd be awesome if bars would host Bachelor nights. They could serve wine, and we could watch episodes with other Bachelor Nation fans.

A great idea, right?

You're welcome.

Our waitress comes over, the low V of her tight black top revealing a small heart tattoo and some major cleavage. I can't

CHAPTER THIRTEEN

help but look and admire, wishing I could pull off a plunging neckline in a similar fashion.

I return her smile and pick up the drinks menu.

I choose a strawberry frozen drink that looks like it belongs on a Mexican beach while Ben orders a beer.

"Is this what Mexico would taste like?" I ask him.

"Hmm, maybe. I think pineapple and coconut are probably more tropical flavors."

"I can't wait to travel someday." I can feel that dreamy expression Lucy laughs at me for taking up residence on my face.

Our drinks arrive quickly, and we order our food and a plate of deep-fried pickles.

"It's like a vacation in a glass, except without the sunburn," I say. Ben chuckles lightly, giving me a comforting smile.

Ben takes a long sip, and I catch him licking his lips as he places his bottle on the table.

I wait for him to finish before speaking, unable to look away.

I can feel heat stirring up inside of me. God, maybe it's just been too long since I've had sex. Maybe Lucy's right, and I need a one-night stand.

I think about tomorrow's date with Blake. He is attractive in his pictures, not Ben attractive, but he still caught my eye. I can't compare Blake to Ben. We're just friends. So, I just happen to have a hot-guy friend. That's all. You don't get to choose how your friends look, and we're just friends, I tell myself a few more times while sipping my piece of strawberry heaven.

I think of Mel, the last girl Ben went out with. I remember how devastated he was when he told me about her. He had just lost his parents a few years earlier, suddenly, and just like that, he woke up one day, and Mel was gone. No talk, no goodbyes, just a letter with two words: I'm sorry.

"So, how's the dating going?" His question breaks my train of thought.

I put my drink down seeing that I was probably drinking it a bit too quickly. As if on cue, our appetizer arrives. I dive right in, taking three very hot, deep-fried pickles and placing them on a small plate, ignoring Ben's question.

I bite in, steam exhaling from my mouth and the pickle alike. I can't chew it. It's too hot. Why do I do this? I find myself just sitting there with my mouth open, pickle and batter unchewable for all the world to see, well mostly for just Ben to see, while I mutter how hot they are and basically do a *'hasafashafsas'* till it cools enough to start chewing. Ben is staring at me, eyebrows raised, with a comical expression I can't describe.

I laugh and cover my mouth.

Ben starts to laugh along with me.

"You saw the steam. Why did you bite in right away?" he asks, still laughing.

I finish swallowing and pick up another piece to bite into. Obviously, I don't learn from my mistakes. "You know me. I have no restraint when it comes to foods I love."

I eat the rest of the pickle with more *hasafashafsas*.

Ben joins in and we are in a fit of laughter as we eat. I don't particularly like to see people chew their food with their mouths open, and I'm not usually one to do so, but such an occasion has arisen. It's just a matter of letting out the steam while chewing.

"So back to my question," Ben starts. "Any more dates planned?"

CHAPTER THIRTEEN

God, he's obsessed. I'm not sure if I'm annoyed or feeling supported.

"Yeah, I have one tomorrow. I'm going Salsa dancing," I say hesitantly, not wanting to give too much information away. Ben starts to respond, but I find myself cutting him off. *"Oh, guess what?* The gas attendant recognized me from the App this morning! How embarrassing. I didn't tell him I swiped left on him. I felt so bad, I told him I would message him, and I have no intention of doing so. How am I going to get my gas filled there now?" I ask, puzzled, then stop for another sip of my drink.

Ben wipes at his mouth. A look of uncertainty crosses his face. "I don't know, Sof. Maybe you could go back to pumping your own gas and stop being a princess?" he says, forcing himself to hide a growing smile.

"Hey!" I say. "I do not act like a princess!" I slap at his hand, knowing he's joking but playing along. He grabs my hand before I can take it back.

Butterflies.

Fluttering.

I look down at our hands. He follows my gaze. I pull away suddenly feeling nervous.

"So, what's new with you?" I ask. "We haven't caught up in a while."

I've been so caught up in the App, and my dates gone wrong, I've kind of been self-absorbed, I guess, not meaning to.

"You know, same old, same old."

Ben has always kept to himself. It's not that there isn't any depth to him. I think he simply holds stuff in because that's how his life has been since he was a teenager. His uncle is great, don't get me wrong, he really helped him out after his

The Dating Debacle

parents' car accident, but he did have a business he was trying to grow, so as time went on, he was busy with other things.

"Come on, give me some dirt," I plead.

"Well, there was something I have been wanting to tell you," he says, blushing slightly.

I shrug, "Okay, you know you can always talk to me. What's going on?"

Our waitress approaches, carrying our dinner, stalling our conversation.

I pull the tomatoes from my wrap, glancing at Ben's burger. "Mm, your burger looks amazing,"

"Want half?" he asks.

"No, no, I will try it next time. I'll suffer with my internal burger envy and watch you eat."

Ben laughs and takes a giant bite.

"So tell me, you have me intrigued. Why the sudden interest in dining with this princess?" I joke.

He laughs. "I like spending time with you."

I smile, feeling warm inside.

We spend the next hour laughing and talking, catching up. We decide against dessert, and Ben drives me home.

He's walking me to the door when I feel a tug from behind. I turn, falling slightly into him, my hands pressing against his chest. His pecs feel hard against my palms.

His face is serious. There's a want about him, and it's sending my body into turmoil. Or lustful, I'm not sure.

His hand makes its way up to my chin, tilting my face towards him. Before I can react, I feel his breath on me, his lips near mine. I can hear the sound he makes as he exhales and can smell the exotic rainforest scent that is him. I pull away, falling into the apartment. I look up at him, confused.

CHAPTER THIRTEEN

"I'm sorry," he says quickly, looking away.

He follows me in.

"No, I..." I don't even know what to say to what almost just happened.

I take off my coat.

"Fuck it," Ben says and walks over to me with an urgency about him. He grabs my face with both of his hands, and his lips are on mine before I can say anything.

My head is swooning.

My lips are pressed tight to his, my body warming, saying yes.

I can feel him pressed against all of me. We're kissing with an urgency, his hands moving into my hair. We back into the wall, and I feel all the butterflies take flight. I gasp as he releases my mouth to move down to my neck. My eyes roll into the back of my head, my body wanting more. He stops suddenly, staring deep into my eyes, his breath rapid. His lips meet mine again, moving in harmony. I feel a tingle from his fingertips, moving slowly down the side of my cheek. He pulls away, and my lips immediately feel the cool air, lonely without his on mine.

He grabs my hand and leads me to the couch.

I follow effortlessly.

"I'm sorry," he starts again, sitting down.

"You're sorry?" I ask. "Why?"

"I shouldn't have kissed you."

My heart stops.

I suck in a breath of air. "You regret it?"

"We can't. I don't want to start something we can't finish."

"What do you mean?"

He rises from the couch and starts pacing the length of my

small living room, his hands on his hips. He looks distraught, his hair tousled in a sexy way. My hands reach up to my own, patting down the flyaways, and then my fingers meet my lips, feeling the tingle that Ben has left there. My lips beautifully raw.

He stops and faces me. "You're dating online. You're writing these articles. You have a contract to complete." His hands fall to his sides. He looks defeated like a child who has been told he could have ice cream only to find out there was none left in the freezer. Okay, maybe Ben looks a little worse off than that.

"What are you saying?" I ask, not sure how that kiss even started or where it came from.

I didn't know how much I wanted it or how I would move forward, knowing what it felt like to taste Ben and not feel it again.

He sits next to me.

"I like you, Sof."

"I don't know what to say, Ben." I cross my legs, uneasy. I'm startled by his words. I never thought of Ben this way, I mean not until recently. "Yeah, I have a date tomorrow night. I need to keep dating. I want to keep dating. I had no idea you felt that way." I tell him honestly.

I'm uncomfortable. God, I like Ben. As a friend, I don't know. Maybe something more? That kiss. Those butterflies. Again, that kiss. I touch my lips lightly, where only seconds ago, they were pillowed under the pressure of his soft touch. I want more, and I'm surprised by that thought.

"Let's forget what just happened," he orders.

I pull back momentarily, well, that's that. We just opened Pandora's box and closed it tightly, key thrown, all in a matter

CHAPTER THIRTEEN

of minutes.

I stand and walk to the door. Disappointment fills my belly where the butterflies were flying moments ago. I can't comprehend what I am feeling. I don't know how I feel about Ben. I know that I can't jump right back into a relationship. As much as these first dates sucked, I'm allowing myself to be open to the possibilities, to meet new people, and maybe find the parts of me I may have lost while with Jake. And I'm getting to write for Lace & Dots magazine. That's sort of a big deal. I'm not ready to give that up. No way, I can't. I accept his order to forget the fact that his lips were just on mine and the perfect chaos it created inside of me.

We hug awkwardly, and I watch him walk down the stairs, silence filling the hall.

I flop face-first onto my cushiony bed. I feel Bob jump up and walk across my back, as usual, making himself comfortable on my lumbar spine.

"Bob... ugh. Why did he kiss me!?" I ask Bob, and he doesn't reply, *obviously*.

I grab a pillow, cover my head, and let out a loud, exaggerated sigh that sends Bob running away.

CHAPTER FOURTEEN

My life is spinning like a tornado.

My head throbs slightly, confused by last night's events. I can't dwell. I won't. I have a date tonight, and that's why I need to keep moving forward.

Before work, I joined Lucy and Briar at Sound Yoga for an early morning class.

I'm rubbing the sleep out of my eyes as I arrive. Lucy and I agreed last year that we would meet with Briar a minimum of once a month for this class. I know it's not much, only coming once a month, but life just seems to happen. Briar is so chill. I really should come more often and work on the equanimity thing people talk about. Respond, don't react. That's tough.

Pushing open the studio door, I find Lucy and Briar already on their mats. Briar looks like a swan, stretching her arms above her head and tilting to the side. Lucy is tapping away on her phone, waiting for class to begin. I claim a spot next to Briar and unroll my neon green mat, dropping my purse and coat beside me. Plopping down, my leggings roll down my

CHAPTER FOURTEEN

stomach. I hike them back over the small roll just for them to do the same thing. Who invented mid-waist leggings, anyway? I need them on my hips or up to my boobs to sit still, not this in-between crap.

Taking a deep breath, I already feel better.

Before I can say anything to Lucy or Briar, the instructor walks in.

We start class immediately with sun salutations, and I feel my body resisting as we do.

By the end of the class, I am damp with sweat. At least the sweat doesn't show through my leggings. I'll give them three stars.

We roll up our mats simultaneously. When we stand, Briar is chipper and humming. Lucy looks distracted by her phone again.

"What's going on Luce?" I ask.

Briar turns to her, but Lucy doesn't seem to hear me.

I place my hand on her arm. "Everything okay?"

"Oh, yeah, sorry. Work is crazy. I have a big pitch tomorrow. I'm not quite ready for it. They keep changing their mind on what they want, and it's making my head spin."

She continues to type on her phone.

We started walking towards the door. I put my coat on, and my leggings rolled down once again. Fuck it, I leave them as is.

We pour into the street and return to our cars.

I dump my stuff in the backseat and walk over to Briar's car, where they're both already seated inside. That was one of Lucy's conditions for joining Briar's class. Briar had to pick her up so she wouldn't bail.

Briar rolls down her window, and I peer inside.

The Dating Debacle

"Why don't we grab lunch this weekend?" I offer. Briar smiles and agrees. Lucy looks up, "Yeah, let's go for brunch, though. I'm craving bacon."

I laugh. "Brunch it is."

I walk back to my car as they peel away.

I'm not sure why I didn't bring up the kiss with Ben. I should have told them already, but a part of me wants to keep it to myself, for now, anyway. Lucy always thought Ben was crushing on me, but I never noticed before. Jake was my priority. I never noticed advances from anyone else.

It's weird that it's already been a few months since Jake and I ended things, and we only spoke that once when he came into the shop. Funny how someone can be your everything, and just like that, you never speak again. I guess that's just how things go.

I shower and get ready for work once I'm home.

I pulled out my little black dress for tonight and hung it from my shower rod, hoping the little wrinkles would magically disappear by tonight.

Bob rubs his side body against my leg, and I make my way to the kitchen.

"Bob, what in the world…" I look down at his bowls.

The water bowl is tilted on its side, water everywhere. There are random food pellets all over, most appearing inflated and soggy in the puddle.

Bob continues to rub against my legs, meowing.

"Bad, Bob," I say, pointing my finger at him and then shooing him away.

He takes off running in that random burst of energy only cats get.

I pick up his bowls and clean up the mess.

CHAPTER FOURTEEN

I can hear the sounds of the Cuban-influenced beats radiating from the large building as I step out of the car. I quickly text Lucy and Briar to let them know where I am and who I'm with and slide my phone into my tiny clutch.

The skirt of my black dress moves wildly in the breeze. I'm happy I chose a dress with a little less flare so I can keep my lady bits concealed. I don't know how much spinning I'm about to take part in, and the last thing I want to do is give everyone a show.

My red peep-toes clack loudly as I make my way up the stairs.

Once inside, I glance around the bar. Some couples are already dancing. I see a few sitting on the sidelines, obviously waiting for class to begin. I notice that I'm one of the few in a dress. Apparently, the internet misled me. I see women in tight skinny jeans, stilettos and crop tops.

The instructor is fiddling with his phone, connecting to a sound system.

I notice the bartender wiping down the bar. My nerves are going wild. I can feel myself shaking on the inside.

And then I see him.

At first glance, he is attractive, maybe more so than in his pictures online. He's not as tall as I imagined. He might actually be the same height as me in these heels. He's speaking with someone as I approach him, and once he notices me, he excuses himself.

His smile appears genuine as he takes my hands in his.

This is a first, not as welcoming as a hug, but friendlier than a handshake.

"Sofia, it is so nice to meet you. You look lovely," he says, his eyes not breaking his gaze from mine.

The Dating Debacle

I smile. "Thank you, it's nice to meet you, Blake." I wipe my palms down the sides of my dress.

I can barely hear him over the music, but I get the gist of what he says over the next few minutes. He tells me that once the class is over, the bar will open, and we can get a drink.

I should have downed a shot or two before coming.

My stomach is in knots, and I am feeling shy.

The music stops, and the instructor appears at the front of the stage.

He calls up a woman from the class and explains that they will show us what we will learn tonight. Everyone gathers closely as he starts the music again. I spend the next minute in awe. My mouth is wide open, and I gasp as he twirls the woman back and forth. Their hips are moving in sync, gliding across the stage. I can feel Blake looking at me.

When the dance is done, everyone claps. I look back at Blake nervously.

Yikes.

He takes my hand and leads me to a spot away from the others, off to the side. I think he wants me a bit out of the way so I don't slam into anyone. Good idea.

The instructor shows us the first eight counts, and we all mimic them on stage.

I'm moving my hips to the music, Blake leading the way. I step on his toes a few times and apologize profusely, but he insists I'm doing great. The instructor goes around to each couple, giving pointers, smiling, and clapping in excitement. We do the same for each set of eight counts. He demonstrates the moves, and then we practice on our own as he makes the rounds. Once we all have it, we add the parts together and practice that set until we move on.

CHAPTER FOURTEEN

Halfway through the class, the music stops, and he allows us to take a water break.

Blake and I make our way to two chairs. He hands me a bottle of water, and I graciously accept. I'm trying to calm my breathing so it doesn't show how out of shape I am.

"You're a really talented dancer," I say. "How long have you been taking classes?"

"Thank you." He's smiling, a crooked smile. "I've been dancing all my life. My parents taught me when I was little. Music always filled the house, and our hips were always moving." His thoughts appear to take him away from me and deep into his memories.

"That's amazing," I say. "My parents were always dancing around as well. We called them our kitchen dance parties." I laugh. "But I have never done ballroom or any couples-type dancing," I say, twisting the cap on my bottle.

"You'll get the hang of it; you are doing great." He puts his water down. "Dancing fills the soul," he begins as he places his hand over the center of his chest. " It's like two people sharing in the creative language, communicating through the art of dance."

When I realize how serious he is about dance, my eyes widen. I'm not sure I'm ready or willing to keep up with him.

He stands and takes my hand once again. He looks me over and asks if I'm ready for more.

I smile and nod.

We spend the next hour dancing, and I'm having a good time. Blake is a true gentleman, leading the way and teaching me the moves. Our hips move closely together, our hands intertwine, we come face to face, and yet - that's it. For as much as we're touching, there should be some sort of spark.

The Dating Debacle

There's nothing.

No feelings.

There is no flirting from Blake. He genuinely helps me learn the moves, encourages me, and we're having a good time. But that's it.

Class ends, and the music level rises. The doors are open to the public now, and the bar has a row of people in front of it. I agree to a drink when Blake proposes the idea.

We take it to a small table at the back, where we can hear ourselves a bit more.

We talk a bit more about ourselves, and I'm enjoying talking to Blake, but I can't stop thinking about how there's no spark. Not even a sizzle from a candle flame being smoldered by wet fingertips.

When we finish our drinks, he suggested we dance again.

"I think I'm actually going to head out," I say.

Blake nods. "Okay."

I smile. "Thank you so much for inviting me and teaching me some of your moves."

Blake helps me off the high stool.

Maybe it's all this gentleness. I mean, I don't necessarily like bad boys, and I'm not a masochist by any means, but there's just this brotherly way about him.

He walks me to the door and waits outside with me as I request an Uber.

"Can I see you again, Sofia?" he asks gently.

I'm smiling but sighing inside. This is hard. He's such a nice guy. "Um, I think there just seems to be something missing between us."

He nods, accepting my answer.

"I'm sorry," I reply.

CHAPTER FOURTEEN

"I appreciate having met you, it's been my pleasure. I wish you all the best."

My Uber arrives.

I can see him waving out the back window.

I have never met anyone my age with so much tact. I mentally wish him luck, and by the time I reach my place, I have mentally friend-zoned him.

I pour out my disappointment in my article for the week. After I finish, I read the comments on the Lace & Dots social media pages, and apparently, many think I should have seen Blake again. I guess sometimes feelings come with time. I don't know. I still feel like I made the right choice. I choose to ignore the comments and close the page. Maybe I won't read any more comments on my future articles.

CHAPTER FIFTEEN

I spin the gold-plated ring on my middle finger.

We are at brunch, Lucy, Briar, and I.

I think it's time to spill the beans about Ben.

Ben has been flat-out ignoring me, even though he was the one who started *and* stopped that kiss. I mean, it was for good reason, and I don't even know how I feel about it all, but still.

I want my friend back, and I need help.

Lucy has been giving us the details on her latest pitch, which went off without a hitch because obviously it's Lucy and she rocks. She'll land the account. She always does.

I don't know anyone in my life who works as hard as her. She's an inspiration. If you want it, you can have it - with hard work. That's her motto.

Briar talks about the kids in her class and then lets us in on the new guy at the yoga studio that she is crushing on. She tells me I should attend a yoga class for one of my dates. I rub the tops of my thighs, my quads tight from yesterday's yoga class and all the dancing the night before. I didn't think

CHAPTER FIFTEEN

that through–two workouts in one day. My metabolism is probably freaking out. I need some hash browns.

I tell the girls about my date with Blake.

"You need a one-nighter," Lucy declares.

Briar laughs.

"No!" I say, not really convincing myself or Lucy.

There's no more avoiding Ben and our kiss. I need to tell them.

"So… there's something that actually happened with Ben the other night…"

"Wait, what?" Lucy asks. "I want details, and why are we only hearing about this now?" Her eyes narrow at me.

Briar perks up in her chair, leaning in.

I sit back, feeling slightly defeated over the situation. I can't explain these feelings.

"Ben kissed me." I put it out there, plain and simple. It's off my chest, but why don't I feel better?

Lucy's eyes widen in surprise. "I knew it!"

"You knew what?"

"He likes you," she says. "He's liked you since you first started working there."

"That's not true, and anyway, it's messed everything up. He regrets it, and now he's evading me at work."

Briar's expression changes. I can tell she feels bad for me. Pity is the last thing I want.

"I just want Ben back, how we were," I say.

"First, tell us everything," Lucy says.

I start by explaining how Ben wanted to go for dinner and how I agreed. It's not like we have never hung out before. I tell them about the little flirts and about him grabbing me from behind, how he almost kissed me right outside my door.

The Dating Debacle

Lucy groans. "Well, nothing happened!"

My cheeks flush. I avoid her eyes.

"What is it? There's more you're not telling us."

"When we got into my apartment, he grabbed my face and just kissed me."

Briar speaks softly, "How was it?"

"Honestly, it was hot," I mutter, avoiding both their gazes. "So lately, um, I guess I have started feeling a little of the feels when he's around."

"Babe, why haven't you said anything?" Briar asks.

"I don't know, I just don't really know if I want to go there. And until the other night, I didn't know Ben wanted to go there either. Plus, I have this contract, and I'm writing again. And although some of my dates sucked, I kinda like this whole dating thing. I've never done this before."

"So, what happened after the kiss?" Lucy prods.

I shrug. "He just suddenly stopped and apologized. He said it was a mistake. He told me he likes me, but he doesn't think this will work while I'm dating other people. I didn't say much, but I agreed with him that I am under contract, and I do actually want to date people. We hugged, and he left. We haven't spoken since."

My heart sinks. I feel bad about the other night. Guilt has been running through me, but I didn't ask for this. I didn't ask Ben to kiss me. I mean it was great, no one has ever kissed me like that. I touch my lips where he left a memory of his on mine.

I feel like I'm on a roller coaster. I can't figure out what I want. But I know what I have to do.

"I want my friend back. How do I get him back as a friend?"

"Is that actually what you want?" Briar asks.

CHAPTER FIFTEEN

"I don't know, but that's what I need right now."

Lucy plays with her fork. "This guy likes you, Sofia. He's liked you for a long time. And you just told him you're not interested in him because you want to date other people. That's got to be hard on him, don't you think?"

My stomach sinks. I hadn't thought of it that way. How would I feel? I'd hate it. I didn't know Ben felt this way, how could I when he's the one asking about my dates.

Our food arrives, and I am saved from answering. Eventually, though, I broach the subject again.

"What do I do, guys?"

They exchange a look between them. They do this, and they know I hate it. This means that they don't technically agree with my decision but will help me anyway.

"You need to talk to him," Lucy says quietly.

"Ugh, can I just act like it never happened? Just go back to normal, as if it was last week."

"You know that can't happen without a talk."

Lucy's right, but I pout anyway. I don't like confrontation.

Briar hoists an eyebrow. "I can't believe he kissed you."

"I know, me either, actually."

"But you liked it?" she asks.

"I did." I think back to the way his eyes hooded as he came towards me or how he licked his lips after he parted from mine. I feel a little sadness overcome me that I choose to ignore, and I shove the memory away. "Anyway, I have to keep dating. I think I might reach out to that cook I was talking to."

Even as I say the words, guilt coils in my stomach. Ben deserves better. He deserves someone who wants him with his whole heart.

Briar smiles. "The chef sounds nice."

Lucy laughs. "Apparently, our girl here doesn't want nice."
I laugh but smack her in the arm playfully.
"I want sizzle," I say.
"Who doesn't?" Lucy agrees. "Maybe he will cook for you?"
"That'd be sweet," Briar says.
I nod in agreement.

We each have another mimosa, order another plate of bacon, and agree to go to another yoga class next week with Briar to check out this man-bun yogi. She sounds elated.

I walk through the front door of Plants, Pottery & Books, holding the yellow box from the donut shop down the street. I decided donuts would be the icebreaker. If in doubt, bring food. Although this is the second time this week I brought Ben donuts. But it should do the trick. Some chocolate and sugar couldn't make the situation between Ben and me any worse, that's for sure.

I can feel the tension coming from Ben when he spots me. His brows furrow. He looks down at the box I'm holding, and I can see his demeanor shift...slightly.

"Hey," I say as I approach him slowly, like a lion approaching its prey.

I'm nervous. I haven't been able to get that kiss out of my head since it happened, despite the attempts at locking it up in the tiny little box in the back of my mind.

I can see Ben contemplating his words. The shop is empty, and there's nothing between us except a giant cactus. I make my way around it, coming up to Ben. I put the box of donuts down and open it for Ben to see his favorites sitting there, facing him.

"You must be their most frequent customer," Ben declares, looking up from the donuts and finally making eye contact

CHAPTER FIFTEEN

with me.

I smile. Okay, donuts were the right option.

"Ha-ha, very funny," I reply. "As a matter of fact, I think they just like the fact that I provide comic entertainment by embarrassing myself every time I go in there. Their display cabinet glass is too clean, and I whack my forehead on it every time." I can see Ben starting to smile.

"Maybe learn to keep some distance between yourself and the donuts," he says, shrugging his shoulders but holding back a smile.

Phew.

Ben takes the cinnamon-covered donut, and I internally sigh with relief. I was really craving the lemon one.

The clock behind the counter shows that I have five minutes before I need to take over for Emily at the bookshop.

I close the box.

"Thanks," Ben replies, holding his donut up in a *cheers* kind of way.

I watch him bite into it and stand back, looking around the room, avoiding his mouth altogether.

"So…" I start, not sure where to go from here. "About the other night…"

"No worries, Sof. It was a bad idea. Let's just move on from it."

I can see a touch of sadness cross his face. I can feel the same sadness throughout my body, from my head down to my toes.

He's right.

Bad idea.

We couldn't possibly start something now. We're friends anyway, and I don't want to lose that. Although a part of me worries that I already have. My mind drifts as I think about

The Dating Debacle

what it would like to date Ben. He's sweet. He really is a great guy. He's kind, playful, and respects me. What is wrong with me? Why am I not jumping at the chance to be with him? No. It's settled, we're friends. I have to put my career in front of love right now. But wait, my career is love right now. Is there a way to try things out with Ben? I halt all incoming thoughts and decide that Ben deserves someone who will put in as much as he would. I can't do that right now. I don't want to. Timing is everything, and now is not the time. It's decided.

"Okay, I'm happy you are my friend, Ben." I force a smile, and I see him do the same. We just need time. Time to forget how my hips kept trying to meet his as his hands were trailing down the sides of my face in a way only someone who cares about you does. Okay so my mind has decided, but it might take my body a little longer to agree.

"Same," he says, finishing his donut.

Okay, good talk. It's a start.

"I'll see you later?" I ask as I walk towards the back of the store.

He nods and gives a small wave.

In the bookshop, Emily is on her phone. She hangs up as I approach the counter, her eyes widening as she sees the box of donuts.

"Oh! What kind did you get?" she asks excitedly. She opens it up and grabs the lemon one. Damn.

"Wasn't sure you'd want one," I say, taking the one covered in sprinkles.

There's never a bad time to eat sprinkles, but I'm eyeing the lemon one she just bit into. I'm having food envy again. This happens a lot. Maybe too often.

"I'm going to the gym, so I need some energy. Was a late-

CHAPTER FIFTEEN

night last night."

My eyebrows lift, questioning. "Oh?"

"Girls night." She replies. No follow-up needed. "How are the dates going?" she asks, leaning her elbows on the counter.

"I went dancing. It was fun."

"Dancing, like to a bar for a date?" she asks, wrinkling her nose.

"Not a bar-bar, well, not initially," I say. "We had a salsa dance class and then had a drink."

"Ooh, sounds like a sexy night."

"Meh, no spark," I reply, taking another bite.

"Ah, too bad. Maybe the next one," she says enthusiastically. I nod. "Maybe."

But I'm thinking about the spark with Ben.

No, stop it.

I decide then and there. I can't keep going back to that kiss.

I pull out my phone, ready to swipe more. But first, I need to message the cook.

Emily grabs her bag. "Well, I'm off. Thanks for the donut, Sof. I'll see you tomorrow."

"Have fun at the gym," I say, settling behind the counter. I open the App and hit reply to the chef's latest message.

Booklover (Sofia): I would love to meet up sometime. What did you have in mind?

GourmetFoodie (Ty): Hey Booklover, been a few days. How are you?

Oh, yeah. Maybe he's already moved on to someone else. I hadn't thought about that.

Booklover (Sofia): Hey, yeah. Sorry, I've been slow at responding. I've been good though.

Am I supposed to tell him I was on a date with someone else

The Dating Debacle

or that I kissed my friend?

No!

And no!

I can hear Lucy in my head, mentally answering me.

GourmetFoodie (Ty): Good to hear. Life gets busy, I understand.

Booklover (Sofia): Yeah, and just at work now.

GourmetFoodie (Ty): I'm headed there myself in a few minutes, but I'd love to cook you dinner if you're interested.

I light up probably more than I should, but dating is kind of exciting.

Booklover (Sofia): That sounds great.

GourmetFoodie (Ty): Great, how's tomorrow night?

Booklover (Sofia): Perfect. Do I meet you at your restaurant?

GourmetFoodie (Ty): I'm off tomorrow. Why don't you come to my place? Do you have any allergies?

It's thoughtful of him to ask if I have any allergies. Not that I do, but I'll give him brownie points there.

Booklover (Sofia): No allergies. Sure, what's your address?

Ty sends me his address, and we confirm the time. I open the friend group chat with Lucy and Briar and give them the basic details.

Lucy: Nice, a girl's got to eat.

Me: Lol

Briar: That's nice. Which restaurant does he work at?

Me: Um, I'm actually going to his place. He's off tomorrow night.

Lucy: No, you're not!

CHAPTER FIFTEEN

Briar: You can't go to some strange guy's house Sofia.
Me: What's the big deal?
Lucy: Do you not listen to murder podcasts?
Me: No, no I don't. Guys, I'll be fine. I'll text you his address and I will follow up while I'm there. I'll just go to the washroom and message you.
Briar: You better.
Lucy: I'll be sitting by my phone, baseball bat in hand. You better update us.
Me: Come on, Lucy. A baseball bat, really? Do you even own one? Lol
Lucy: Yes, and I'm not afraid to use it.
Me: Plus, you guys have my SNAPCHAT Location, so you can track me. If you see me going for a swim in the river, know that I am not swimming, and my body might have been pushed overboard.
Briar: Not funny, Sof.
Me: I'll be fine, but thanks for the concern.

A young woman enters the bookstore, eyeing me as she sees me texting.

I smile at her. "Hi."

She replies, 'Hi,' not making eye contact, and makes her way to the young adult section.

Me: Guys, I've got to go. I have a customer. Talk later! xo

I put my phone down and approached the girl.

"Can I help you find anything?" I asked in my friendly, customer service voice. I didn't think I had 'that voice,' but Ben laughs at me and tells me I do. He says I 'turn it on' as soon as someone walks in.

"Just looking." Her fingers trail the spines of the books as

The Dating Debacle

she looks at them one by one.

"I've got a great enemy to lovers, a fantasy that just came in by the front desk. Looks like a fun read," I say. "It's by a local author."

Her expression perks up.

"Sure, I love fantasy."

"I've got an entire table of them here, but this is the new one." I pick up one of the copies that was just brought in. My hand glides over the dark cover.

She takes it and scans the back cover. She opens it up to the author's bio. "I want to be a fantasy writer one day," she admits.

I smile. I know what that feels like.

"That's great," I say. "You should totally do that."

"I'll take it."

She pays for her book and heads out the door. I see Ben peering through the entrance as she is leaving.

I open my laptop and look at the shop's calendar. Emily and I have been saying we should host a writing seminar. I think one for young adults would be a great idea.

I spend the rest of my shift helping customers and planning a writing workshop for the following month. I text Emily, and she's in.

I prepare a mass email and send it to everyone on our mailing list. I print a few posters and bring one to Ben for the plant shop.

"Hey," I say as I approach. He's playing in the soil. I know this is his favorite part of the job. Planting seeds so he can watch them grow. "Can I put up a flyer?" I ask. Expecting the answer is already yes, I make my way to the bulletin board at the store's entrance.

CHAPTER FIFTEEN

"Sure, what's it for?" he asks, taking his hands out of the dirt and wiping them on a cloth beside him, pieces of dirt crumbling to the countertop.

"Just a sec," I say, and I pin up my poster. When I see that it's straight, I return to the store.

I walk around a couple arguing over how many plants to buy. I think back to when Jake would argue that I spent way too much money on books. You can never have too many plants or books.

I approach Ben. "We're having a writing workshop for young adults next month."

"That's a good idea. I'm sure you'll get a lot of interest."

"Yeah, I sent an email over to the local high school too," I say as I head towards the door to the bookstore. "Gotta go. I'm alone this afternoon. Thanks!"

He nods in understanding and grabs another pot, fingerprints of dirt now marking the sides.

CHAPTER SIXTEEN

I'm digging through my jewelry box, looking for my small gold hoops. My feet are all warm and cozy in my short ankle boots. They match the dark blue mom jeans I'm wearing with a cropped green sweater. I put on a pair of long, dangly boho earrings and gaze into the full-length mirror.

Nerves run through me. I think I let Briar and Lucy get into my head. What are the chances I will actually get murdered on this date? I would think it's slim. I check that I have my travel-size hairspray in my bag. It's not pepper spray, but that shit burns the eyes. It's something. Something is better than nothing.

How am I going to let him even offer me a drink? How will I know if he's slipped something into it? Oh. My. God. My mind is running like a hamster on its wheel. I'll only drink water, I decide. I blame Lucy and mentally curse her. Obviously, she is just looking out for me, but she knows I have anxiety. I'm an overthinker, and not in a good, productive way.

CHAPTER SIXTEEN

Okay, now I am going back and forth. Do I cancel the date? I'm spiraling.

Fuck it.

I'll chance it. I am not going to get kidnapped or murdered today.

I'm a ball of nerves when I look at the time and realize it's almost time to go.

Why is dating so hard? Why do you have to assume everyone is a liar, a thief, a murderer, or even sixteen years old? Okay, if I had to choose to be catfished, I am one hundred percent glad it was by a sixteen-year-old and not some random creepy old man. I shudder at the thought.

Okay, Sof, you're not helping the nerves with these thoughts.

I turn back to the mirror.

I am open to new experiences; I am open to love, and I will enjoy myself tonight.

Satisfied with my affirmations, I head to the couch and sit beside Bob. He immediately stands and sits on my lap. Leaning my back against the couch, I sigh, petting him lightly. He purrs, and I focus on the sound and the vibrations. I inhale, and I exhale. I suddenly feel maybe two percent calmer. Okay, that's as good as it is going to get.

Lucy is no nonsense when it comes to dating. Her intuition guides her constantly. I don't think I have one of those. An intuition. I think I may be gullible or naïve. So I'm told.

"Okay, it's time, Bob." I pet him one last time and gently try to shoo him off of my lap.

He doesn't budge, and he just looks up at me.

"Bob, I gotta go," I say, a little annoyed this time.

Nothing.

I go to stand, and he slides off my legs and scatters as soon

The Dating Debacle

as he hits the ground.

"Sorry, dude." He's in the hallway now, glaring at me.

"See you later. If I don't get murdered." That last part comes out in a whisper.

Turns out Ty lives less than ten minutes away from me. If things go well, that's definitely a bonus. Traffic here sucks to get across town.

I pull up to a brown brick home. Large trees surround the house. It's a friendly-looking bungalow. I see a blue SUV in the driveway. Oh, thank god, he doesn't have a trunk to stash me in.

Before I get out of my car, I text Briar and Lucy that I'm here. I take a picture of his SUV with plates, just in case, and send it to them. The thoughts in my head are getting out of control.

I want to turn around the minute I step out of the car. But I don't. This is all part of the experience. I wonder why I have to feel moderately terrified to meet a new guy—to date. I doubt my parents had to worry about this when they were younger.

I hear my phone chirp and look down. Lucy responds with a thumbs up.

The spring gardening has already been done. The flower beds are ready for planting, and fresh ground lays still. I'm walking pretty slowly, taking in my surroundings. I make my way to the side door, and I ring the doorbell.

Nothing.

I wait.

How long should one wait before they ring again?

Is this a sign?

Do I run?

CHAPTER SIXTEEN

I wait another minute. I ring again.

I hear a loud but muffled "Come in" from inside the house.

Oh, he's cooking and probably has his hands all dirty or something with chicken.

I open the door slowly, peering in before I commit to stepping inside.

"Hey Sofia, come in." I hear it louder this time. I close the door behind me. "Sorry, my hands are full," Ty calls out.

Called it. Chicken. I knew it.

I start up the steps and make my way to the landing.

I halt. I can see Ty standing behind an island, hands in oven mitts. He's setting down a casserole dish of food, steaming.

My eyes dart to the apron he is wearing. It's bright red and says 'Kiss the cook'. Okay, cute. Must have been a Christmas present or something. But that's not what's got my attention.

He's shirtless.

Ty is cooking shirtless.

"Come in, come in," he says, smiling brightly. "It's so great to meet you. Sorry I couldn't come let you in - just a second."

He's taking off his mitts. I'm waiting, hanging back a bit, wondering what my intuition will tell me. You know, if I have one. But I do notice one thing, and it's not my intuition speaking.

This man is HOT. He is so much cuter than his pictures. And that chest. I'm now staring at his broad shoulders. I have yet to mutter any words of greeting. Nothing. I'm standing here like a deer caught in headlights.

"Hi," I utter and take a step closer. Ty is making his way around the island, and I stop short.

Ty isn't shirtless.

I was wrong.

The Dating Debacle

Ty is NAKED! As in N-A-K-E-D. All except his bright red apron, which hits his upper thighs, barely covering his man parts. His legs are dark and muscular.

No.

Stop it, Sofia. This is not okay.

"Um..." I start.

He's walking right up to me as if this is nothing. As if he doesn't realize he is naked.

Does he know he is? Did he get so preoccupied with cooking that he forgot to get dressed?

He's almost reached me when my hand goes up without thinking in a kind of talk-to-the-hand type of way.

The words are coming out of my mouth before I can stop them.

"Oh, HELL NO," I say.

He frowns but stops dead in his tracks.

"Not doing this," I mutter. I turn on my heels, and I am out the door in ten seconds.

I don't look back until I'm in my car and lock the doors.

This has got to be a record. Two dates that lasted less than five minutes.

I back out of his driveway and thank my lucky stars that he didn't decide to follow me out the door and make a scene. I don't know what I'd have done.

As soon as I'm home, I open the group text.

Me: Guys, I'm home.

Lucy responds right away.

Lucy: What'd he do? I've got my bat ready.
Me: He didn't do anything. But he was naked!
Lucy: So why aren't you in bed with him right now?
Me: Are you kidding me?

CHAPTER SIXTEEN

Lucy: Well, I mean, he probably wasn't going to murder you if he was naked.

Me: Ugh, I let you get me all caught up in my head, and I was so paranoid, and he was naked. No, not okay. This isn't how I want to date. I want to date-date. Not just eat and hook up. It's too soon to laugh about this, but I'm sure one day I'll be wondering why I turned down a free meal and a hot, naked guy.

Briar: Glad you're safe, Sof. Good idea. Glad you got out of there. Who knows what could have happened?

Lucy: You girls don't know how to have fun. JK.

Briar: Come on, Luce. Lay off.

Lucy: I'm just kidding. Glad you're home safe too. Don't give up hope. Lots of fish out there.

Me: Thanks guys.

We chat a little longer. I give them all the deets from the time I arrived to the time I left, including the 'kiss the cook' apron and the toned legs.

I'm back on my couch, peppermint tea in hand, and a menu for Chinese food. I still have to eat.

While I wait for my dinner to arrive, I decide I may as well start my article.

So, I decided to date online...
by: Sofia Daria

So, I decided to date online... and he was naked.

You might be wondering, WHAT?
Yup, I showed up for our date, and my date had nothing on except a 'kiss the cook' apron.

The Dating Debacle

Again, I haven't been spending a lot of time chatting up people before meeting them. Maybe this is a bad thing? Or is it a good thing because I'm not wasting my precious time on dudes who are underage, are rude, or, um, only want a hook-up?

I think I'll keep it as is. I might as well find out the cold, hard truth as soon as possible.

So, let's go to the beginning...

I wrap up the story with a positive spin on how I'm ready to keep going, to keep swiping. But right now, I'm too exhausted to even think.

CHAPTER SEVENTEEN

I cross my right leg over my body, resting on a large pillow. I think the instructor called this a bolster. My back is pressed firmly into the ground, my arms stretched, head turned to the right. I'm facing Lucy's back. I think my eyes are supposed to be closed, but my mind is wide awake, and therefore, so are my eyes.

Beside Lucy is Briar. Beside Briar is Aiden.

Aiden, Briar's new love interest, has his hair tight in a bun on top of his head. He's wearing these cool boho baggy pants, and I want some.

I'm looking around the room. There are only about ten people. A restorative class. Briar says this will relax me mentally and physically from my recent sporadic energy coming from online dating. My body feels pretty good at the moment. My mind is another story.

I dreamed of Ben last night. Ben in the kitchen, as naked as Ty was.

I woke up with a curious feeling in the pit of my stomach.

The Dating Debacle

My subconscious mind took my almost date with Ty and turned it into a full-on sweat fest with Ben.

I walked into the kitchen as I had with Ty, and in his place, Ben stood with the famous red apron, wearing nothing underneath.

I'm not sure what my subconscious is trying to do to me, but I'm only human.

I noticed his strong, tanned legs as he approached me.

He took me and placed me gently on the kitchen island, and then all this pre-sex stuff happened.

I shiver at the thought.

I remember the dream in little slivers of memories. Like clips or a trailer for a movie.

I can still see us kissing. His hands, touching me, running over every inch of me.

Roasted baby potatoes rolling across the counter, some landing on the floor as he lays me down.

I snap back to reality when I see Lucy change positions. Zoning out, I didn't hear the instructions. Following her lead, I turn onto my stomach, bringing my left leg up beside my body. I turn my head to face the opposite direction.

I breathe in; I breathe out.

I close my eyes, thinking back on the past few dates. Thinking of last night's dream. Thinking of Ben. The butterflies haven't stopped. Ben came into the bookstore yesterday, and he helped me carry some boxes that had been dropped off. When he took the box from me, I felt his hand touch mine briefly. Our eyes met, and I felt it. The spark. I think he feels it too. He glanced away, the spark fizzling.

We both know nothing can happen between us. I'm dating other people.

CHAPTER SEVENTEEN

I have a meeting with Miriam next week, and she wants me to date a bit more before we meet.

I hear movement and open my eyes. Everyone is shifting legs, and I follow along.

I close my eyes again and let my mind settle. I add last night's dream to the closed box in the back of my mind, and I try an affirmation to stop the racing going on inside my head.

This moment is for me and me alone. I welcome peace and tranquility.

It must have worked because the next thing I know, class is done and Lucy is shaking me. Oops. I think I fell asleep.

I pack up my mat and let my hair fall loose from my small ponytail.

Briar informs us she's going out for coffee with Aiden and that she'll talk to us later. Lucy and I walk out of the building into the fresh air. The sun is shining. We decide to go to breakfast at the diner down the street. I notice store owners setting up shop as we pass. An older couple is sitting on a bench in front of the bank. Lucy's talking about work and her new client. I bring my attention back to her as we make our way into the small restaurant and choose a booth by the window so we can people-watch.

We order our breakfast and get comfortable.

"I need some new clothes." Lucy starts as she pulls off her sweater.

"Let's go shopping after this," I suggest.

"Can't today, but maybe this weekend?"

"Yeah, sure."

She looks at me with intent. "Any more dates this week?"

"Nothing yet," I admit.

"Take out your phone. Let's look at some of your options."

The Dating Debacle

I do as she says and take my phone out, opening the App. There are a few new matches and a couple of messages I have yet to read. I open the first one. Meh, not feeling it, I tell Lucy that exact thought.

"What kind of guys are you swiping on?" she asks, taking my phone from me.

"I don't know, cute ones." I lift my shoulders, feeling slightly embarrassed. "I read their catch line and swipe based on that and their looks combined," I say, trying to make myself sound better. "The feeling I get from looking at their picture. But obviously, I can't seem to read people right." I think back to the matches I've made so far.

"Okay, so you have to open their profile and actually read it, Sof." She's tapping on a profile. "This will help you rule out some, and you might find that you're interested in someone you might not normally have swiped on."

"Okay."

She's right. Maybe I have been a little shallow. I'm certainly reaping the rewards of shallow pics.

"Check this guy out." Lucy indicates a profile. "He loves trivia nights, road trips, reading, and hiking. He is looking to meet someone who enjoys similar things. You love trivia nights. I'm swiping on him."

I peer over her shoulder and see that he isn't someone I would normally swipe right on. He's got limp, untamed hair and a gentle smile. He looks kind, but his hair would have been enough to turn me away.

Our breakfast arrives shortly after having read a few more profiles. I've matched with a few others, and I promise Lucy I will send them messages when I get home. All of them being guys that I probably wouldn't have swiped without her help.

CHAPTER SEVENTEEN

She tells me I have walls up and that maybe I have been keeping myself closed off to potential matches because I'm not ready to meet the right guy. She could be right. I am picky, but isn't that just having standards and knowing what I want?

We spend the next hour finishing our breakfast, talking, and people-watching as the shops on the street open and the sidewalk crowds. I purposely veer away from any talk about Ben, and I keep last night's dream shenanigans to myself.

The waitress brings us our bills, and Lucy grabs mine to pay. I learned a long time ago not to fight this with her, to thank her, and to remind myself to grab the bills first next time.

"Thank you." I smile. She side-hugs me in the booth.

"You're welcome."

* * *

Swipe left. Swipe left. Swipe left. Swipe right. Swipe left.

I think I'm giving myself carpel tunnel. Rotating my wrist, I stretch out the length of my fingers. I've matched with several guys and have a few messages to respond to.

I learned that one of them hates the beach...deal-breaker.

One is a heavy gamer and doesn't work...deal-breaker.

I caught one in a lie...deal-breaker. He started by saying he is pretty quiet, reads, and enjoys breakfasts and game nights with friends. He sounded very similar to me.

Almost too similar to me.

I asked a few questions about his friends and work, and his answers contradicted what his profile said. No one has time for that.

I start talking to Callum, an athlete and a personal trainer. He appears confident in his messages but not cocky. He tells

The Dating Debacle

me he has season tickets to the local football games and asks if I have ever been to one. I told him no, but that going to one was actually on my bucket list and that I would love to go. Callum tells me there is a game on Saturday night and that he would love to take me to dinner and then to the game. I can't wait to see the cheerleaders, if I'm being honest. To see the girls throw themselves into the air would be pretty cool.

We spent the next few days chatting. I'm working every day until Saturday, but I find myself daydreaming and gradually getting excited to meet him. I learn that Callum is an only child, like me, and that he loves animals and also has a cat. We bond over our feline's quirks.

Booklover (Sofia): I don't really play sports, except for badminton. I'm sort of afraid of the ball...

Trainer1997 (Callum): I need to hear more about this lol

Booklover (Sofia): There was an incident back in fifth grade during a very aggressive game of dodgeball lol

Trainer1997 (Callum): Oh, no! Lmao. Kids either love the game or hate. Depending if you're the easy target or the cocky jock.

Booklover (Sofia): I think we both know where we each stood back in 5th grade when it comes to dodgeball Haha

Trainer1997 (Callum): Hey, not cocky! I just had a good arm lol

I was definitely the someone who spent a lot of gym classes running back and forth, trying to avoid being hit by the ball in a state of panic.

I'm probably jumping ahead, but talking to Callum, I get the impression I'd feel safe around him. Like he is a hero from a movie that would wrap me in his muscular arms, tell me

CHAPTER SEVENTEEN

everything will be okay, and kiss me gently on the top of my head.

When Saturday comes and I see him standing at the entrance to the restaurant, my eyes run over him, noticing his broad shoulders, tall stance, and clean-shaven face. Maybe Lucy was right. Maybe getting to know someone's personality immediately makes them more attractive. He is incredibly attractive, but I wouldn't have swiped right based on his appearance alone. I tend to go towards the dark-haired, stubbly type.

As I approach him, I feel my smile growing. He notices me and hurries forward, embracing me in a big hug and lifting me right off the ground. My legs wrap around his waist. We hug as if we are already romantically involved.

Did I just have one of those moments only seen on *The Bachelor*? Where the woman runs into their arms, and they greet each other with full-on body contact? Huh, I didn't expect myself to be one of those. I think I like it.

He sets me down, and his voice is deeper than I imagined when he tells me how excited he is to meet me. He takes my hand in his, and I feel tiny next to him. Callum leads the way into the restaurant, and the hostess shows us to a table. Opening our menus, we glance over them but spend our time talking, continuing conversations that we started by chat.

When our waitress stops by for the third time, we decide we should order our food so we aren't late for the game. Conversation with him is easy. We talk about everything and anything. He listens intently as I speak and acknowledges every word I say, appearing to soak it in. I feel the love goggles sliding onto my face. I'm in lust. Maybe this is love at first sight? I notice his strong jawline, and although he is quite

The Dating Debacle

health-oriented, he orders fries and eats every last one of them. He explains to me how he believes in moderation and treating yourself.

We finish our meals, and he requests the bill. Once he has paid for our meals, I decide to run to the washroom before we head to the game since it's a few blocks away and we're walking. I'm returning to the table, and I see him on the phone. I stand back to give him some privacy, but I hear him mutter the words *I love you* into the phone. He hangs up, and I slide back into the booth. A lump has formed in my throat.

He looks surprised.

I raise my eyebrows quizzically.

He knows I heard him and starts explaining how his mom just called, and he thought since I was in the washroom, he wouldn't be rude by answering. I smile and tell him, of course, and ask if everything is okay. The lump melts, and I can swallow again. He tells me he's close with his parents and that his mom checks in from time to time when he's out. I think that's sweet—to hear him tell his mom that he loves her and that she checks in. I think I've got myself a good guy.

It's gotten cooler with the sun setting, and I pull on the hoodie I brought with me for the game. Callum takes my hand as we walk, and I feel the tender touch of his thumb stroking my hand in his.

I feel them. The butterflies.

We have amazing seats. We sit, and I can see the players warming up on the field without squinting. The cheerleaders are dancing at the center of it all. I'm in awe and feel a different type of excitement in my chest, one that I haven't felt in a while.

Callum explains a bit more of the rules to me, and the players return to their locker room to get ready for the game.

CHAPTER SEVENTEEN

The cheerleaders take their spots and start a fresh routine. I'm watching with pure delight. Callum's hand slips from mine, and I watch from the corner of my eye. He's pulled out his phone from his pocket, glancing at the screen. I see 'mom' light up. He silences it and returns it to his pocket, grabbing my hand again.

That's weird, isn't it, his mom calling again? It hasn't even been an hour since we left the restaurant.

I push the thought aside since Callum doesn't seem to be bothered by it, and we enjoy the game.

When intermission starts, Callum stands. "Let's get some drinks." I watch as he stretches his long legs, and I'm suddenly reminded of Ben's toned ones from my dream. I internally sigh and tell myself to stop. I shake my head and bring my attention back to Callum, willing myself to enjoy this date with Callum. He's a great guy.

"Yeah, sure."

I hear a phone vibrating as we stand in line, and once again, Callum is taking his phone out of his pocket. He apologizes and tells me he'll just be a moment, stepping out from the line.

I hope that there isn't some sort of family emergency.

He returns just as I'm reaching the counter, and he orders and pays for both our drinks. I thank him, and we return to our seats.

"My mom's a bit overprotective," he admits as we sit.

Three times in less than two hours. Three calls. That can't be normal.

I let it go as the game starts up again. This has got to be one of the best dates I've had.

Callum is gentle and attentive, and I am excited that maybe there will be a second date. Our hands link together

The Dating Debacle

effortlessly, and I lean into him.

When the game is over, he invites me to share an Uber since we live somewhat in the same direction. I say yes, smiling. I'm suddenly aware of how soft-looking his lips are. How they curve up when he looks at me. His piercing blue eyes, sun-kissed hair, and his deep voice that stirs things deep within me.

The Uber arrives, and he asks me if I want to go to his place for a drink. I know what this means, and I nod yes, the butterflies stirring inside me. Turns out, I'll Netflix and Chill if it's the right guy.

We hold hands the length of the car ride. "I had such a good time," he says.

"Me too," I respond as the car pulls into a driveway.

I'm shocked by the size of the house.

It's a two-story with a brick façade. The front yard is large and full of beautiful trees and flower beds with freshly planted flowers. I see a stone path leading around the house and an in-ground pool lit by fairy lights on the fence enclosing it. I imagine there's a hot tub nearby, and I see a pool house at the back of the property.

I had no idea a personal trainer in his early twenties could afford such a house.

"Your place is amazing," I say.

"Want a tour of the pool?" he asks.

I notice how much I like him leading me. Like he is a man who would take care of his woman.

The pool is even more amazing up close, and I see the hot tub further back near the pool house. "The pool is heated, so we opened it quite early in the year."

He sits on one of the lounge chairs and pulls me down onto

CHAPTER SEVENTEEN

him, the tour ending before it really began. Our lips are nearly touching when I turn to face him, and he releases his tight arms from around me. We stop and have this moment. I can feel heat building just through our eye contact. A shiver runs down my spine.

I can feel him underneath me, and that creates this want inside of me. Before I can react and kiss him, his lips are on mine with a heat and passion I can't explain. We kiss hard, his hands sliding up and down the sides of my body.

I hear his phone vibrate. We ignore it and continue kissing as if we're long-lost lovers and it's been years since our lips met. I turn my body, lifting my leg over him until I'm straddling him. He picks me up, and my legs wrap around his waist.

We're walking, and I'm not sure where he's taking me, but I feel safe in his arms. I trust him. Our lips part as he walks up to the pool house, and he opens the door. I'm in his arms, and he's still carrying me as if I am nothing more than a feather. I feel glorious. He sets me down on a bed in the middle of the room and asks me if this is okay. I nod, unable to speak. I look around the room. It seems to be like a small bachelor apartment, everything all in one room. He takes off his shoes, looking at me.

"Do you want to go in the hot tub?" he asks.

CHAPTER EIGHTEEN

My heart is pounding, and my hands are shaking in excitement. I peel my jeans down around my ankles and toss them onto the nearby chair with the rest of my clothes. I'm left in a strapless bra and underwear. Callum is already in the hot tub. When he asked if I wanted to go in, I couldn't think of a reason to say no.

I want this.

I want Callum. Maybe this is what I need to push the thoughts of Ben out of my mind for good. I turn my thoughts back to Callum.

He's watching me with fire in his eyes. I can tell he feels what I'm feeling. There's a mutual want. My feet tingle as I step into the steamy water. The air is cool on my skin, prompting me to move a little quicker. I can see him watching me, watching the effect that the air has on my skin as the tiny hairs on my arms stand. I sit across from him and give him a sexy smile.

"Are you okay?" he asks.

Okay, maybe I need to work on my sexy. He's asked this a

CHAPTER EIGHTEEN

few times since I agreed to get into the hot tub. I tell him I'm perfect.

I can hear his phone vibrate from his pants on the nearby chair. My mind is quickly brought back to him as he moves closer to me. I can't help but watch him as he stands, taking in all of him as he closes the gap between us. Once he's sitting next to me, I turn towards him, my lips wanting his. He is only inches away, and I wait for them to touch mine when I close my eyes. I'm surprised when I feel them touch my neck, kissing me slowly at first. I press my hand against his chest, soft curls between my fingers, tilting my head toward him.

He stops, and his lips are on mine for a moment. I feel him scoop me up with little effort, and I'm back on top of him. I love this. We're kissing, hands touching, sounds escaping when I hear a noise. Again, my attention is brought back to him, his arms wrapped tightly around me. Then I hear a voice nearby. I pull away quickly, startled.

"Did you hear that?" I ask, my breath hard and raspy.

He takes my mouth again, and between kisses, he tells me no.

"Callum!" I hear someone call his name and pull back, further this time. I can tell he heard it this time, too.

"What the fuck?" he asks no one in particular. I look into the darkness, and suddenly, I see a shape forming at a distance brought on by the overhead fairy lights.

"Oh my God," I say in a start, and I'm off his lap in seconds, sitting low in the water, hiding. "Who is that?" I ask quietly, turning towards him.

I see him squint into the darkness. "Oh, that's just my mom," he says.

What in the actual cheese and crackers did he just say?

The Dating Debacle

"Your mom?" I ask, confused.

"Callum." the shape takes more of a form as it reaches the pool. I can see a woman. "Callum, I have been calling you. Why aren't you answering?" she asks, walking right up to the hot tub, paying me no attention in particular.

"Mom, I'm on a date. I'll see you inside later," he replies.

I see his mom glance from me to my bare shoulders, to our clothes spread across two lounge chairs. I'm quiet, unsure where to go from here. I say nothing. His mom turns back to me, acknowledging me with a disapproving frown.

"When I call you, Callum, I expect you to answer, regardless of whether you have a *date* or not," she says, and my eyes widen in shock. She says *date* as if she thinks I'm only here for a hook-up.

I sit up a little taller.

"Get rid of her and come clean up the mess you left in the kitchen." She turns swiftly, and I watch her until she turns back into a shadow, and suddenly she is out of sight.

"I'm sorry," he says. "But you gotta go. My mom's pretty pissed."

"What?"

He stands, getting out of the hot tub, then grabs a nearby towel.

Again, I say, "What?"

"Look, my mom doesn't seem to like you, so this isn't going to work."

I'm in shock. All rational thinking has left my brain. I'm at a loss.

"Do you live with your parents?"

He nods, pulling on his pants. "Yeah, I don't pay rent. I have access to this sick pool and hot tub anytime I want…" He goes

CHAPTER EIGHTEEN

on, but I stop listening.

"Maybe you should add that to your profile," I say. "Mama's boy who still lives at home."

He throws me a towel, "Look, I'm sorry she doesn't like you, but I can't be with someone she doesn't approve of." I catch the towel as the ends dip into the water.

He turns away from me. "Get dressed and go, please."

He walks away as I sit there, stunned. Utterly mortified that I have put myself in this situation. The nerve of her! The nerve of him!

I wait till his shadow is gone before I exit the hot tub. I dress quickly and turn on my phone, requesting a car.

I'm home and in bed within the hour.

Well, I think to myself, that was HOT until it wasn't.

***

I'm still at a loss for words when I think about last night. I'm keeping busy re-arranging the books on the shelves in the shop. Ben's been in to water the plants, and I've made sure not to make any comments about what happened on my date. I didn't tell him I was going on another one. We both know I'm talking to guys and dating, and that's all that needs to be said.

I've been thinking about how I'm going to write my next article.

I called Lucy after I got into bed and fell apart. I just started crying, and I know I did nothing wrong, but I felt horrible inside by the time I washed my face and pulled on clean PJs. Why is dating so hard?

Lucy listened as I spoke. I told her how I was really

excited about Callum. He had so many pros and so few cons. Obviously, the fact that his mom was a B is one of them. The fact that his mom calls him every twenty minutes is kind of a bit much. And that he lives with his parents with no intention of moving out is a deal-breaker. I'm still upset. It was a great date till his mom showed up.

Lucy reassured me they wouldn't all be like this, and by the end of the call, I was feeling better.

I'm just getting off the phone with a local author when Ben walks in. I love those calls. My heart has grown two sizes. Ben asks what's up.

"I sold all our copies of a new book recently published by a local author, and I just got off the phone with her. We now have a wait list started and need more books. She was ecstatic. I'm so happy for her!" I clap my hands together and exclaim, feeling overjoyed.

Ben smiles and leans on the counter. "That's amazing. That will be you one day."

"I know," I say, my smile diminishing. I'm not sure if I quite believe that. Not at the rate these dates are going.

Ben hangs out a bit more, and he tells me about this new hybrid plant he has been working on. I like seeing him excited and happy. He deserves to be happy, and that makes my heart sing a little.

When he leaves, I finish arranging books, dust a little, then settle on my stool. I'm working till close, and it's always quiet after supper, so I take out my laptop and start thinking about my article. I open a new document and let the words fall through my fingertips and onto the keys.

So, I decided to date online...

CHAPTER EIGHTEEN

by: Sofia Daria

So, I decided to date online... and I met his mom on the first date.

I opened my heart this time. A little, at least. Maybe I even let myself dream, imagining a second date, even a third, maybe even dating this guy long term.

Was I wrong to do so? Am I supposed to keep my walls up, have a guard, and not fall so easily in lust or attraction?

My friend Lucy would tell me, and she would tell you too, that yes, fall. Whether it be in lust, love, or just plain old attraction, do it.

You can't live these joyful moments if you don't let yourself be you. If you hold back and are only a small version of yourself, you're only going to get to live a small version of lust, love, or attraction.

So, I did it. I let my guard down, and I had an amazing date, that is until his mom showed up.

After detailing the humiliating encounter, I ended with: *I refuse to let this one leave a bitter taste in my mouth. This won't be my only wonderful date. This was just another hiccup in the road, leading me to the person I am meant to grow into and the person I am meant to be with, eventually.*

CHAPTER NINETEEN

I've been sitting across from Miriam for the last hour as we go over the articles I have already submitted and her goals for me in the following weeks. I stand and pick up my greige suede bag, sitting it high on my shoulder.

She reaches across the desk and smiles at me. "Keep your chin up. There are many more men to meet out there."

I can see the scar above her right eyebrow where she once wore an eyebrow ring.

I tell her how I have three dates this week.

Yikes!

I need to go shopping.

I call Lucy as I step outside and start making my way the three blocks to my car. The parking garage was full when I arrived. I can feel the wobble of my skinny heels underneath me.

"You still need some new clothes?" I ask as she picks up.

I hear her mutter, "Sorry, just out of a meeting." A door closes. "Yeah, want to meet at the Outlets in the morning? I

CHAPTER NINETEEN

need some summer clothes."

The sidewalks are full, it's late afternoon on a Friday, and people are finishing up work early for the weekend. The temperature has been rising, and more and more people are venturing into the sunny weather. A woman bumps into me as she passes.

I switch my phone to my other ear, trying to squeeze through the crowd. I can feel my thighs chaffing under my leather skirt.

"Yes, I have three dates, and I could use a closet refresher," I say. "I'll call Briar and see if she can meet us."

Once home, I sit at my desk and pull up my calendar when a text comes in. It's from Ben.

Ben: Want to watch that new superhero movie tonight?

Me: Yeah, okay. I guess I can watch a superhero movie for you.

Ben: Oh, yeah. You only watch chic flicks, I forgot.

Me: Haha, you're so funny! I'll have you know that I also watch reality TV.

I smile to myself, knowing Ben will probably laugh at that.

Ben: LOL

See.

I go back to my calendar and see that I'm meeting Alex first on Sunday, for brunch. He's a game developer, super nice so far, and maybe a little quirky. Quirky is good in my books. I think it's better if I date people who are weird like me. It's just easier when you don't have to explain why you are the way you are or why you do things the way you do because, honestly, you don't even really know. They just happen.

Another message pops up on my screen before I can look at the rest of the week.

The Dating Debacle

Ben: So, a movie?
Me: Yes, I'd love to.

I mean, this is good. We can hang out as friends and get over the weird hump.

Me: Bring me Doritos, please. If I'm going to have to watch an action movie, I need food.
Ben: Got it. See you in an hour?
Me: I'll be here.

I pull up my calendar again.

So, Alex is on Sunday, and I'm meeting Tom, a paralegal, on Tuesday night. I think we're going to a comedy show at a pub. I scroll through the days and see that Friday is my date with Harper. Harper is a nurse. If I associate each guy with their job, I won't mix them up when talking to them. One can hope. Again, I think dating is hard. It can get complicated. But I'm also learning that dating can be fun and exciting. I mean, yes, my dates have kind of sucked, but getting ready, going out, and trying new things has brought me a little out of my comfort zone. A tiny bit, anyway. And those kisses the other night, that feeling with Callum, I want more of that.

I put my laptop away and fed Bob supper.

Ben arrives exactly sixty minutes later. He walks in with a pizza box, a bag of Doritos, and two iced coffees. I also see some sort of plant poking out of a mesh veggie bag.

My stomach growls as I inhale the scent of the pizza. My saliva glands go into working mode.

He's standing there, performing a balancing act as I stare at him, thinking about the food.

"Oh, sorry, I was kind of daydreaming for a second," I say and take the drinks and bag of Doritos from him.

I hear him kick off his shoes and follow behind me.

CHAPTER NINETEEN

He places the box of pizza on my countertop and starts opening the mesh bag. I turn to see what he has in his hands.

"Are you trying to win over Bob?" I ask.

Bob, hearing his name, jumps off my bed and saunters in slowly, looking up at Ben, clearly annoyed by his presence.

Bob sees the grass and starts walking in circles around Ben's legs, rubbing his head as he passes, the annoyance leaving him as he sees Ben is holding some greenery that he now wants.

"Hey there, Bob, I got you some cat grass." He places the mesh bag on the counter. "Do you have a plate I can put this on?"

I grab a small dish from my cupboard as Ben sprinkles a bit of water through the top. Bob meows at Ben, now impatient for the grass he's about to get.

I take out two plates and set them beside the pizza, then open the large cardboard box. Ben grabs a plate and leans over me for a slice. The cheese is pulling, leaving a trail behind it. I feel the warmth from his body next to me, and I am briefly reminded of the heat I felt in my dream.

"Hey," I say, "I wanted that slice."

Ben laughs. "There are seven other slices to choose from, and this is the one you wanted?"

"Yeah, it's the biggest."

He offers the plate to me.

"It's fine. Your fingers are all over it now." I make a disgusted face and laugh so he knows I'm half joking and pull a slice out of the box.

He grabs his iced coffee and carries it out of the kitchen to my living room.

I'm washing my hands, and I can hear him turning on the TV.

The Dating Debacle

"Which movie are we watching?" I ask loud enough for him to hear me from down the hall. He mutters something I don't hear. I close the box of pizza in case Bob decides to jump on the counter. I take my plate to the living room. "Which movie?" I ask again as I sit next to him.

"The new one with Blake Hennely," he replies as the movie comes up on screen.

"Thanks for the pizza, by the way. So good."

"Of course."

Getting comfy, I lean back, my plate on my lap. I notice Ben relaxing, and the feeling I get when the side of his thigh presses up against mine is electric. I turn back to my pizza and take another bite. Ben finishes his.

"Should I just bring the box in here?" he asks.

"Yeah, for sure."

He stands, and I reach over to pause the movie.

We spend the next hour and a half locked in a state of anticipation. Ben talks during movies. Usually, I would find this annoying, but I respond with similar thoughts. As the credits are rolling, I grab the bag of Doritos. I open it noisily as I return, and Ben picks out a fifth slice of pizza.

"How about another movie?" I ask. "I'm wired from the caffeine and won't be going to bed anytime soon."

He nods, his mouth full. I put on a romantic comedy before he can argue otherwise. As the music starts up, I feel joy spark through me. The only thing better than a good rom-com is a good romance novel. The movie plays out exactly how you'd expect, and it's fantastic. I'm smiling, feeling all the feels by the time it's done. This excites me.

I see Ben stretch his arms above his head and turn to face him, pulling one leg up onto the couch and settling in.

CHAPTER NINETEEN

"So..." I say.

He raises his eyebrows. "So..." he responds.

I refuse to let us be awkward anymore.

"Any plans this weekend?" I ask.

He lays his head back on the top of the couch, staring at the ceiling. "Actually, I ran into Mel yesterday."

"Oh, yeah?"

"Yeah, we're going out for coffee tomorrow."

"You don't say." Huh, feeling a little something something inside of me. Mel broke his heart. And he is going out for coffee with her...years later! "How do you feel about that?" I ask, secretly hoping he doesn't want to go.

"It'll be nice."

That's it? That's all he's going to give me?

"Nice?" I repeat his one-word answer. "She broke your heart. Do you think it's a good idea?"

"I'm well aware she broke my heart, but people change," he says, rubbing his forehead. "It's just coffee."

"Huh." Not sure what else to say, I leave it at that. I pull my knees to my chest, making myself into a ball.

I think I'm jealous.

I've got absolutely no reason to be jealous. Ben's not mine. We're not a couple. We're not dating. I've got a date with three other men this week. I'm hardly one to have any feelings of jealousy.

"I'm going out for brunch on Sunday morning," I blurt.

Ben is eyeing me. "Cool, Sof. I hope he works out."

Okay, this is awkward. I hear a horn blast from outside, and I'm pulled out of this wrecking ball that's happening inside of me.

"Thanks, he's a game developer." I force a smile. "We'll see."

The Dating Debacle

Ben smiles back at me. "Thanks for watching the movie with me."

"Thanks for the food," I say, biting into another chip loudly, crumbs falling out of my mouth. "Oops."

"Is that how you eat on dates?" Ben asks.

My eyes widen. "Um, probably?"

He laughs, "I'm joking. I love that you're always yourself."

"Is it that embarrassing, the way I eat?"

"No, no, I'm just playing." He's laughing a little harder now as I stuff more Doritos into my mouth. I can't help it.

I hit him playfully in the arm. "That's not funny. I'm going to be paranoid eating now on my date."

"God, no, Sof. I was just kidding. And if a guy can't handle watching you eat, maybe he's not your guy."

My heart skips a beat. Is Ben my guy?

I swallow. "Thanks."

"So, do you think you would ever get back together with Mel?" I ask, curiosity killing me.

"It's just coffee, Sof. We'll see where it goes."

My chest tightens, and I wonder if this is how he feels when I talk about my dates.

He pushes his sleeves up and stands, picking up the empty pizza box. "I'll put this in the trash out back."

"Thanks," I say, standing up too, rolling the bag of Doritos closed.

He bends to put his shoes on. "I'll see you tomorrow?"

"Yup, I'm going shopping with the girls, and I'll be in later in the afternoon."

He leans in to give me a hug. I feel his breath on my neck. It's warm and comforting somehow, and I feel my body melt a little against his. I hug him tightly, and he lets go first, so I

CHAPTER NINETEEN

step back.

"Thanks again for the pizza, and thanks on behalf of Bob."

He nods as he opens the door, and he's halfway down the steps before I turn to go back inside and close the door.

* * *

I pull open the thick white velvet curtain acting as a changing room door and step out. I walk up to the large mirror facing the rooms and join Lucy.

Briar calls out from her room, "Guys, this is way too small."

Lucy decided we all needed a new going-out outfit and chose one for each of us to try. I'm standing in a pair of tight brown leather pants and a beige cropped tank. The tag scratches my skin, making it blotchy red as I pull it out, and my eyes widen. "I don't think these pants look good enough on me to spend this," I say, turning back to the mirror and meeting Lucy's eyes.

We both raise our gazes in the mirror as Briar comes out of the room behind us.

"Damn, girl," Lucy hollers, whistling.

Briar is wearing a short red skirt. It's so tight that she is almost waddling. But she looks amazing. "Luce, I can't even walk in this. How am I supposed to dance, or sit, or, I don't know, live?" she asks, laughing and pulling at the material.

Lucy comes up to her and grabs her hands. "You look gorgeous. Aiden won't be able to keep his eyes off of you."

"These pants are a no for me, Luce," I say, returning to the changing room.

"Same, it's a no for this skirt." Briar waddles away.

"You guys are boring," Lucy says, turning back to the mirror.

"I'm okay with boring," I yell as I struggle to pull the velvet material closed.

I pull off the pants and check what I have left to try on. I see the solid black jumper with a low neckline and take it off the hanger, pulling it on. Grabbing my heels, I step back into them. This time, I decided to squeeze through the curtain door instead of wrestling with it.

Briar steps out in a cute and flowy floral dress.

"Briar, you look so sweet," I say. "You should def get that."

She does a little twirl to the side, smiling. "I love it. I'm going to get it."

I'm adjusting my bra in the mirror. We're the only three back here, so we have the place to ourselves. The bonus of waking up early on a Saturday to shop. Worth it.

Lucy steps out in another incredible outfit.

"I think I'm going to get this jumper," I say, "What do you think?" I turn, trying to visualize my butt from the back.

"You need a necklace, but yes, get that. It looks great," Lucy comments.

I smile. I feel like I look good. The three of us are all standing side by side in such different outfits. We are so different. It's what makes us…us.

We let the saleswoman ring us up, and we spend the next two hours going from shop to shop. I've spent quite a bit, but I love my new stuff. Lucy got a lot of stuff too, but Briar settled on just the one dress. She's a minimalist. I could learn from her. I shove my bags into the back of my car.

"Wear the jumper to brunch tomorrow," Lucy calls out from her car.

"It's not too much for a breakfast?"

Briar chimes in, "Wear the jumper!"

CHAPTER NINETEEN

I smile. "Okay, thanks!"

I cross to Lucy's car and give her a quick hug goodbye, and then I hug Briar next, and then Briar and Lucy hug. We're a huggable group. We laugh as we do the switch.

"Talk to you guys later," I say, waving as I get into my car. I look into the backseat. I can't wait to get back home and try it all on again.

I look at the clock. Crap. I have to get ready for work.

CHAPTER TWENTY

I'm five minutes late for my date. I shove open the door to the restaurant and make my way inside. My heel catches on the rug in front of the hostess' desk, and I feel myself falling. Oh, God. I'm about to go down. Strong, sturdy hands grab my waist from behind, sliding down my butt, trying to catch me. I'm not sure if I should feel violated or grateful.

"Whoa," I exclaim as I'm suddenly back on my feet. I turn to see whose hands just had the privilege of meeting my ass today.

He's the same height as me in my heels. I recognize him. It's Alex. He pushes his glasses back up his nose, and I see his eyes are a deep brown, hiding behind thick black frames. He glances down.

"Sorry about that," he starts, obviously embarrassed by manhandling me before we've even started our first date.

"Alex, hi," I say. "Thank you for catching me. That could have been a lot more embarrassing had you not been there." I laugh, but it comes out louder than I expect, and I see a few

CHAPTER TWENTY

people turning to watch. My cheeks flush, and I ignore them.

"I was waiting in my car for you and saw you arrive. I guess I just happened to walk in at the right time."

"Well, thanks again," I say, smiling. Alex is cute. And obviously kind but shy.

The hostess is waiting for us to approach her. "For two?" she asks.

Alex nods. "Yes, please."

We follow her to a table in the center of the room. It's pretty crowded.

Alex waits for me to sit first, so I do. I can feel him watching me. I bring my hands up to my hair, setting it back into place from the disaster that almost just happened.

I can tell I am already going to like Alex. He has a good feel about him. He has a quirky charm. He's witty throughout our conversation and tells me about the game he is working on.

I admit to him that I have never played a video game before.

His eyes light up as he explains his favorite game, his gaze unwavering. I imagine what he's describing: a world all on its own. He tells me more about his job, and it's nice to see someone speak with so much passion. It feels good to be around him. I'm opening up and telling him things about me, about my dream to write a book one day.

"You're going to do it," he says confidently with a genuine smile.

"I will," I reply. I know I will. It's just not time yet. "Thanks."

The waitress returns, and we order our breakfast. I order a peppermint tea and convince Alex to try one, too.

The waitress returns in what seems like seconds with a small pot of hot water and two tea cups as if we are about to have tea with the Queen. There are tiny flowers outlining each cup.

The Dating Debacle

Lifting the pot, I pour and manage not to spill a drop, feeling proud. I admit this to Alex. I always spill the water out of those damn little teapots, often feeling like I could use a few etiquette classes.

He takes a small sip, his lips barely meeting the cup, as if I filled it with poison, and I laugh. He smacks his lips together. "That's pretty refreshing, but I think it's too hot still."

I agree, smiling. Our food arrives, and we dig in. I'm starving, and I see Alex pick up his fork with determination. I'm eating my scrambled eggs and see Alex doing the same. We admit that you always start with the eggs and finish with the hash browns. I plop a big glob of ketchup on my plate and offer it to Alex, which he takes.

I don't feel nervous or awkward and when I'm eating, I don't think about how I am probably embarrassing myself. I notice I feel completely at ease with him. Maybe it's because I started out this date with a minor mishap, or maybe it's because he is a lot like me. I don't know.

We finish our breakfast, and Alex finishes his peppermint tea. "So, how was it?" I ask, waiting impatiently for his verdict.

"I liked it," he says, putting his cup down.

I take a sip of water and eye him questionably. "How long have you been online dating?"

He pauses. "I just started. My older sister just sort of convinced me." He looks up to the ceiling as if contemplating telling me something.

"What is it?" I ask, "Is something wrong?" I can sense his uneasiness.

He's playing with his napkin, folding it and unfolding it as he thinks about answering. I let him have the space he needs and take another sip of my water.

CHAPTER TWENTY

"I don't want you to take this the wrong way," he starts. "But I don't think I'm really ready to date."

"Oh my God, Alex, that's okay!" I exclaim a little too loudly as the couple next to us turns towards me. "Oops." I smile at him. "It's okay, really. I think you're great. We can be just friends," I finish, and he looks relieved.

"I don't have many friends, well definitely not any 'girl' friends. I just, I don't know." He hesitates, trying to find his words. "I just started my career, and I just, I'm not ready." He pushes his glasses up. "My sister thinks I spend too much time alone."

I grab his hand, reassuring him. "That's cool, Alex, seriously. I should probably tell you something too."

His eyes widen with what looks like fear.

I splay my hands. "Nothing bad, I promise!"

He chuckles lightly, not convinced. I let go of his hand. Our eyes lock, and I sense his discomfort. "To be honest, I signed up on the dating app because I was offered a writing job."

I glance up quickly. I don't want to hurt his feelings.

His gaze shifts. "What do you mean?"

"I want to date, well, I didn't at first. I mean, I do want to date. I want a boyfriend." I realize this as I am saying it. I pause before continuing, "I only started because I was offered a job at a magazine. My friends convinced me to do it, and well, it has sort of been a roller coaster, but I am enjoying dating."

"Do you write about your dates?" he asks, worried.

"Yeah, kind of."

He shifts uncomfortably. "You're going to write about our date?"

"I sort of have to. I write about my dates from my perspective. I don't give out any names," I assure him.

He looks like he is going to throw up a little. I notice again how similar we are.

"Look, Alex. I like you and I really want to be your friend, and I am okay that this is all we'll be. I won't write anything bad about you, I promise. This was the best date I've had so far. I feel at ease around you." I grin. "Even though you grabbed my butt in the first thirty seconds, and I nearly fell on my face."

Alex begins to laugh, pushing up his glasses. "Sorry about that…again."

"You saved me."

I can see him relax. We stay at the restaurant for another hour, talking about everything and anything. I tell him more about the bookstore, and about Lucy and Briar and the yoga classes, and he admits he has wanted to try one.

"You should definitely come with us!" I exclaim excitedly. "Briar's the only pro. Lucy and I are beginners. It'll be fun." Alex doesn't seem convinced, but he doesn't say no.

He tells me more about his sister, and I tell him about Ben and our recent lip match, and I'm finding it super easy to talk to him. By the time we pay the bill, we decide to split it. I've convinced Alex to come into the bookstore, and I agree that he can teach me to play a video game.

We walk outside, and I make sure not to trip on the overly thick rug at the entrance. Alex holds the door for me. He gives me his phone number, and I tell him I will text him so he has mine. We hug briefly.

"I'll send you a copy of my article," I say, "once it's written. It'll be good, I promise."

He smiles. I think he believes me.

We say goodbye, and I walk to my car, smiling.

CHAPTER TWENTY

I take out my phone.
Me: Here's my number :)
Alex: Got it :)
I turn up the music when I hear a song I know come on, and I sing loudly the entire way home.
Lucy: How was the date with Alex?
Me: Was great! But we're just going to be friends. He's going to come to yoga with us sometime!
Lucy: Okay, cool :)
Briar: Yes! Another new yogi to create!
Me: LOL
Lucy: I don't think you will create a yogi out of me.
Briar: In time, my dear, in time :)
Lucy: LOL we'll see. How's your yogi hottie?
Me: Yes, spill. What's going on with you and Aiden?
Briar: He kissed me last night.
Me: Yay!
Lucy: No down dogs?
Briar: Lucy!
Me: LMAO
Lucy: I've got to run, but will talk more later?
Me: Sounds good :)
Briar: Have an amazing day!!

So, I decided to date online...
  by: Sofia Daria

So, I decided to date online... and I made a new friend.

Everyone talks about online dating. They talk about bad dates, the X-rated pics, the liars, the hookups, and catfishing. But no one talks about meeting new people and becoming friends.

This week I decided to run for it. I booked three dates! With still two to go, I am not disappointed one bit in my Sunday morning breakfast date. Was it entertaining, yes! Were there embarrassing moments? Again, yes! Obviously... it is me we're talking about here. Did I make a new friend? Hell yes. Let me tell you about it.

So, although my date didn't end up with butterflies flying, or an awkward first date kiss, I did get to second base unintentionally, and I made a new friend. What more could a girl ask for?

After relaying all the details while being careful not to say anything that will be embarrassing for Alex, I end with, *Stay tuned for more adventures in dating...coming up!*

CHAPTER TWENTY-ONE

I spotted her as soon as I walked into the bookstore.
An island princess, maybe? Someone who looks like a cross between Barbie's BFF and an exotic fire dancer. I nod to Emily, who's talking to another customer. I place my bag under the counter, and when I look up, my eyes meet hers, and I am lost in a sea of green haze. I think I just got my first girl crush.

"Hi," I say. "Is there anything I can help you find?"

She smiles, showing pearly white teeth through large, red-stained lips with a speckle of glitter. I notice her long, dainty fingers as she presses the novel she's holding tight against her chest.

"I found what I was looking for," she says. "But thanks."

She continues to browse the shelf in front of her. I force myself to turn away. Let's not be a creeper today, Sofia. But isn't this just one woman appreciating another woman's beauty? Meh, I've got things to do. I turn to my phone and see a text from Alex. We've chatted a few times since Sunday,

The Dating Debacle

and he came into the store yesterday and hung out for a bit. I introduced him to Ben, and they got along right away. Ben talked about plants, Alex talked about video games, and then they went at it, discussing superheroes and which was stronger and faster. I got bored and left them to it. The store got busy after that, and before I had a chance to talk to Ben, it was closing time, and he was gone when I locked up.

I'm opening up my laptop when the beautiful creature of a woman places two books on the counter.

I scan them and hand them back to her. Before I can ask her how she is paying, she takes out her debit card. I hand her the machine to tap, and the receipt prints out.

I'm just about to wish her a good day when I see Ben stroll in behind her.

"Hey, Sofia." He smiles over her head.

"Hi," I say as I notice the green in the woman's eyes grow bright with excitement. Clearly, someone liked what she saw when shopping for plants. I can't blame her.

And then it hits me. Right in the chest.

Ben stands next to her, and his arm slips effortlessly around her waist.

What?

She turns to him, looking up, a pout of red glittery lips puckering for him.

And then it happens. My heart stops.

Ben leans down and kisses her right on the mouth. The mouth! And in front of me.

Ben doesn't have any sisters or any friends, really, except for me. He's kind of a loner, so who the hell… Fucking Mel. It dawns on me. This is Mel.

Ben manages to pull his lips away from her, and a sad, puppy-

CHAPTER TWENTY-ONE

eyed look crosses over her face.

"Sof, this is Mel." I feel Emily behind me. "Emily, Mel."

"Nice to meet you, Mel," Emily says, her voice revealing nothing more than the automatic customer service voice she's perfected over the last year.

Shit, how am I going to pull that off?

I have a sinking feeling that makes its way through me, down to my chipped purple nail-polished toes.

"Hi, Mel," I manage. "It's nice to meet you. Ben told me you were grabbing coffee on Sunday," I say, not sounding jealous at all.

"Yes," she replies, leaning into Ben's hard torso.

The outline of his broad shoulders takes form through his t-shirt as he moves his arm to press her even closer to him as if trying to become one.

She looks up at him again. "Was nice to catch up," she says, letting out a tiny laugh as if there is this secret only he is aware of.

Ben's laugh matches hers, and I want to throw up. "Did you find the books you were looking for sweetie?"

Puke, I just puked in my mouth and swallowed it. *Sweetie?*

"Yup," she answers, then turns to me. "I'm just addicted to these psychological thrillers right now."

Emily points to the top one on the counter. "That's a good one."

"Well, I better go."

"I'll walk you to your car," Ben nods in my direction, mentally communicating that he'll be back.

"Wow, Ben managed to get himself a hottie," Emily says as she snaps her laptop closed, oblivious to my seething jealousy.

"Yeah," I muster.

The Dating Debacle

Emily takes off, leaving me alone with a pile of books to shelve and nothing but my thoughts and the heavy weight in my heart. He kissed me, but I was too busy dating other people to notice that we might have actually had something. And now it's too late. I'm not sure how I feel about that, but I do know I am not happy to see him press lips against another girl, especially a goddess like Mel. I'm seething.

* * *

I'm closing up the cash and Ben hasn't been back in to see me, so I'm surprised when I hear him call me out from the hallway.

"Want to grab a drink?" he asks, his form taking up space in the doorway to the bookstore…and my heart.

I lock up the cash drawer and grab my stuff.

"Can't," I say, dropping a bag as I round the counter.

"Let me get that for you." He bends down, and I notice the pull of fabric across his back, and then his…

"You got a date?" he interrupts my thoughts.

"Yeah," I say, not revealing anything further. "Mel, she's beautiful," I admit, "I guess coffee went well?"

"You could say that."

Ben follows me as I turn towards the door. We make it to my car, and Ben dumps the bag in my backseat for me.

"I just hope she doesn't hurt you. Do you know her intentions this time?" I ask, knowing this is none of my business, but I can't seem to stop the words from spilling out of my mouth.

"She's not going to hurt me. Plus, I think I can handle the disappointment," he says with a snarky tone.

"What's that supposed to mean?"

CHAPTER TWENTY-ONE

He averts his eyes. "Nothing,"

I feel a lump building in my throat. "What did you mean, Ben?"

"I mean, I tell you I like you, and your response is that you're going to keep dating other people."

"Ben…" I start.

"No, don't…"

He has a point. I nearly collapsed in a fit of jealousy when I saw his arm around Mel. What must it feel like for him to read my articles every week? To read about my encounters with other men?

My back is pressed against the passenger door. "I don't know what you want me to tell you."

"That you feel the same way as I do," he says as he takes a step closer to me, closing the large gap between us.

The cool Spring air circles around us. I feel my breath catch in my chest. I see him let out a sigh, his chest heaving slightly.

"You know…" I start but can't seem to finish my sentence. "I've got to go," I say, breaking the silence between us as I push past him. "Have a good night with Mel," I add sarcastically.

I don't know why I am jealous; I have my own date tonight. I'm on my own path. But I find it difficult to suppress my longing for his touch and his kisses. The way it felt when his mouth trickled down the length of my neck.

Fuck.

I put the car in reverse and back out. I see Ben standing under the streetlight, watching me as I go.

* * *

I change quickly, and I'm just adding some lip gloss when I

The Dating Debacle

see the time. I have to go. I'm meeting Tom at a comedy show downtown.

I pull up with only a few minutes until the show begins. I'm not usually late like this, but Ben had me all flusterfucked after the conversation in the parking lot. Two for two. I was late for Alex's date.

I walk into the crowded bar, and I see a guy waving me over. I told him I'd be wearing a red shirt so he could spot me. I'm glad I did because I don't know how I would have recognized him or found him through this jungle of people. I approach the table and see we'll be sitting in the first row. Does this guy know anything about comedy shows? You never sit in the first row unless you want to be picked on. I cringe, uncomfortable.

I force a smile, and Tom stands, giving me a quick hug.

At first glance, Tom's on the thinner side. A little lanky, with brown curls on top of his head. He looks a little ruffled. Like maybe it was a long day at the office.

"Have a seat," he says, motioning.

I feel nervous. I don't feel at ease.

I tell him it's nice to meet him, and he doesn't really reply.

There's something about him that I can't quite put my finger on it.

"The show's about to start. Have you been to a comedy show before?" he asks, barely glancing at me, distracted by the people on the small stage.

"Yeah, it's been a while, but I usually sit towards the middle to back." I laugh out of discomfort.

"Nah, these are the best seats," he says.

We don't have much time to talk before the host of the evening is on stage. We really should have met up a little earlier before the show. I know nothing about Tom besides

CHAPTER TWENTY-ONE

what he wrote on his profile. I remove my sweater and place it on the back of my chair, revealing the new cropped top and a pair of high-waisted jeans. I see Tom glance at me, not looking at my eyes. I feel his stare linger a little too long for my liking, so I adjust my top, snapping him out of his daze. He turns towards the stage. He sticks his finger in his ear. What's he doing, digging for gold? He pulls his finger out and sniffs it.

I gag.

I think I just got the ick.

The host is finishing up, and people are clapping. Music starts playing.

I hadn't heard of this comedian before, but I love to laugh. I try to shake the reaction my body is getting from sitting next to Tom.

With the chairs so close together, the sides of our arms touch, sending shivers down my body. Not the good kind.

I try to shake it off and clap as the comedian comes out.

She gets right into it.

I start to forget who I'm here with until her eyes meet mine.

Look away, I will her with my mind. I wish I had the superpower of mental persuasion.

She's cool so far, funny. I like her style with her low-rider jeans and halter top. She has long red hair and sass. We could be friends, but not tonight. Not as the audience member she is about to call out.

I see her turn to Tom as our gaze breaks.

Phew. Close call. I'm safe…for now.

"Hey," she says. "So, you're on a date with this girl here?"

Fuck.

"Yeah, I guess you could call it that," he answers.

Seriously?

The Dating Debacle

"You could call it a date?" She laughs, turning from me to him. I show no emotion. I am not going to be sucked in. "What is it if it's not a date? You guys just friends? Friends with benefits?"

Tom sits up a bit taller. "Not yet." He laughs.

Oh. My. God.

She turns to me. "So what do you say, are *you* on a date?"

"I was."

She laughs, and the crowd starts to laugh with her as she repeats my answer. "You were? Not anymore?"

"I just met him a few minutes before the show, and I mean, if he's just looking for friends with benefits - I'm not interested. Plus, he kind of gives me the ick."

I sink lower in my seat, hiding my face from the onlookers.

Tom is looking at me. Again, not at my eyes.

"She got eyes, bro," she calls him out, then turns to me. "Wise choice, my lady."

Tom calls out to the comedian, "Hey! What's this ick thing?"

She looks at me.

"Well..." She pauses. "Come on, ladies, y'all know what the ick is, right?" The women in the crowd are laughing and clapping. A few men join in. "So, how can I describe it? Let's see... the ick is something you do—" She crouches, looking at Tom, "—that stops a woman from ever wanting to get laid by you. Bro, bottom line, you made her cringe. You're never going to bake her potato. Let's just say there's not going to be any belly-bumping, no boinking, no boning, no bow-chick-a-wow-wow. You get what I'm saying?"

The crowd is roaring. I find myself laughing along. Tom is sitting there, confused as hell.

"So tell me. What did he do? We all want to know."

CHAPTER TWENTY-ONE

"He stuck his finger in his ear and then sniffed it."

She grimaces. "What, like you guys sat down, and he just sticks his finger in his ear and sniffs it right in front of you?"

"Yeah."

"Dude, sorry, but I think this 'date' is over for you. What were you hoping to smell? A field of daisies?" She has to practically yell over the roaring crowd. "You guys ever hear about…"

I slip out of my seat and walk to the back of the bar. Date's over. I'm grabbing a drink for myself when I see Emily waving me over.

"Hey, Em!" I say as I slide into the seat next to her.

She introduces me to two of her friends. "I thought that was your voice up front, but I couldn't see you."

She invites me to stay and watch the show with her friends, so I do. I'm not going to let this night go to waste.

The comedian starts in on another couple. "So, I already broke one couple up tonight. Let's hope I'm not setting a pattern here."

Everyone laughs.

CHAPTER TWENTY-TWO

So, I decided to date online...
  by: Sofia Daria

So, I decided to date online... and I got the ick.

Have you ever gotten the 'ick'?

Ick - An expression of disgust, an unpleasant feeling that runs through your body. Like eating cold, chunky oatmeal.

I had yet to experience this so-called ick people talked about until I did.

I shudder as I type a description of the encounter, right down to the comedian's humiliation of Tom.

Sounds like a terrible night, right? Turns out my coworker was there with some friends, saw me, and invited me to hang out with them. All in all, it ended up being a great night with friends, and it reminded me - listen to your intuition!

I guess I do have an intuition after all, I think smiling to myself.

CHAPTER TWENTY-TWO

* * *

Alex sent me a text shortly after reading my article online. I'm not sure if I am turning him off dating even more than he already was, but I reassured him that finding love one day would all be worth it. We made plans for him to come to yoga next week.

I'm reading a new mystery novel, snacking on chocolate-covered almonds, when Ben walks into the bookstore to water the plants. Our eyes meet, but he doesn't say anything. I look back down at the page I was reading, but I'm just staring at it, unable to focus. He clears his throat, so I look up.

Ben walks over to me and rests his elbow on the counter. He runs his hand through his already tousled hair, leaving it a bit messier, giving him an I *just rolled out of bed* look. He's sexy as hell.

I imagine what it would be like to be in bed with him. Sheets tangled between our legs, our limbs intertwined, our hearts beating fast. I snap myself out of the dead-end road my mind wanted to travel on.

"What's up?" I ask casually, glancing back down at my book as if I have better things to do. I'm so immature.

"I read your article this week." He's put the watering can down on the counter next to him.

I'm surprised. I didn't think Ben would read my articles since he was so against it, but I get why now.

"Oh, yeah?" I ask again, showing little interest.

"You need to be careful, Sof…" he starts, but I don't let him finish.

"Thanks, Dad," I say, knowing my maturity level has just fallen even further. But Ben doesn't back off or pull away. I look up at him, and there is concern in his eyes.

"Sof…"

"Where's Mel today?" I'm trying to change the subject, but I'm also nosy and jealous.

"She's in class."

"So, how's that going?" I ask in a tone that might be a little sarcastic.

I can't stop myself. I feel a fight brewing. My emotions are about to take over my mind, body, and soul, and there is nothing I can do about it. I glare at Ben. Poor guy, he doesn't deserve this, and yet, here it is.

He leans further on the counter so that his face is right in front of mine. His eyes are peering deep into my soul. I see the gold flecks, and I'm in a trance. My breath is speeding up. Is he aware he does this to me? Does he know he sends my body into sweet convulsions, making me feel all syrupy and gooey inside?

I snap back to reality. Mel. Yes, she is with him, I'm not. I wait for his response.

"It's been a few years. We're just reconnecting," he says.

"Reconnecting. Is that what they're calling it these days?" I ask, laughing.

"Sof."

"Funny how you can kiss me out of nowhere. Tell me you like me, and a week later, you're in bed with someone else."

He pushes himself off the counter, standing tall. "Weren't you in a hot tub with a random stranger just a few days ago?"

Huh, so he is reading all of my articles.

He's not wrong. I was in a hot tub, making out with a rando, and I've been on other dates too. I have no reason to feel this way or act like I am.

CHAPTER TWENTY-TWO

"I guess we're even," I say, closing my book and standing.

"This isn't a competition, Sofia."

"Isn't it? You tell me you like me, and then what? Because I'm dating, you feel it necessary to get back at me and flaunt your sexy mermaid of a woman in front of me?" There it is. I let it all out on the table. "I've got work to do, so if you're done watering the plants, I should get to it."

I pass Ben, and he grabs my arm, turning me towards him. Our eyes lock. I pull away.

"Don't," I say, and I march to the restroom.

Once inside, I place my hands on either side of the sink, feeling the cool marble under my palms. I face off in the mirror, willing my reflection to come at me. I feel riled up. I wish for just a moment that I didn't wear makeup. I could be one of those women in the movies who splash cold water on their face and it changes their entire mood. They instantly calm down. Who am I kidding? I'm not about to start neglecting my eye makeup on the off chance I need to splash cold water on my face.

When I emerge, Ben is gone. I spend the afternoon reeling in a mix of emotions until Emily arrives. She distracts me with stories about her night, and we decide to order sandwiches from the deli down the street for lunch. I ordered a few chocolate brownies, obviously to feed the jealous beast lingering inside me.

CHAPTER TWENTY-THREE

I look down at my freshly painted toenails, a mellow shade of yellow.

It's officially warm enough for sandals, so Lucy, Briar, and I painted our toenails after yoga last night.

Alex left after class, not wanting to join in on the pedicures. The girls liked Alex immediately. I think Briar managed to convince him to come back for another class.

The afternoon sun is beating down on me. It's 2:03 p.m., and I'm supposed to meet Harper at 2:00 p.m. I managed to be on time today. I take a sip of my iced latte and look around. We're meeting by the water, and I'm sitting on the only free bench.

Harper is a nurse. I guess he works at the local hospital in Emerg. I think. We're just going to sit, talk, and go for a walk if things go well.

I'm people-watching while I wait. I don't feel as nervous as I did the night I met Tom. I don't feel overly excited, either. I think I'm still thrown off by all the emotions I get when I'm

CHAPTER TWENTY-THREE

around Ben. It's distracting. We've been avoiding each other again. I hate this. I miss my friend. I want to get off this roller-coaster ride. But Ben is with Mel, and I am going to keep dating. At least for now.

I'd be lying if I hadn't thought about what it would feel like to date Ben.

I notice a young guy approaching me. He's wearing green cargo shorts and a baggy beige shirt with a stain on the chest. Or where his chest would be if the shirt fit him properly. Is that mustard?

"Hi, Sofia?" he asks hesitantly.

"Harper?" I ask back.

"Nice to meet you," he says, smiling. His smile doesn't quite reach his eyes.

"Yeah, same." I look back down at the dark spot on his shirt. He looks like a teenager who half-assed his way to school.

There is more than just appearances, but if he won't make an effort on our first date, will he make an effort with anything if we start a relationship?

"Did you just finish work?" I ask, thinking maybe that accounts for his shabby appearance.

"Nope, I'm off today."

Oh, okay.

"It's beautiful out, eh?" I ask, feeling awkward.

"Yeah, yeah." He looks around us, then back at me. "I thought you were a little taller," he says.

"Oh, my profile says I'm five-two. I kick out my legs in an attempt to show my high wedges. "But I'm more like five-five since I'm almost always in my heels."

I'm the only one laughing. Clearly, I'm no comedian.

"Okay, okay. You just looked thinner in your pictures."

Did he just?

Before I have time to say anything, he adds, "You know it's important to take care of your body and eat healthy."

I look down, glancing at the outfit I took time to put on. I'm wearing cute wedges and an old school type dress, maybe slightly baby doll style, which I guess does make me seem like I have a little bit of a belly, but like, WTF, who says that on a date? A first date. I'm not skin and bones… but that's beside the point. I'm fired up.

"And that mustard you have on your shirt, was that hot dog healthy?" I ask. I'm now in a mood, and I stand.

"Whoa, whoa. I don't eat hot dogs," he replies, glancing down at his shirt as if seeing it for the first time.

"You don't change your clothes for a date either, I guess." I'm pulling my purse over my shoulder. I'm out. Some things you just can't force. "This isn't going to work. I'm going to take off."

I leave before he can say anything.

I find another bench a few minutes away and plop down heavily. I let my purse fall off my shoulder beside me. I feel the warm wood under my thighs and adjust my dress to cover my knees.

Emotions stir inside of me. What is happening to me? I'm embarrassed by the way I spoke to him. But I'm even more ashamed of how I spoke to Ben the other day. I close my eyes and take a deep breath. I count to four and then exhale. I repeat this, feeling the sun on my face. I let myself feel the slight breeze through my hair. As I continue my four-count breath, I hear a dog bark nearby. I open my eyes, and that's when I see him.

He's gorgeous.

CHAPTER TWENTY-THREE

He looks so familiar.

He's passing the Frisbee to his dog right in front of me, the dog barks, runs, and catches it mid-jump. I'm in awe of both the dog's abilities and the fine creature standing before me.

His hair is pushed back in an I-don't-care-way that must have taken a lot of time to achieve. His shorts slide up his legs as he runs to his dog, revealing tanned, toned thighs. My gaze drops to the tattoo on his calf.

Why does he look so familiar? I'm trying to place him.

I can feel myself staring, pulling a Tom, but there's something about him.

"Fuck."

"Excuse me?"

Shit. Did I say that out loud?

He's approaching. "Are you okay?"

He lifts his hand to cover his eyes, blocking out the sun. His dog follows him, running up to me, but sits just before he reaches us.

"Oh, yeah, sorry. That was nothing."

This man is beautiful.

"I could have sworn you swore at me," he says.

"Oh, God no, I'm so sorry," I mutter, utterly embarrassed. Is that just what I do now, embarrass myself over and over?

He sits next to me. This is unexpected.

I should tell him. But what do I say?

He offers me his hand. "I'm Cole." I shake it.

"Uh, Cole, this is going to be really weird, but I should tell you something," I admitted hesitantly. "There are pictures of you. Online."

His face does something I can't explain. "Is that what the whole 'fuck' thing was for?" He laughs.

The Dating Debacle

I laugh. "Uh, yeah, sorry."

"So, where are these pictures of me?"

"Um, I'm on a dating site, and I was talking to you, well I thought I was talking to you, but it ended up being a kid. I was catfished. He, well, was sixteen..."

"Wait, what? There are pictures of me on a dating site?" He leans against the bench, tilting his head to the sky as he rubs a palm down his face. "Are you sure it's me?"

"Yes, it is definitely you."

I relay the story, making sure to mention the pizza parlor where we met.

"That must have been some shock," he says sincerely.

"That's one way of putting it!" I laugh again, and I can feel his body relax beside me.

I hear a fart. It DID NOT come from me. I look at him.

"That was not me, I swear." He wiggles his toes under his dog, who looks up with a sheepish grin. Ha, I never saw a dog grin that way before. I laugh.

"Sure, is that why you take your dog out with you, so you can blame him for your mishaps?"

He shakes his head, laughing, and leans down to pet the soft golden fur. "Poor Brutus is a little gassy after getting into the kitchen garbage last night."

My hand flies up to my mouth. "Oh, no," I mutter.

Our eyes meet, and another laugh escapes me.

"Well, thanks for letting me know about the whole dating site and my pictures. I better go pay that kid a visit," he says as he stands.

"Yeah, no problem. I mean, it's weird that I actually ran into you. I was kind of wondering who you were."

Brutus lumbers over, and Cole ruffles his fur. "You can pet

CHAPTER TWENTY-THREE

him."

I put out my hand gently, and he sniffs me before rubbing his head on my knee. "Oh, you're so sweet."

"Thank you," Cole replies.

I hoist an eyebrow.

"Yeah, yeah." He smiles, revealing a dimple on his left cheek. "Hey, this might be weird since, technically, you've already had a date with me…"

I laugh again.

"But did you want to maybe go out sometime?"

I stand, "Oh, okay, uh, yeah, I'd like that."

"Good," he says.

We exchange numbers and make a plan to meet up in a few days.

I watch as Cole and Brutus leave.

I feel the excitement rise in me.

This is what dating should feel like, right?

* * *

I rock back and forth, trying to adjust myself on my mat. I'm not sure why Happy Baby Pose is supposed to be oh-so-good. I'm not sure if it's because my thighs are too thick or if it's the fact that I'm not flexible, but this doesn't feel good. I look at the woman on one side of me; her eyes are closed, and there's a smile plastered on her face. She is the picture of calm. I don't feel calm. I think Happy Baby is making me an irritable baby.

"Let's start rocking side to side," The instructor indicates from the front of the room.

I rock a little too hard and land on my side. Whoops. I roll back onto my back and extend my legs. I think I'll just wait for the next pose. I close my eyes.

After leaving the park, I decided I needed to check myself. I've been letting whatever this is with Ben affect me way too much. I'm irritating myself with how I've been reacting, which is how I ended up here. I open my eyes and see the sun setting through the window. The sky is forming a beautiful mix of pink and orange.

I'm thinking about work. I need to write my article about my date with Harper. What do I even say? I'm embarrassed by what I said. Did I overreact? I mean, he didn't exactly call me fat or anything. Was it just my ego?

I sigh.

Regardless, he couldn't even put a clean shirt on for our date.

I bring myself back to the present moment when I hear the instructor, "Gently let go of your feet, bringing your legs down to the mat for *Savasana*, corpse pose."

I widen my legs and arms so they're not touching my body and close my eyes again.

I hear a singing bowl, and I let the sound run through my body. I exhale a sigh, releasing to the mat. It feels like I've been lying here for hours when I hear, "Thank you all for coming, *Namaste*."

I blink my eyes open, but my body isn't ready to move yet. I'm rolling to my side when I see Aiden hand in hand with a short brunette. Behind Aiden I see a tall silhouette I would recognize anywhere. Briar. I sit up quickly grabbing my mat, no time to roll it. Briar spots me.

"What are you doing here?" she asks.

"You know, I just needed to Zen out, and you're always

CHAPTER TWENTY-THREE

saying how good yoga is for you." I lift my shoulders and drop them, then indicate Aiden. "What happened?"

Briar moves me towards the back of the room. I'm struggling with my open mat crushed into a ball. Briar takes it out of my hand and starts rolling it up like a pro.

"Aiden, yeah, wasn't going to work out. It's Okay." She smiles, a warm smile, letting me know that she truly is okay.

"Do you want to grab a tea?" I ask.

She looks from me to Aiden and considers it. "You know what? Yeah, I'd love a tea."

We walk a few blocks towards a little cafe. The sun has set, but the streetlights provide a soft, warm glow overhead. The street is quiet, and I find myself feeling calm, finally.

"So what happened?" I ask as we drop into the soft, worn, dark brown leather sofa.

I let my yoga mat and bag fall to the floor, then lift the warm mug to my nose, breathing in the refreshing peppermint.

"We only went out a few times. It really is no big deal."

"You sure?" I ask. Briar is such a sweet person. She doesn't really date, but when she does, I know she puts her heart fully into it.

"Yeah, I think I was more excited about the idea of him. He had the same hobbies as me, so I guess I was excited that we could share that together." She takes another sip and pauses. "But if I'm completely honest, I don't think I really liked him like that."

"Okay, I get that. But I'm here," I urge. "Anytime."

"I know." She puts her mug down and gives me a quick side squeeze. "How are things going with you?"

I shrug. Where do I even begin? My throat is constricted. I pull one of my legs under me to face her.

"You going to tell me why I found you at yoga?" she asks. "It's not exactly your thing." She winks at me.

"I know, I know. I've just been feeling…I don't know…a lot of feels lately. The crap kind."

"What's going on? Ben?"

"How did you know?"

"Sofia, I've always seen the way he looks at you, and then you tell us he kisses you and just walks away? I know you like him. It's okay to like him."

"Well, it doesn't matter anymore. He's back with his ex."

"Who's his ex?"

"A beautiful redhead, Mel. She broke his heart years ago, and apparently, they're an item again." I stop for a second, trying to keep my emotions in check. I won't let that yoga class go to waste. "She was in the shop the other day. They kissed right in front of me."

"Oh, I'm so sorry, Sof." She rubs her hand lightly on my arm, her eyes showing concern.

"It's okay, it is. I mean I'm still dating for the article. Plus, something kind of weird happened today."

I fill her in on all the deets from the morning. My date with Harper, the guy from the catfishing, Cole giving me his number.

"Wow, that's a lot," she agrees. "You know, Sof, just because you're writing these articles and dating doesn't mean you have to fall in love."

I think about this.

"And just because Ben is hanging out with Mel again doesn't mean he still loves her."

She's right.

Of course, she's right. It's Briar, the smartest woman I know.

CHAPTER TWENTY-THREE

"You're right on both counts."

"One day at a time."

"Yes, one day at a time," I agree.

We finish our teas and talk a little bit about our plans for summer. Briar's signed up for a two-week retreat in Costa Rica.

I'm so happy for her, living her best life. I wish I could do a retreat like that, but I think I would be bored with all the calm, peace, and quiet.

I glance at the large clock above the fireplace in the corner and tell Briar I better get going. We stand and walk back to the studio, where we're both parked.

"Thanks for the tea and chat," I say as she wraps her arms around me, taking me in for one of her friendly hugs. I watch her as she crosses the street to her car, waving as she drives away.

CHAPTER TWENTY-FOUR

So, I decided to date online...
by: Sofia Daria

So, I decided to date online... and I met the mystery man.

Am I wrong to expect my dates to put in as much effort as I do? I get it, men are from Mars, and women are from Venus, but there should be some effort, right? Does it make a difference if your date is at a restaurant, or set for a stroll in the park?

I get it, different scenes, different outcomes, HOWEVER, I think some effort should be made. If a guy can't even put on a clean shirt for a first date, it has me wondering, how much effort will he be putting into himself three months from now, or a year from now?

AND, if he doesn't put any effort into himself, how much effort will he put into a relationship?

Maybe I'm overthinking this. You might be thinking, what if the guy can't afford new clothes, or what if, what if... but the lack of a clean shirt, and the words that came out of his mouth with

CHAPTER TWENTY-FOUR

little thought brought out the 14-year-old insecure teen in me, and I rebutted in an immature way...

Have I got your attention now? You want to know what happened, don't you?

Well, here it is...

Reliving the horrible date makes me feel a little better about myself. The guy was a little off, and I did wind up meeting someone better.

...So although my date ended with a different man than it began with, I got to meet my mystery man... And I got his digits!

Only time will tell now, so until next time, I'll leave you with this....

Always put on a clean shirt, date or no date. You never know who you will run into!

CHAPTER TWENTY-FIVE

I step out of Cole's Lexus. This is the third time we have seen each other since that day at the park, and things are going great. I'm ecstatic.

I step forward, and he comes around the car to close my door. He insists on opening and closing the door for me as if he were some kind of man from the medieval concept of chivalry.

"Thank you," I say. He grabs my hand, and we walk up the pathway to Lucy's front door. I see she has recently painted it a bright shade of turquoise.

I'm a little uneasy about tonight. I have mixed emotions. Lucy bounced into the bookstore a few days ago to invite me to a game night. Ben was there, and she felt the need to extend the invitation to him and Mel. So, I had to ask Cole to come. I couldn't be the third wheel on a Ben date.

I mean, it should be fun. It'll be Alex, Lucy, Briar, Cole, Mel, Ben, and I.

And I love game nights.

CHAPTER TWENTY-FIVE

I just don't know if I love game nights with Ben and Mel.

I knock lightly and open the door, letting myself and Cole in.

I see the pile of shoes and know that we must be the last to arrive. I hang up my sweater on the railing and take a few steps into the open-concept kitchen, Cole close behind me.

Lucy loves to entertain. They're all there, sitting around her large dining room table. I set the bottle of wine I brought on her countertop and retrieve two glasses.

"Guys, I'm so happy you came. Cole, it's so nice to meet you," Lucy says, pulling him into a hug he wasn't prepared for.

I pour our wine and head over to the table behind her, holding Cole's hand as if he were my life support.

Ben's eyes meet mine, and I see a look of, was that jealousy? Nope. I'm not playing that game, Ben. I relay this through my skills of clairvoyance. I don't think it works because he continues to stare.

I introduced Cole to everyone.

"It's nice to see you again, Mel," I say as Cole pulls out my chair.

I'm sitting between Alex and Cole but across from Ben and Mel. Lucy and Briar are at each end of the table.

I see Lucy watching Ben, who is watching me. I look up at Cole beside me. He doesn't seem to notice.

"So, what are we playing?" I ask the group.

Briar pushes back her chair and stands. "Alex brought us a game."

Alex fiddles with his own paper plate. "It's just Pictionary, sort of." His cheeks flush.

"Oh, I love Pictionary." I can't draw worth crap, though.

Lucy laughs. "Oh, this isn't your average Pictionary."

The Dating Debacle

Alex looks down, a shy laugh escaping his mouth.

Briar chimes in, "We're playing dirty Pictionary." She's beaming. She looks flushed with wine.

"Alex! You own dirty Pictionary? I'm impressed!" I laugh, and Alex's red cheeks deepen slightly. Lucy cackles.

"It's my sister's. I thought it'd be fun. It's called 'Uncensored Sketching.'"

"Hell yeah," I reply and pump my fist into the air. Alex laughs beside me. "I'm glad you're here," I tell him quietly.

"Me too. Thanks for inviting me."

We pour ourselves more wine and set up, dividing into two teams. We make our way to the living room to get comfortable. I feel Cole's hand run across my bottom as I walk beside him. He smiles down at me. I feel a little twinge of anticipation.

Lucy, Cole, Alex, and I are on one team, so we huddle at the end of the long L-shaped sofa. Ben, Mel, and Briar are on the opposite side.

Cole sits and pulls me onto his lap. I laugh as he squeezes my waist.

Alex takes out the timer and sets up a board with paper.

I can feel my body flushing from the warmth of the wine. I look across the room at Mel, whose body is nudged close to Ben. They're whispering, and I look away.

I give Cole a quick peck on his mouth, and I feel him stir underneath me.

"Alright, guys, let's flip a coin to see who goes first. Whose calling it?" Lucy stands, taking a coin out of her pocket.

"I call tails," I shout as I stand abruptly. I'm slightly competitive.

Ben holds up a hand. "You have to wait to call it."

"Oh."

CHAPTER TWENTY-FIVE

Lucy flips the coin in the air, and I call out tails again.

"Big surprise." Ben laughs as he sits back down next to Mel, who takes his hand in hers. I see her eye me, and I look away again.

Lucy examines the coin. "Tails it is."

"Yes!" I huddle with my team.

Alex unpacks the timer, and I take out the cards. Lucy grabs them from me. "You suck at shuffling," she says.

"Hey!"

"She's not wrong!" Briar exclaims from the other side of the couch as she takes a sip of wine from her glass.

"Okay, okay," I say, and lean against Cole. "So, who's drawing first?"

"I will!" says Lucy. She places the cards back in the box, facing down, so we can't see what's on them.

"You have one minute to draw while we guess. You can't write any words, draw symbols, or talk," Alex says in an authoritative voice, very different from his regular demeanor.

Lucy takes the card from the top and lifts it right in front of her face, making sure we can't peek. "Oh. My. God." She is laughing uncontrollably.

"Luce, come on," I urge her to get started. Alex hands her the drawing board.

"Are you ready?"

She says no as she tries to catch her breath. "I have no idea how I am going to draw this." she looks back at the card. "Okay, I've got it."

I slide off Cole's lap so Alex, Cole, and I can all see her drawing. I pick up my legs, and hug my arms around them, digging my toes into the soft cushion of the couch, waiting.

Alex flips the timer. "Go."

The Dating Debacle

We're all watching Lucy, and I start yelling out random words. I think the wine is hitting me a bit hard. She's drawing a bowling alley, pins, and ball in the gutter.

"Balls!"

"Balls in the gutter!"

"Blue balls!"

She keeps drawing beside the pins. I see the shape of a head. She's drawing a brain and circling it.

"Brain."

"Balls, brain."

Alex joins in my random words and yells, "Brain, thinking, mind!"

I nudge him. "Those aren't dirty, Alex!"

"Time is running out!" Briar hollers.

"Uh, uh, uh, Cole, help!" I hit him playfully in the shoulder.

"Dirty mind."

"Mind in the gutter!" I shout.

Lucy stops just before Briar yells out, "Time!"

We high-five Lucy.

She clutches her chest. "Geez, I thought you guys weren't going to get it. Get your minds in the gutter!"

Briar pulls out the next card and smiles at Alex. He blushes. Huh. Alex may be crushing on Briar.

Alex takes the timer back. "Ready?"

"As I'll ever be." Briar flips to a fresh page.

I watch Ben and Mel huddle together, and I squeeze Cole's hand.

Briar starts drawing a phone. Ben and Mel start yelling out.

"Phone."

"Call."

"Cell."

CHAPTER TWENTY-FIVE

"Text."

"Sexting." I look at Mel. Do her and Ben sext?

Briar starts drawing a peach and circling the peach.

"Fruit."

"Peaches."

She draws the back of a person and circles the butt.

"Butt!"

"Booty!"

Then Ben calls out, "Booty Call!"

Briar cheers and returns to her seat.

Ben nudges her playfully. "Good one."

I grab a card. "My turn!" and then I look at Alex. "Sorry, do you want to go first?"

He passes the board to me. "No, no, go ahead."

"Oh, fuck," I say as I look down at my card. Here goes nothing.

I start drawing a boat, I think it's more of a sailboat, but then I sketch a pair of boobs.

Cole stands. "Motorboat!"

"Yes!" I wrap my arms around him.

"Did you guys cheat?" Ben asks, "You got that one pretty quick." He eyes Cole.

"Lucky shot," Cole replies.

Ben goes next. "Ready," he says.

I lean over so I can see better. He's drawing a photograph, like a Polaroid-type picture. I see him draw a stick figure inside the picture.

"Picture!"

"Camera!"

He starts drawing what looks like a garden and plants.

"Grass!"

He goes back to the picture and starts adding books to the stick figure. Mel and Briar are silent.

"Time's running out," Alex chimes in.

Ben scribbles over the grass.

"Time!"

"What in the world was that, Ben?" Mel asks, squinting at his drawing.

"Dirty Pictures," he says and plops back down.

Mel pats Ben's hand and gives him a quick peck on the cheek. "We'll get the next one, babe."

Ben stands. "Hold up, I'm just going to grab more wine."

I look down at my glass, "I want some."

Lucy hands me her glass. "Fill me up."

I notice Cole isn't drinking much. "Want something else?"

"I'm good." He sits back on the couch and starts talking to Alex.

Ben has the wine so I hand him the glasses. "I thought you'd be better at drawing."

Ben's smile doesn't reach his eyes, but he lets out a slight sound. He hands me the two glasses, filled halfway. "Hey, little more," I urge, and he tops off our glasses as much as they'll allow for safe travels back to the living room. I rest them on the counter and wait for him to fill his own. "Having fun?"

"Yeah," he says. "It's good to get out and do something different for a change."

I nod, and we head back in. Cole pats the spot next to him, and I hand Lucy her glass and sit. Alex is talking to Briar, and Mel is picking at a hangnail.

"Ready?" I ask.

Alex picks one, and his ears go pink. "Ready."

Briar turns the timer, and I stare at the board as he draws.

CHAPTER TWENTY-FIVE

He's pretty good, actually, but he's drawing a teapot.

"Teapot, tea, cup."

He draws something else.

"Bag, balls."

Cole is quiet again, and Lucy and I are on our own in guessing.

"Tea-bagging!" Lucy shouts and lifts her arms in victory. She lifts her shoulders. "What can I say?"

We all laugh.

"Three to one," says Briar. "We have to get this one, guys."

Mel pulls at the cards and picks one out. I see her wink at Ben.

"Hey, hey, none of that." Lucy points to Ben and waves her finger back and forth. "No, secret eye reveals."

We spend the next hour going back and forth and end on a tie. I'm on my third glass of wine, and I feel my limbs going numb and my mind settling into a peaceful haze. I notice Alex and Briar have some sort of spark between them. I caught them eyeing each other a few times between rounds. The more I think about it, Briar and Alex would be amazing together. Briar's pretty private, so I'll wait for her to confide in me.

I grab a handful of dill pickle chips and stuff them in my mouth, leaning back into Cole. I smile at him. He takes a few chips himself, and I feel relieved. I'm not the only eater in the relationship. I guess this is actually date number four. I haven't been to his house yet, but he's been to my apartment, and he's supposed to stay over tonight.

I think tonight might be the night. Maybe I should sober up a bit. I take another sip instead. I'm having such a good night. I mean, it's a bit weird to watch Mel and Ben, but I'm happy with Cole, and that's what matters. I've forgotten about

The Dating Debacle

the kiss we shared. I haven't thought about it at all in the last week. I pucker my lips at Cole, who returns the kiss. We've shared a few hot kisses, but that's it so far. He leans in, and his breath tickles my ear as he whispers something I can't hear. My body shivers anyway.

I can't wait to get back to my place, so I call out, "One more round for a tiebreaker?"

I down the rest of my drink. Everyone nods in agreement.

Cole is next. He goes at the board in a fierce, competitive mode. He started out pretty quiet, not jumping into the game so much until the last half hour. He's drawing a foot, paying extra attention to the toes.

Lucy is on a roll. "Feet, toes, pedicure, foot fetish…"

He starts drawing a mouth, and Alex joins the guessing, "Mouth, lick, suck…"

"Toe sucking!" I yell out, and Cole drops the pencil, coming in for a hug.

Alex, Lucy, and I all high-five. We collapse in a fit of laughter as Lucy lifts her freshly pedicured toes and teases Alex with them in fun.

Ben's up at the board.

"Okay, this is it, we have to get this one," announces Briar.

Alex starts the timer as Ben starts drawing. I see him draw two stick men. Well, he draws one with spiky, short hair, and the other is wearing a dress, standing side by side. He pauses and looks from Mel to Briar, who looks back at him.

Mel calls out, "People, lovers…"

Briar joins in, "Couple, relationship…"

Ben draws two lips kissing.

"Time's almost up," calls Alex.

Silence fills the room. Ben circles the lips, then the people.

CHAPTER TWENTY-FIVE

Alex is pumping his fists in the air in excitement. *"Time! We win!"*

We all stand and jump up and down.

"Well, what was your card?" asks Mel.

"Friends with benefits," replies Ben, sitting next to her.

"Next time," says Briar, leaning in and patting his knee.

We start clearing up our mess. Alex puts all the pieces of the game back in its box, and then we're at the door, saying our goodbyes.

I hug Lucy, Briar, and Alex. "Thanks so much for having us."

I'm buckling up in Cole's car as he turns the radio on.

I watch as Mel and Ben get into an Uber. Alex and Briar are still inside as we leave.

I turn to Cole. "I'm so happy you came." I admit, "I can't wait to get back to my place," I add suggestively.

Cole winks at me and presses his hand on my leg, squeezing my thigh. I feel it stir up a want inside of me.

We pull into the parking lot, and he shuts off the car. Cole leans in and kisses me with heat. His hand slides down from my temple to my chin, tilting it to join him in a harder kiss. I feel his other hand tightly on the back of my neck. He's a little more aggressive than I'm used to, but I find myself wanting more.

I can feel he wants the same as I run my hands over him.

The windows start to steam, and I mutter about going upstairs in a blur of wine and a fiery want for what's to come. We make it up the stairs in a hurry and are back to kissing in my front hallway. He picks me up, and my legs wrap around him as he presses me into the wall. This is hot. This is probably the hottest makeout sesh I've ever had. Ben comes to mind, but I quickly push him out of my head as Cole's lips meet my neck. He starts walking me into the bedroom when his phone starts ringing.

He pulls away from me with a sheepish grin, but the fire is still in his eyes. "Sorry, I gotta take this."

He sets me down, and I quickly start picking up random pieces of clothing and tossing them in my closet.

Cole is in my doorway, one arm raised up, leaning on the frame. "Hey, so I, uh, gotta go. A friend needs me."

Man, he's sexy as hell.

"Oh." I try to hide my disappointment. "Everything okay?"

"I'll make it up to you," He leans down and kisses me gently on the mouth and then on the forehead, and my heart swoons.

I walk him out and make my way back to my room. Bob jumps up to join me on my bed as I flop back and let out a sigh. "Well, that sucks, Bob."

CHAPTER TWENTY-SIX

So, I decided to date online...
    by: Sofia Daria

    So, I decided to date online... and I'm not sure what I'm doing.

So, I haven't exactly been swiping the last week because I have been busy dating Mystery Man from my catfish days. But technically we met online, but also in a park, if you know what I mean.

    Am I confusing you yet? Go back to my recent articles and catch up on some reading.

    It has been a fun week. I'm getting to know him in person, there's some flirting going on, we've gone on a few dates, and even had a game night with some friends of mine.

    So what is the problem Sofia?
    I don't know.
    Well, for one I said I wasn't going to be pulling any type of How To Lose A Guy In Ten Days sort of thing, and here we are. Four

dates have passed, and I haven't come clean on the fact that I am writing these articles. Please don't hate in the comments, this is hard!

It's not that I don't want to tell him, it's that I feel like I've missed the opportunity to do so. It's like when you forget a neighbor's name and suddenly a year goes by, and it is just too awkward to admit you don't know their name, so you avoid calling them out altogether. That's what's happening here. Maybe I'm just trying to talk it out with you when I should be talking it out with my therapist. But here we are. I'll tell him. I promise.

On another note... I am going to let you in on a little secret, something pretty personal to me.

You all know I am new to the whole online dating thing, well I'm also new to the whole dating thing in general.

Yes, I have had a few relationships, but more long-term. I have never dated this way before. I have never done the whole hook-up thing, and I don't know what I am doing.

Part of me feels by admitting this, half of you will think, Go Girl, Get It! And perhaps the other half of you may be thinking, how can you go from guy to guy? I know we are in a world right now of no shame. And I will be the last person to Booty-Call shame anyone, but I feel like I've been on a season of The Bachelorette, and I'm just going around kissing everyone. Again, there is nothing wrong with that!

Don't get me wrong, part of me is LOVING this. Who doesn't love some hot chemistry, flirtatious vibes, and wandering hands? Is this too much? My editor will tell me, I guess, Ha-Ha. In all seriousness, I have yet to hit a home run or bake the bread, if you know what I'm saying, but yes, I have kissed multiple guys in my recent past.

I'm not sure why I am letting this take up space in my brain, but

CHAPTER TWENTY-SIX

I can't help it. I am. It's new to me.

I guess what I am saying, or perhaps just writing out what I should be writing in my journal and not for the world to see - but I think you need to test the waters a little bit to see if there is a connection, right? I think chemistry, passion, and physical connection are important in a relationship. It's what takes you from the friend zone to the girlfriend zone, am I right?

So, in conclusion, what have we learned about my online dating this week? I need to be honest with Mystery Man and tell him I'm writing about him. It's only fair. Secondly, I need to give myself space to be me and explore relationships I want to explore. Physical or not.

And I think you should be doing the same, exploring your dating life in a way that feels true to you. But be safe out there!

I send Miriam my draft, and she approves it almost immediately. I tell her that I know I haven't been swiping but that I like Cole. She admits that the readers are interested in me now, and they want to know what's going on in my dating life, and if I've caught the feels, I should be exploring that. But I do still need to write about it. I have just a few articles left to hand in.

So I need to talk to Cole.

I'm waiting for him to pick me up because we're going to dinner and a movie. It's been a few days since I've seen him, and I haven't really spoken to him much since he left so quickly after game night.

I'm waiting by the window overlooking the parking lot when I see him pull in. I can see he's talking to someone, and he doesn't shut off the engine or get out right away. I'm watching him as he runs his hand through his hair. He looks a bit angry.

I turn away, I shouldn't be watching, but then I'm back at my window. My nosiness outweighs my thoughts on doing the right thing.

He sits there another few minutes, and I can see his mouth moving a mile a minute. Who is he mad at? I hope his friend is okay from the other night. I sent him a text saying the same thing the next morning, and he replied to my other message but skipped over that one. Maybe he is just protecting his friend's privacy.

That's sweet. I mean, we just started dating. Trust is built.

I'm peering into his car, and I can see something that looks like a car seat for a baby. My stomach dips.

I see him open the car door, and I quickly move away from the window before he catches me. I feel like I'm doing something wrong, but isn't this the same thing as creeping into his social media accounts? Which, by the way, I can't find. Nothing. Zilch. Is this a red flag that I am going to choose to ignore? I mean it's really odd for someone now a day to not be online somewhere, anywhere, right?

I thought maybe he just wasn't a social media person, but then again, I think of the pictures that were used online to catfish me. They had to be stolen from somewhere online.

I hear a knock and run to meet him. Someone must have let him in since he didn't buzz me first.

"Hey," I say, smiling widely as he pulls me into a tight hug.

"Missed you," he says, muffled into the depth of my neck, where my hair tickles my shoulders. "You ready?" he asks as he pulls away. I see his jaw square with tension.

I hesitate. "Yeah, I'm ready. I'll just grab my bag."

I say goodbye to Bob. I like that Cole has a dog, we're pet people. It's good.

CHAPTER TWENTY-SIX

He opens the car door for me, and I slide into the warm leather seats.

"I see you have a car seat, any kids I should know about?" I ask jokingly, trying to sound light without sounding accusingly.

"Oh, right, yeah, no. No, it's my buddy's. He left it in here the other night." He starts the car and signals to exit the lot.

"Oh, cool. How's your day been? I haven't talked to you much the last few days."

"Work's just been crazy. I've had some overtime to do."

He drives us a short distance to the restaurant. A small, intimate place where they serve the best pasta. I order the chicken fettuccine, and he decides on the lasagna. I think now is probably the time to come clean as we wait for our food to arrive.

"I, uh, have something to tell you," I reveal to him slowly.

He nods in my direction and reaches for my hand across the table. I don't know why, but this always makes me nervous. I just don't think I'm someone who likes holding hands on top of a table…even when Ben did it. It's like when people kiss the top of your hand. It's weird to me. I'm not a princess, I don't need to be addressed with hand kisses, and we can hold hands after we're done eating. I feel irritable. I should have had a snack. I can feel my hangry setting in.

I see him waiting patiently for what I have to say. I nibble on a piece of garlic bread, trying to work up the courage.

"Okay, so you know I told you when we first met that I was online dating…"

"Yeah, are you still dating other people?" he asks, pulling his hands away from the one that's not holding the giant piece of bread.

"No, no. I'm only seeing you. I think I mentioned to you that I'm a writer. Well, the thing is, I started to date online for a series of magazine articles."

"I don't get it. What are you saying?"

"I go on dates, and then I write about them. The readers are following my online dating journey. Kind of giving them an inside scoop on what it can be like dating online, or for me anyway, my experiences." I pause, and when he doesn't say anything, I continue, "What I am saying is that I've written about you."

"You what?" he asks with a little more hostility than I like.

"I haven't given out your name or anything, I promise. I haven't even said your dog's name. No one knows it's you. But I have to keep writing about us, I'm on contract, at least for the next few weeks, so the dates we go on, I have to write about them."

"Except no one knows it's me?"

I nod. His shoulders slump, and relief washes over his face. "as long as no one knows I am dating you."

"I mean, my friends know. Don't your friends know you're dating me?"

"I'm kind of private. I'd rather wait till I know we're the real deal, you know?"

My stomach flops in disappointment. I mean, he's right. We just started dating. It's not like we're an official couple or anything.

I pick up a forkful of salad. "Okay."

The rest of dinner feels a little off, but I know I surprised him with the whole article thing, so I think that's why.

He takes me to a theater on the outskirts of town where they have these leather Lazy Boy-type recliners, and I spend the

CHAPTER TWENTY-SIX

next two hours cuddled into him. By the time the movie ends and he's driving me home, I forget about the angry call he had before picking me up, I forget about the no social media thing, I forget about his reaction to telling his friends about me, and I'm left wanting more of him.

CHAPTER TWENTY-SEVEN

Our pinky fingers are hooked together as we climb the stairs to my apartment. Silence fills the air, and I'm hoping Cole can't hear my heart beating in my chest. Cole has been keeping some distance between us, but I have a feeling that's all about to change. I can see it in his eyes. He wants me.

I want him.

Yes, I tell myself, this feels right.

I unlock the door, and turn, meeting his gaze. There's a pull between us that I can't explain. Once inside, Cole wastes no time in kicking off his shoes, and I follow suit. As our eyes meet once more, a surge of anticipation fills the air.

Cole walks up to me, and I feel myself fall into a trance. I'm hesitant to disrupt the darkness by turning on the lights, especially when the streetlight outside radiates a soft, yellow glow that fills the room, emphasizing the outline of Cole as he draws nearer.

His lips are on mine in a matter of seconds, and I bring

CHAPTER TWENTY-SEVEN

my hands up into his tousled hair. My skin tickles with goosebumps as his hands slide down my arms, to my waist, down to the curves that fill my jeans.

I feel his body press into mine, and without hesitation my body is dancing with his as we stand in the radiant light.

Our kiss deepens right before he pulls away and places his soft lips on the curve of my neck. My head tilts back allowing him space to move freely over me.

I feel the urgency in him as his body starts to move harder against mine. I pull away, and take his hand, leading him down the hallway. He follows without a word, our fingers intertwined with him only a step behind.

As we enter the frame of my doorway, I'm pulled back into him. His lips meet my neck once again for a moment before his hands scoop the end of my top, lifting it over my head. I feel the dainty straps of my bralette slide down my shoulders as the palms of his hands trail over me, removing me for his touch. His thumbs graze my bare skin, and I harden in reaction.

I turn to face him when I can't take another moment without his lips on mine. We walk towards my bed without disconnecting. His body is heavy on me as I press into the mattress.

Thoughts about the articles, about Ben and Mel, all my crappy dates flutter out of my subconscious as Cole takes me into another dimension.

I unbutton his shirt with trembling hands as he stares into my eyes. I keep my gaze locked on him as he rises, removing the remaining fabric that separates our bodies. I feel his gaze linger on me, igniting a fire within.

The next hour is lost between our bodies as our mouths collide, and our hands explore one another until our breath is heightened to the point of no return.

* * *

I feel myself smile the moment I wake. Last night was incredible. I turn to face Cole and rub the sleep out of my eyes before registering that I'm alone in bed.

Sitting up I try to focus and scan my bedside table for my phone. When I don't see it, I stand realizing it must still be in my purse from the night before. I grab a T-shirt from the floor beside my bed and pull it over my head as I walk out of the room.

"Cole?" I call out, wondering if he is still here.

When I reach my purse, I can conclude that Bob and I are the only ones here.

I pull out my phone and see that I have a few messages, one of them being from Cole. He informed me that he had a great time but had to rush off due to an early meeting today. I reply letting him know that I also had fun and wishing him an amazing day.

I can't help but feel a bit of dissatisfaction from waking up without him by my side.

My stomach grumbles, and I choose to focus on last night's events instead of the sinking feeling in my belly. I'm just hungry.

I walk into the kitchen and feed Bob breakfast before starting on my own.

CHAPTER TWENTY-EIGHT

I feel a tap on my shoulder.

I turn quickly, slightly startled, and see Ben towering over me with those sparkly eyes of his.

"You didn't hear me say your name?" His voice rises in question format.

"Sorry, I guess I'm distracted."

"You were humming, annoyingly, I might add."

I roll my eyes at him and turn my attention to the couple that just walked in.

"Hi," I greet them with a warm smile. I see them holding hands, and I feel my heart soften. I turn back to Ben.

"Game night was pretty fun the other night, right?"

"You could say that."

"I said it."

I'm not sure what's going on, but I feel something's off with Ben. He's still hovering close to me. I take a step back so that I can breathe without inhaling his intoxicating scent. I mean I like it, but I will myself not go there. Not with him. He's with

The Dating Debacle

Mel, I remind myself, and I am with Cole.

"Cole looks familiar," Ben says.

"Oh, yeah?" I ask. I don't wait for a response. "I probably showed you his picture when I thought I was meeting him at the pizza parlor that time."

"That's not it. I think I've seen him around here before."

I bring my focus back to the couple who are looking at the self-development aisle. "Is there anything I can help you find?"

"I'm just looking for some..." She doesn't finish her sentence and is pulling out a book.

"That's a great one!" I say.

Her boyfriend leans over her shoulder to see what she's looking at. "Yeah, I've read a lot about her online."

She smiles at me.

I return to Ben.

"So, do you think Cole is a keeper?" he asks, his eyebrows raising. I see him inhale abruptly.

"I don't know, I like him, if that's what you're asking."

"I saw your last article."

Okay, where is he going with all of this? "And?"

"I'm just saying."

"Okay, Ben. I have work to do, is there something you wanted to ask me?" I feel bad immediately. I mean, Ben is my friend. I just don't know what he wants from me, really. This is all one big mess. We never should have kissed.

"I still think about that night I kissed you," he admits, lowering his tone, glancing at the couple still browsing the store.

"Ben..." I start.

"Look, you don't have to say anything. I still like you, Sof. It's you. I want you."

CHAPTER TWENTY-EIGHT

I bring my hands up to my temples and rub them slightly. He closes the gap between us, stopping just inches away from me. I can smell the minty scent coming from him as he exhales slowly.

I place a hand on his chest, stopping him from coming any closer. "I'm with Cole."

My mind is swirling in confusion. I feel my palm pressed against his hard chest, knowing that if I ran it down further, I'd feel his contoured abs that dip low. I step back again. "You're with Mel."

I pull my hand away, shaking it as if trying to rid it of the heat that Ben flares inside of me.

"No, no, I'm not."

"What do you mean? You were just with her a few nights ago," I say bluntly with fascination. I'm shocked but relieved. I feel wrong for feeling this way.

The heat is building between us, the way his eyes meet mine. I wish I could peer into his soul and see it all for myself, his thoughts, his feelings. I must remind myself that I'm with Cole. This can't happen between Ben and I. We missed our chance.

Ben drops his hands to his sides, making him look, I don't know, almost hopeless. I expect him to come closer to me, but he steps back and makes his way to the small table, sitting down. "Things will never work out with Mel. There's too much pain there from the past." He starts picking at his fingernails, a habit of his that has always annoyed me. I walk closer to him. "I mean, I forgive her, and I'm over that part of my life. I don't want to go back there. I don't love her anymore."

"Wow," I say, stunned, not sure what to say to reassure him.

The Dating Debacle

"How did she react?"

"She saw right through me, through us. She knows I'm into you."

I press my hands on the table beside where Ben is sitting, "There's nothing going on between us, Ben." I lean further into my hands, feeling it stretch my wrists.

"I know, but I want there to be."

He looks up at me, straightening his body, and I notice the curve of his shoulders. He's wearing green again. It brings out the color in his eyes. I shrug. He rubs the lines that are taking up residence on his forehead.

"I don't know what to say, Ben. I like you too, but you should have told me this before."

"I did, Sof. I told you when I kissed you."

"I mean, you should have told me before I agreed to write the articles."

He looks back down, seemingly defeated. "I tried, I tried so many times, Sofia, but there was never the right time. I didn't want to lose you, and I feel like I *am* losing you."

I push off the table, making a face. "Maybe all we are meant to be is great friends. You're a good friend, Ben." My stomach is in knots. This is all just so fucked up. I've really started to care for Ben, but I put my career ahead of us. Things just didn't work out. The timing wasn't right. And now I'm with Cole.

I haven't heard much from him the last few days, but I know he is busy.

Something feels slightly off.

I feel the same disappointment I felt when Cole wasn't there the morning after. Ben would never have left me. I close my eyes and shake my head. I'm with Cole, not Ben. So that's a

CHAPTER TWENTY-EIGHT

thought I cannot entertain.

My thoughts are in a state of turmoil.

He studies me for what feels like a long time. I feel the feels. I will them away and think about Cole. I'm starting something fresh with someone. I can't stop it. I don't want to stop it. But I care so much about Ben. I think of the heat between us, the laughs we've shared. Life is good with Ben, as a friend. It could be great as a couple, but do I want to risk throwing away what I'm starting with Cole? Ugh, I feel so torn and confused.

I've spoken to Miriam, and I only need to submit two more articles. Things are coming to an end. If I wasn't with Cole, would I take a crack at it? I think back to his lips on mine, wandering down my neck.

"I'm sorry, I just needed to tell you," he says, standing.

I glance at the clock. I feel like time has stopped. Like it's only Ben and I in the room. I scan him, his face, those shoulders, the V that I know is under that dark green shirt. I see the shoes he's wearing, the ones that I suggested he buy that time we were out. I run my hands through my hair, feeling awkward, like I'm not sure what I should do with them, until I realize my hair is clipped back, and I've just messed it up. I take the soft pink clip out and readjust it, peering at the mirror behind the counter.

"It's just bad timing," I say, seeing the hurt cross his face. He places his hands on his lower back and stretches.

"I think you need to be careful with Cole," Ben says suddenly.

I scrunch my forehead. "Why are you saying that?"

"I don't trust him, Sofia, and if I can't be with you, I want you to be with someone good." He places his hand on my arm and runs it down slowly. I pull away.

"Don't do this," I say, catching him off guard.

The Dating Debacle

"What am I doing?"

"I turn you down, so you want me to bail on Cole? After a few shit dates, I meet someone pretty great, and you don't like the thought of that."

I sound egotistical as I say it, but I don't care. I turn to the couple to make sure I'm not making a scene, and I catch them stealing kisses between the stacks of books.

"Whoa, come on, Sof, you really think I'm like that?"

I start to walk away from him. "I don't know, just kind of convenient timing, you think?" His face flushes slightly. I feel awful. I think I've hurt him. "I'm sorr—"

"I gotta get back to the shop. Be careful, Sof," he says and turns away before I can reply.

My stomach plummets as if I've just swung high on a swing set. I grab the counter to hold myself up a second as all the emotions of what Ben has just said hit.

Why is he warning me off of Cole? Is it because he is jealous or because things didn't work out with Mel? I walk around the back of the counter as the girl approaches carrying a stack of books. I take them from her and start scanning them. He said he wanted the best for me. I think back to the party. Lucy or Briar would have surely noticed if something was off about Cole and told me.

I feel an emptiness inside of me I can't explain.

The customer hands me her reusable bag, and I start stacking the books snugly inside.

Have I just been so desperate for a date to work out from the App, desperate for a good article to write, that I'm missing something that is going on with Cole? No, I refuse to let Ben flood me with insecurities. I'm happy, and Cole seems happy with me.

CHAPTER TWENTY-EIGHT

I say goodbye to the couple and rest my chin in my hands. I hear my phone ping, and I pull it out from under the pile of books next to me.

Cole: Thinking of you ;)

I place my phone down, not responding. See, he's thinking of me. And he's not afraid to tell me so, unlike Ben, who withheld his feelings for God knows how long. Cole's good. He's a good guy, I convince myself. I think back to our few dates and the way he looks at me. He may not make my heart jump like Ben does, but it's close. It'll come. I don't know him like I know Ben, it only makes sense that it could take a little bit longer to feel those butterflies in the way I do with him.

I pick my phone back up and hit reply.

Me: Thinking about you too :) Want to come over tonight?

CHAPTER TWENTY-NINE

Our legs are intertwined, and we're spread across the length of my couch. My toes curl into the plush material beneath me. We're watching a thriller, Cole's pick, and the last hour has been spent in a mix of kisses and of me covering my eyes like I'm twelve and watching *The Conjuring*.

Cole teases me slightly at the scary parts when I cover my eyes, but he insists I'm being cute and not pathetic.

Bob is on the carpet, all curled up, watching me with judgment.

My lips pull away from Cole's, and I turn my attention back to the movie, resting my head on his arm.

"I think I missed something," I admit. "I don't really get what's going on."

"I wonder why," Cole replies, laughing and tilting my head towards his again, kissing me deeply.

We part ways, and I lean towards the coffee table, grabbing a few chips.

CHAPTER TWENTY-NINE

"Pass me some?" Cole asks, and I lean over again, this time grabbing the bowl. I squirm out of his grasp and manage to sit up, at least a little.

We watch the TV as the suspenseful music begins to rise, and I prepare my palm over my eyes, my fingers opening slightly to reveal a fraction of the screen.

Someone jumps out, and I shriek loudly, sending Cole into a fit of laughter.

"Hey! It's not funny," I squeal as he grabs my waist, pinching me slightly with the roughness of his large hands, tickling me slightly with the grasp.

I manage to wiggle out of his hold, but he catches me with his lips once again.

We finish the movie, and Cole stands. "Well, I better get going."

"What's the rush?" I ask, sending him my cutest puppy dog eyes.

"I have to get home. I have an early morning tomorrow." He starts putting on his shoes. I grab the bowl of chips and head into the kitchen.

"That sucks," I say honestly. "I mean, you could always stay here, and you could still wake up early," I reply suggestively as I walk up to him and press my chest into his abdomen as I look up into his eyes.

He leans down and kisses me. A single peck on the lips. "Maybe another time."

"Okay," I say, and he turns to leave. "Bye."

I watch him walk down the steps and turn to put the rest of the snacks away. I pick up my phone and notice I have a couple of messages from Lucy, so I sit to reply.

Lucy: How are things with Mystery Man?

Me: They're ok.

Lucy: Just ok?

Me: We hang out, we laugh and have fun, and I like him...

Lucy: But??

Me: I think I let Ben get in my head.

Lucy: What did Ben say?

Me: He told me to be careful, he gave the impression he didn't like Cole.

Lucy: Ahh, I see.

Me: What? Tell me.

Lucy: I don't know. There's something about him.

Me: Oh, not you too!!

Lucy: Well, what are your worries, what's going on with him that has you hesitant?

Me: It just feels like we're not really going anywhere. He never wants to stay over.

Lucy: Maybe he just likes to take things slow, it's not a bad thing.

Me: No, you're right. I should just enjoy things as they are and go with the flow.

Lucy: I know, you're not exactly a go-with-the-flow girl, but you got this. Things will work out. So what's with Ben?

Me: He and Mel aren't together anymore.

Lucy: Oh?

Me: It's not happening Luce.

Lucy: Okay, okay, I believe you ;)

Me: I better clean up and wash my face for bed. You good?

Lucy: I'm fantastic, let's catch up for yoga on Friday.

CHAPTER TWENTY-NINE

Me: Let me check my schedule tomorrow, and I'll let you know.
Lucy: G'night.
Me: Night.

* * *

I walk into the bookstore and see a familiar, yellow-colored box sitting on the counter. There's a sticky note attached. "Friends?" It says.

I open the box and see two of my favorite donuts and smile. My mouth waters at the sight.

I close the box and go in search of Ben. I see him at the cash register, helping an elderly lady put a few succulents into a box so she can carry them out. I lean against the door frame and watch him.

I look at the large clock on the wall as I approach him when the customer leaves. I have twenty minutes before the bookstore opens.

"Thanks, " I say, lifting up the yellow box. "Want one?" I ask, making my way to the two bucket chairs facing the sidewalk of Main Street.

"I guess that means we're still friends?" Ben asks, eyeing me questionably.

"Definitely friends," I respond and take out a donut, passing him the box with the second one in it.

We stare at the cars passing on the street and the crowds walking the sidewalks.

We used to people-watch all the time before the bookstore got busy, and I couldn't escape quite as easily.

I lick some of the cinnamon off my bottom lip before taking

The Dating Debacle

another bite.

I feel my cheeks flush in embarrassment. "I'm sorry for how I acted the other day."

"I'm the one that's sorry."

I see someone familiar, and I squint my eyes as if trying to make them focus. Ben sees this and follows my gaze. "Is that Cole..." Ben starts.

"Yup," I reply. "I mean, he told me he had an early morning. He must be helping his friend out again." Cole is pushing a blue stroller with a small toddler inside. I can see the tiny legs dangling, confirming there's a small body in there. "I didn't ask if he was working or anything."

Ben shoots me a look I can't quite describe.

"What?" I ask.

"He's been helping a friend with his toddler?"

"Yeah, I think so. He had a car seat in his car a few nights ago."

Ben turns back to Cole and the stroller.

"What's he waiting for?" I ask. "I feel like such a creeper right now."

"You don't feel like a creeper when we people-watch, same thing."

"Yeah, I guess, but..." Before I can say anything else, a tall blond woman emerges from a shop and settles her bags underneath the stroller before smiling widely at Cole. "Maybe that's his friend?"

My ears buzz. There's no way that's just a friend.

They talk for what feels like forever. All the while, his hand glides up and down her arm, over and over again. She throws her head back, laughing, and I suddenly wonder what could be so funny.

CHAPTER TWENTY-NINE

We watch them for a few more minutes in silence, I hear Ben finish his donut as he places a friendly hand on my knee, as if in comfort.

"I mean, we don't know that they're not just friends yet," I say to myself more than to Ben.

Ben's quiet. I know that things are over with Cole. I can feel it. I'm about to witness something I don't want to see, but I force my eyes to stay on them. I need to see it. I grab Ben's hand from my knee, and I hold it. He lets me and doesn't say anything.

I watch as Cole gently gathers the woman in his arms and kisses her. Not a quick peck on the mouth, but a good kiss. One you share with someone who matters to you.

I watch for a second before turning away, letting myself sink into the bucket chair and feeling the weight of what I just saw. It feels like I've just gotten off a roller coaster and I feel disoriented. As a headache forms, I pinch the skin between my eyebrows.

"He's married, Sof," Ben says out of nowhere, focusing on the couple. "They're both wearing wedding rings."

The woman is fussing with the toddler in the stroller, leaning over, Cole watching her every move. When she's done, they walk hand in hand while Cole pushes the stroller.

I watch them walk away.

I watch Cole walk out of my life. Wincing, I try to remember the day we met, if he was wearing a ring.

Ben turns to me. "Are you okay?"

"You were right," I say, staring straight ahead, too uneasy to look him in the eye. He places his hand on my shoulder, and I flinch. He pulls back, but I remain still.

He takes a deep breath and speaks softly. "You couldn't have known Sofia. I didn't know. And that's not the point. You put your heart out there and took a chance."

I feel a tear slide down my cheek. I guess I didn't expect this to happen. I look up at the clock again. Ben follows my gaze as I stand.

"I've got to open the shop," I say numbly.

I make my way slowly around the tables filled with plants and feel Ben take my hand from behind, turning me towards him into a hug. My body melts against his, and I allow a few more tears to escape.

I let myself feel safe in his arms for a few seconds before pulling away.

"I'm sorry, Sof," he says as I nod and walk out of the plant shop.

I turn the corner towards the bookstore and prop open the door between the two shops to allow customers to come back here. I take a sip of the water bottle I left at the cash last night and wipe the small tear stain from my cheek as I look into the mirror to my left.

I plunk down on the stool and pull out my phone. I see that I have an unread message from Cole. Was he messaging me while he was with his wife? I feel sick to my stomach at the thought. I would never allow myself to be the other woman. I hate that I unknowingly did this to his wife. I take back the words as soon as I hear myself say them. No, I won't put the blame on me. I had no idea he was married. This is all on Cole. I feel awful for his wife, but I can't take the burden of responsibility when I had zero clue.

I deleted the message and then opened my contacts to block Cole's number. I don't even think twice about it.

CHAPTER THIRTY

So, I decided to date online...
 by: Sofia Daria

So, I decided to date online... and he turned out to be married.

There's not too much to tell this week, but I will debrief you on the latest events of my life in online dating.

So as you know, I left you with the thoughts of, do I tell Mystery Man that I write these articles or not? And, well, I decided to tell him. I didn't think much of his answers at the time, but now things are making a bit more sense.

So, I met Mystery Man in the park, the guy from the catfishing date. Things were going great. They were progressing, I think. We went out for maybe only two weeks, but it actually felt longer. Does that ever happen to you? Where you just put everything into it and spend lots of time together, and suddenly it feels like you have known each other for months, but you have to remind yourself to come back down to earth because it's only been days? I felt that, in some ways, with him.

We hung out a lot, and I got to know him, but I realize now that I only got to know the sides of him he let me see. There was a whole other part of him I knew nothing about, like the fact that he was married and had a child! A Child! A wife!

Parts of me still can't quite believe that someone would do this.

How does one cuddle, kiss, and confide in someone when they have someone waiting at home for them?

I dislike very much the fact that I became the other woman in someone's life without knowing. I wouldn't have chosen this for myself.

Bottom line, it's over, and I guess I'm back to swiping. I may just need to mend my heart a little from the deceit first, but I know I will come out stronger in the end.

* * *

I call Miriam and tell her what's happened. I'm not feeling up to dating online anymore, but she insists I go on one more date and that I find one more guy. So here I am lying in bed, days after the sidewalk reveal in front of Plants, Pottery & Books, swiping left and right.

I haven't been on the App in a few weeks since pursuing Cole, so there are a few new men on here, but with every picture I look at, I'm wondering, are you a cheater? Are you a cheater? Are you a cheater? It's not going well.

I roll onto my back and stare at my ceiling. Bob decides that now is a great time to settle down on my stomach, focusing mostly on my spleen. His face is close to mine, and he's just staring at me. "I know what you're thinking, Bob."

CHAPTER THIRTY

I feel the judgment in his eyes, but I'm pretty sure he's probably only thinking about the fact that I have not given him a treat yet today.

I hear a ping, and I lift my arm in the air above me. I'm careful not to drop my phone. I've learned my lesson from the time before when my phone fell smack on my face.

I see I have one new message on the App. I sigh, not really wanting to look at it, but maybe I should just get on with the date and let this cycle of my life come to an end.

I feel blah. I haven't allowed myself to think of Ben in any other way than still a friend. I have to finish what I started, and my commitment to Miriam. Plus, if I am being honest with myself, I don't deserve Ben. I haven't been there for him with Mel. I brushed him off so quickly, and I put work first. I messed everything up, and I think that for right now, the best thing to do is to let Ben live his life, and hopefully he meets someone great. Because he's great. Despite feeling sad, Cole's impact is still affecting me, and I need time to get my head in order.

I open the message. My heart's just not in it, but I'm going to suck it up, and get the job done.

Friendly001 (Henry): Hi Booklover. Read any good books lately?

Booklover (Sofia): Good morning Henry, I do have a romance on the go right now, how about you? Do you read?

I look through his profile quickly and decide, I will talk to him and see how things go. I don't see any red flags, but then again, I guess I can be pretty naive at times.

Friendly001 (Henry): I actually just finished a good mystery. Do you work weekends?

Booklover (Sofia): I do, yes. Not every weekend, but I go in this morning. What do you do for work?

I'm not ready to tell him where I work just yet. Way too soon. I think I'm getting better at evading questions. Is that a good thing? I'm not so sure. Maybe in this circumstance only?

Friendly001 (Henry): I actually own my own company, I build and install fences. I try and take weekends off and make it a Monday-to Friday-job, but it doesn't always work out that way.

Booklover (Sofia): Oh, that's pretty cool.

Friendly001 (Henry): I took some construction classes, and just sort of really liked building things with my hands. It feels great when you can take a step back when the project is done and admire your work. It's a great feeling.

Booklover (Sofia): Yeah, I bet, that would be a great feeling.

Bob adjusts himself from my spleen, moving down to my thighs. I shake my legs, trying to make him fall off, but he's committed to my left leg. I spend the next ten minutes talking to Henry until I realize I'm going to be running late and I have to shower. I tell him I'll talk to him later if he wants, and I log off.

I swipe at my phone, opening a music App. Standing, I allow myself to move to the rhythm.

I turn on the shower while yelling out the words to the song, letting all the frustration from my time with Cole out in an unpleasant-sounding tune, but I don't care.

***

CHAPTER THIRTY

I look out at the small crowd filling up the bookstore. It's a pretty small space, but we've managed to set up a little table to have a local author do a book signing. Ben took out the small round tables we had here to create more room.

I'm watching from behind the counter as Avery meets and greets her book fans. There are piles of her books everywhere, tastefully placed. I absolutely love prepping for book signings. I think I get just as excited as the authors do themselves. I read her book last month when she approached me about taking in some copies to sell. A sweet little contemporary romance, a friends-to-lover, fake-marriage read, and I loved it.

I pick up one of the bookmarks she had made for the event, and I let my fingers run along the edges. It's a bookmark that's been shaped into a couple that is embracing, depicting her two main characters. It's cute, and I'm here for it.

I smile at a woman who picks one up and then grabs a water bottle. We have a few little refreshments and water displayed on the counter, as well as a few other things from the novel. The tiny little succulent that Boe gave Mary in the first chapter and some little stickers with quotes from the book.

I see Emily walk through the door and wave. We're always two for these events, in case sales get busy.

"Looks like you have things under control here," she says, dumping her bag on the extra stool. "What a great turnout!"

We both watch as a teen she's been talking to lifts her camera to take a selfie with Avery. Avery is holding up her book and looks so genuinely happy.

I want to write my book, I think to myself. I sit back and let my thoughts drift back to my mom and dad's relationship. One I always hoped to have for myself. One that would inspire me to write a novel worthy romance. I see Ben poke his head

The Dating Debacle

into the doorway, giving me a thumbs up while raising his eyebrows as if asking if everything is okay.

I smile and mimic his thumbs up, letting him know that we're good. He nods, and I'm grateful for his check-ins. I can feel some of the tension that was building between us slowly dissipating, and we can finally be ourselves again.

When I came in this morning, and he was helping me with the set-up, I told him that Miriam wanted me to go on one more date, and Ben was supportive. I think we're just going to accept that we are friends, and that's all we will ever be. It's better that way for both of us. I think part of me is trying to convince myself of that, but he hasn't said anything further to lead me to believe that he doesn't accept this.

I'm still messed up a bit from Cole. I've decided that I will have my last date with Henry, because why not? He seems nice, and I guess you never know, but a part of me does feel bad, like I'm using him for work. I think back to Alex and how that date has led me to such a great new friend. My friends welcomed him into their lives as well, and it's like he's always been a part of us. Ben likes him too. I think they actually got together one night to play video games.

I'm grateful I met him. And he seems to be just as appreciative. Plus, I think he and Briar have a little spark between them that they're not quite ready to explore, but you never know. Only time will tell.

"Excuse me, miss, but do you have any Grey Poupon?"

I look up at the sound of her voice and laugh. "Oh, my God, Lucy, you have got to let that go. No one knows who *Wayne's World* is." My head tilts back as I laugh. Last year, Lucy and I dressed up as Wayne and Garth for a 90s party we were invited to. Briar, Lucy, and I made a night out of it and

CHAPTER THIRTY

watched *Wayne's World, Pretty Woman*, and *10 Things I Hate About You*. Briar dressed up as Julia Roberts in *Pretty Woman* after she had her makeover.

"How's the book signing going?" she asks.

"It's going great, as you can see. Have a bookmark." I pass her the one I've been holding on to. Lucy makes her way behind the counter and gives me a hug.

"I'm sorry about Cole," she says, signs of sympathy displaying on her forehead.

"It's fine, it's fine. I'm just glad I found out now and not after a few months." I shrug. She takes Emily's bag off the second stool and props herself up on it. "Thanks for coming," I say.

"Hey, I may not read, but I will always support my BFF in her endeavors." She gives my knee a squeeze. She tells me about the big project she has been working on and how one of the guys on the team has been driving her mad with his condescending tone. I know Lucy is strong and won't take crap from anyone, but I hate that she is going through that.

"It'll all be worth it in the end when I get my promotion," she says.

Lucy hangs out a little longer until Emily makes her way back. The store is pretty busy now, so we hug, and I tell her I will call her later. I grab a pile of books from a box on the floor, and I bring them over to Avery, setting them down beside her since I see she is running low.

"You're doing great," I say, giving her an encouraging smile.

"It's all been feeling so surreal, to be honest."

"Enjoy it," I say, and I mean it. I stand next to her and talk to a few customers, and the rest of the day passes in a blur of pure joy.

CHAPTER THIRTY-ONE

Henry is tall. I mean, not just tall because I'm short…
but tall. Six foot five tall.

He persuaded me to meet him at the driving range on Sunday afternoon. The sun is shining, the birds are chirping, and I'm feeling cranky as hell. I've spent the last few days wallowing in my own self-pity.

I'm not feeling very dateable right now.

It's 4:00 p.m., and the plan is to hit some balls and then go out for something to eat across the street at the Wing place.

I choose a basket full of bright pink balls, and Henry takes a basket full of green ones. He pays for the two baskets, and we head out to grab our clubs.

"Are you left-handed or right? He asks, pulling out various sizes and handing them to me to see which would be best.

"Um, right-handed, but I think I hit both sides."

"Both sides?" he asks, chuckling.

"I'm not very good, whatever way feels like I have a better chance at hitting the golf ball," I say. He pulls out a club for

CHAPTER THIRTY-ONE

himself.

"I'll teach you." He winks at me flirtatiously, and we walk towards the large pond that faces numerous people already there practicing their swing.

Henry finds two empty spots side by side, and we set down our baskets. He immediately starts stretching out his hamstrings and triceps, pulling his arm over his head, down the center of his back. I do the same as if this is normal practice for me. He smiles at me. I think he knows I'm a fake.

He makes his way around the divider between us. "Okay, let me show you the right grip." He shows me how to place my hands by coming behind me and leaning into me. I feel like I'm in a rom-com in a classic guy-trying-to-hit-on-a-girl move. "Okay, part your legs a bit more," he says kicking my left foot, separating my two feet a bit wider.

"Yes, sir." I do as he says. I pull my sunglasses down from the top of my head, shielding the sun from my eyes.

I feel Henry's hands come on top of mine, forcing me to swing my club upwards and back down a few times, practicing. "Ready to hit some balls?" he asks, backing away to his own space and basket.

"Yup." I stand and watch him for a few minutes before I get started. He honestly looks like a pro. I don't feel any initial spark with him, but I think part of it is my mood. I'm just not feeling this date, but I turn to my side and start hitting balls.

A half hour goes by, and we're both hitting balls. We stop a few times to watch the other. I managed to hit a few past the 150-yard mark and feel happy with my progress.

When we've emptied our baskets, we head back to the little store to return them and our clubs. Henry takes my hand as we cross the street to the restaurant.

The Dating Debacle

We're sitting in a large booth meant for six people, but I put my purse on the seat beside me and enjoy the extra space between us. "What kind of wings do you like?" he asks as I peer at the menu in front of me. There seem to be over fifty flavors here.

"I've only ever had mild or hot," I say.

"Let's order a few different flavors, and we can just share."

"Sounds good," I say. I order a beer to go with the wings.

I look around the restaurant, and I see a group of people about my age doing shots and eating a giant pile of nachos not far away from us. One girl is wearing a crown, and I smile, seeing them all happy and laughing. It reminds me of Lucy, Briar, and I.

When my drink arrives, I find myself taking a giant gulp. I see Henry watching me.

"Thirsty?"

I answer by taking another long sip. We chat awkwardly while we wait for our food to arrive. He tells me about a trip he recently took to Mexico with some friends and about his job, the books he's read, movies he likes, and I'm bored. I'm half-listening when the server comes with serving plates full of wings. I order a second beer, one they have on draft, and I'm excited when I see it arrive in a larger mug.

"I don't really like these honey parm ones," I say as I bite into my third one.

"I think I like pineapple honey the best." He takes a sip of his own drink and wipes sauce off his lips with his napkin.

"Mm, these ones are good," I say, licking my lips and taking another large sip. I feel my toes tingle and my body warm from the alcohol.

Our conversation dwindles as we eat. We have enough

CHAPTER THIRTY-ONE

wings here for four people, but I know I'll finish whatever he doesn't eat. I finish my second drink and order a third from the server as he passes by. Henry takes a second one, and his eyebrows lift when I let out a small burp, "Oops," I say, and let out a small giggle. I notice he doesn't say anything when I excuse myself.

I turn to the crowd, the girl with the crown, and slightly wish I was drinking with them.

"Feeling good, are we?" he asks as I notice I start to slur a few of my words.

"Sure am," I say. I don't bother to meet his eyes as I continue to eat.

We exchange funny dating stories, but then I start to tell him about Cole. I haven't revealed that I'm a writer, and I don't intend on it. There are no feelings between us, and I can tell he feels the same way. It's like we have a mutual agreement to finish this supper and go our separate ways. To be honest, I'm having more fun with this large glass of beer and licking the peppercorn ranch sauce off my fingers.

I'm starting to feel a bit riled up, the crankiness from earlier returning. I think of Cole and picture him and his wife on the street. I haven't heard from him, obviously because I blocked his number, but he hasn't come by my apartment either, thank God. I'd really rather just forget about him and never see him again.

"You never confronted him?" Henry asks when I finish the whole Cole story.

"No," I say, wiping my face with a napkin. I try and focus on him, my eyes blurring a little. Kind of like that commercial for drunk driving. I feel like I'm looking through an empty glass. I'll have to get a cab home.

"Don't you think he deserves to know why you're ghosting him?"

My jaw literally drops. "Are you freaking kidding me?"

"He deserves to know why he isn't hearing from you."

"Hell, no, I owe him nothing," I'm kinda pissed now.

If I was cranky before, the monster within me is starting to rise. I finish my drink, and I pull out my phone. I don't usually take out my phone on a date, but I don't even care right now. I want my girls.

I send Lucy and Briar a text, asking them to meet me here for drinks. I look up and see Henry staring at me.

"Want to split the bill?" I ask.

He dishes out a $50.00 and stands. "This should cover more than half," he says.

I eye him as he tucks his shirt back in. I feel my body sliding sideways and steady myself on the table by propping up my elbows, supporting me. I hear my phone ping and grab it to check my texts.

Henry narrows his gaze at me. "Alright, it's been great. I'll see you around."

I'm glad he's not the one writing the articles. I see him out of the corner of my eye and lift my arm to wave.

Lucy and Briar are on their way.

The server comes over, and I ask for another beer. I feel like this will probably be a mistake, but I take a sip when it arrives anyway. I hand the server the $50.00 before he hands me the cheque, and he tells me he will be right back with the bill.

I hear Lucy and Briar come in about twenty minutes later. I've joined the party table and have been having a blast making new friends. Cole, Henry, and online dating are now a thing of my past.

CHAPTER THIRTY-TWO

So, I decided to date online...
by: Sofia Daria

So, I decided to date online...and I think I lost myself a little.

I'm not even sure where to begin for this last date of mine, but I sabotaged it. I never even gave it a chance. To be honest, even if I had given him a chance, it wouldn't have worked out with some of the comments he made towards the end. However, I did learn how to properly hit balls at the driving range, and I did eat some pretty fantastic wings. That's got to count for something, right?

I went back online for the purpose of these articles instead of following my gut. Who was I kidding? I wasn't ready to get back out there after the deceit I felt from Mystery Man. But I did it anyway.

I write as much as I remember from the "date."

Now, I sit here, slightly hungover, and I am contemplating the last few weeks.

The Dating Debacle

Maybe online dating just wasn't for me. I mean, I am super happy that I got to experience most of these dates, I met someone who's become a really great friend to me and my friends. I got to experience different activities I'm not sure I would have done had it not been suggested to me by a date. Salsa dancing, a football game, the driving range.

Or maybe the online dating thing was never going to work out for me because I wasn't ready. Or maybe because there was someone in front of me the whole time.

I'll leave you with this...Go out, experience things, laugh, love, and be vulnerable. You never know where life will take you or who you will meet along the way. Just be safe, and follow not only your gut but your heart.

Thank you for following me on my journey.

* * *

I'm sitting in a park, the same one where I met Cole, facing the water and watching the ducks. I have my laptop with me, and a notepad.

Miriam contacted me right after I sent her the article. She wants to meet, and I'm not really sure what this is about, but I mark it in my calendar.

I feel like my head has been in a fog the last week. She says the way I left the article, mentioning that maybe I had someone in front of me the whole time, has left the fans of my articles wanting to know more. I can't tell her more right now. I don't know what's going to happen—if anything. I just know that I need to get my head space back to normal.

I dangle my legs and move my feet around until my flip-flops slide off and tuck my feet underneath me. I pull my notebook

CHAPTER THIRTY-TWO

onto my lap and close my eyes.

I feel the hot sun on my face. I let myself listen to the sounds of the ducks, the birds flying overhead, and the kids playing at the splash pad nearby. I let my mind wander as I breathe in and out slowly. I'm working on soothing some of my anxiety. Life is moving too fast, and I don't want to spend it caught up in the fog I've been flying through, just slightly above the ground.

I place my hands on my notebook and let myself feel it, bringing me back to this moment without getting too caught up in my head.

I asked Emily if she wanted a few extra shifts this week and decided to take a few vacation days. She was thrilled to have the extra hours.

I haven't seen Ben in a week, just between our schedules and my impromptu time off.

But I'm not thinking of him right now. I'm thinking of me. I think back to the proposal from Jake. I wonder if I was so caught up in my anxiety back then, and that's why I didn't really expect it or see it coming. I never noticed how I was the one drifting in the relationship. I became so self-absorbed with my own issues, thoughts and dreams, that I wasn't really present for others in my life, not the way they deserved me to be.

Including Ben.

I need to see the beauty that lies all around me. I open my eyes and look around at the flowers planted nearby. I need to really appreciate my friendships and relationships.

I'm not saying that I haven't been, but man, am I ever lucky to have my friends.

I open the notebook and look down at something I wrote

last year.

My First Novel

I take out my purple pen. It's time.

I've put my dream of being a writer on the back burner, waiting for life to happen in the way I wanted it to. With a life, and romance like the one my parents had shared so many years ago. But maybe I have something better right now. Maybe the love that my friends and I share is enough.

I've decided I'm going to write. Maybe someday I will write about a great romance that will be inspired by one that I get to live, but maybe right now, I can find inspiration in the world around me.

I spend the next hour making notes. I come up with character ideas, a plot that has been circling my brain for the last few days, and a few settings. I think about the kind of story I'm going to write. I mean, obviously, it will have some romance, but I think it will be based on three best friends.

I'm in the zone when I feel arms wrap around me from behind, and I scream as if I'm about to be murdered. My heart pounds hard in my chest.

I hear light laughter and a loud cackle.

"Oh. My. God. Lucy! Are you trying to give me a heart attack?" I say, grasping at my chest. Briar comes around until she's in front of me while Lucy remains where she is, arms around me.

"I told her not to. I told you, Luce, that you'd scare her to death." She picks up my laptop and sits beside me in its place. "How's it going?" she asks.

I'm still trying to get my heart to calm down, and between breaths, I manage to tell her about the notes I've made so far. Lucy lets go of me and comes around, joining us on the bench.

CHAPTER THIRTY-TWO

She gives me a side hug.

"I'm so happy for you," she says, smiling.

I close my notebook and decide that's enough for now. I note the picnic basket Lucy set at her feet. "What kind of goodies do you have in there?"

"Well, let's see. Briar brought some sandwiches she made on ciabatta buns with some of that good cheese, and I packed up some watermelon and cantaloupe. Oh, and some green grapes."

"Sounds perfect," I say. "Let's make our way to the spot."

Lucy and Briar stand simultaneously.

"Yup, I'm starving," Briar admits.

I pick up my bag, and we head to this little spot to the left of the river, where there's a small clearing. We came across this spot accidentally a couple of years ago when we were out for a walk, and it's like a setting in a movie. The perfect spot for a picnic. So we agreed that day that we would have at least two picnics in this spot, our spot, every summer. It's not quite summer yet, but the temperature has warmed up enough that the ground doesn't feel too cool under the large quilt I pull out from my bag.

I set my bags down as I fan out the quilt until it's sitting perfectly on the ground, and I kick off my flip-flops again. Lucy and Briar do the same, and we sit barefoot, crossed-legged around the picnic basket.

Lucy opens the basket up and starts handing out our sandwiches. I'm not much of a sandwich type of girl, but Briar makes the best kind. I take it out of the reusable plastic Ziplock and see that it's filled with creamy avocado, her white bean spread, tomato slices, and baby spinach.

I take a large bite. "This is so good, Briar."

The Dating Debacle

We manage to eat everything, with only a few green grapes left over. But they look a little sketchy, so we decide against finishing them off.

Briar tells us how she's leaving for her trip in less than five weeks. She only has four weeks left of school. Sometimes, I wish I had gone the route of becoming a teacher, but it would have been for the wrong reasons. It would have only been so that I'd have the summers off. I would not make a great teacher.

She shows us pictures on her phone of Costa Rica and where she will be staying for the retreat. "You're going to be right in the middle of the jungle," I exclaim. My eyes widened at the beautiful pictures.

It's like what you would expect—yoga mats all laid out in a single file across a golden floor in an open hut. It overlooks acres of rainforest, and just passed the beautiful forest, you can see the ocean.

"I'm so excited. You have no idea," she says, her eyes lighting up.

I place my hand on her knee. "I know you've been saving up for this trip. It's going to be amazing. You deserve this."

Lucy rests her chin on my shoulder as she peers over me at Briar's phone. "So when are we having your going away party?" she asks.

Briar laughs. "Better idea. Let's have one of our sleepovers!"

It's been quite a while since we had a sleepover. After we moved out of the dorm and into our separate apartments after college, we had weekly sleepovers. They've kind of dwindled over time.

"Yes, let's!" I agree, and Briar nods.

She puts her phone back down on the blanket and closes

CHAPTER THIRTY-TWO

the picnic basket, moving it to the side and stretching out her long legs.

Lucy and I follow, leaning back on our elbows and peering up at the blue sky.

I knock the side of Lucy's foot with mine. "And you, when are we celebrating your big promotion?"

"It's not mine…yet."

"You'll get it."

"I know I will. We're almost done with this account, and it's going really, really well," she says. "There's a dinner with the clients in two weeks, and the announcement will be made then."

"So, are we invited?" Briar asks.

We used to crash all of Lucy's client events. There are so many people who attend, as long as you look the part and wear some swanky dress; no one even notices that you shouldn't be there.

"Hell, yeah!" she says.

We all laugh, and I look from Lucy to Briar and take this moment in fully before letting myself fall onto my back, eyes closed, sun on my face.

This is my happy place.

CHAPTER THIRTY-THREE

I'm cleaning out my bedroom closet when I hear the buzzer go off in the living room. I look around at the piles of clothes that are now scattered everywhere, floor, bed, dresser. There's not an ounce of space left untouched in my bedroom.

I hop my way out of the room as if I'm a kid trying not to touch the lava.

I press the intercom. "Hello?"

"It's Ben."

I step back from the intercom, hesitant. No, this is good. We're friends again. There's been no mention of that kiss we shared or the fact that we're both single. Just friends. I can do this.

"Come on up."

I watch him make his way up the flight of stairs. I look down and suddenly realize that I haven't even showered yet today. My hair is pulled back in an old headband with wisps flying everywhere, and I have on an old Toronto Blue Jays top and

CHAPTER THIRTY-THREE

some spandex shorts.

Too late, I can't possibly shower, wash my hair, and change before he makes it up the last three steps.

"Hi," I say when he enters my apartment. "What are you doing here?"

He crosses his arms, his biceps straining the sleeves of his blue t-shirt.

"I just thought you might like some company," he says.

"Oh, okay," I say, closing the door behind him. "Yeah, it's just…" I point towards my bedroom and turn as he follows me. "I was kind of trying to de-clutter and get rid of some stuff."

I see his expression change as he looks around my room. He starts roaring, and it catches me off guard. I turn to see what he's laughing at, and I notice Bob's tiny face peering out of a mountain of clothes. He must have dug his way through.

"Oh, Bob," I say, laughing so hard my body is shaking. "You're so freaking cute."

I make my way over to his tiny face and pet between his eyes - where his eyebrows would be if he had some.

Ben walks in, making his way to my bed. I see he is also walking as if there is lava everywhere. He pushes a pile of clothes to the side and sits. I like that he can make himself at home here and with Bob. Feels like we have definitely grown closer in the last few months. I keep looking down at his chest. I can't help it. I'm still attracted to him.

But friends, we're just friends. I remind myself.

"You have a shit-load of clothes," he says.

I laugh. He's not wrong.

"Well, I'm trying to remedy that." I motion around my room. "I'm guessing you're rethinking the random stop-in?"

I walk to my closet and disappear inside. My apartment might be on the small side, but at least I have decent closet space.

"No, not at all. Let me know what I can do to help."

"Seriously?"

"Seriously," he says, standing.

"Okay, that pile there are all donations, if you want to fold them and place them in some garbage bags?" I feel bad for asking, but I hand him two garbage bags.

He takes them and starts folding my sweaters without saying a word.

I turn on some music.

I start taking out the empty hangers and look at my closet. I'm singing softly to myself when I notice that Ben is doing the same. We spend the next hour taking turns playing songs, and my room is coming together quicker than it would be if I were alone. I look at the clock beside my bed, my body telling me I haven't eaten in a few hours.

"Want pizza?" I ask.

"Sounds good."

He's placing my jeans diligently on hangers. It's funny to see him sitting on my floor, legs crossed, folding and organizing my clothes. He's made a few comments about some of the random pieces that I've purchased throughout the years. But it's Ben. What does he know? He only knows jeans and t-shirts.

I step over the few remaining piles that need to be hung back up and around three garbage bags of donations. It feels good to get rid of stuff that is just taking up space. Plus, I like to donate my clothes to the women's shelter a few blocks away. Then I know they're helping out women directly.

CHAPTER THIRTY-THREE

I order a large pizza because who doesn't want leftovers for breakfast, and I also get a Caesar salad and bread sticks. When I get back to my room, I stop and find myself staring at Ben.

We're just friends.

We are just friends.

Friends.

But then, why do I want to walk right over to him, grab his face, and kiss him?

How could I have been so blind? He is the sweetest guy I know. Sitting here with me, he seems to be the happiest person in the world, as we go through my clothes and spend time together.

He turns to me, catching me staring at him. He smirks, and I wonder for a split second if he could hear my thoughts.

He's quiet, but his eyes don't leave mine. His fingers have stopped folding my pink cashmere sweater. Time stops for just a minute while we share this same space. The pile of hoodies beside him starts moving, and I see Bob attempting to climb out. We watch as he finally takes a jumps and makes a dash for the hallway as if he has been held captive for weeks, and his freedom has now been returned to him.

We hang up the rest of my stuff, and I'm just closing the closet doors when the buzzer rings.

I meet the pizza guy halfway up the stairs. I pay him and take the warm boxes up.

"This is a lot of food," Ben says, grabbing two plates from the cupboard.

"I want leftovers, plus I'm actually really happy you stopped by and helped out. I'm pretty sure I would have given up by now and would have just joined Bob in a pile of clothes and wished for a Genie to grant me three wishes. One of those

The Dating Debacle

wishes being to go back in time before I felt the need to clean."

We take our plates to the living room. "Wouldn't it be better to wish that the room was de-cluttered and cleaned instead of going backward?"

"But the Genie wouldn't know what pieces I'd want to keep and which to donate," I say, biting into a slice of pizza.

"I guess that makes sense. What would your other two wishes be?"

"Hmm, I'm not sure." I finish my slice and pick up a mouthful of salad.

"Remember, a Genie can't bring anyone back from the dead, can't kill anyone, and can't make someone fall in love with you."

"Well damn, what's left?" I say, laughing. Ben smiles. "I don't know, what would you wish for?"

He puts down his empty plate and leans back against my couch. "I wish I could buy out Plants, Pottery & Books. I know my uncle would love to travel the world, and I'd like to do that for him. But also, I'd really love to own it."

"Has Jeffrey talked about handing it over to you one day?" I ask, matching his positioning on the couch.

"He's made comments about the future..." I can see Ben processing his thoughts on the subject.

"Maybe one day you will be able to," I say and place my hand on his thigh in comfort. I glance down at my hand, and I see Ben do the same. I pull it away quickly. I stand and make my way back to the kitchen. I can feel his eyes watching me as I walk away. "Want another one?" I call out.

"No, thanks." He whispers behind me.

Unaware that he followed me to the kitchen, my body tenses. I close the pizza box as his hands come to my waist. And I'm

CHAPTER THIRTY-THREE

frozen, unsure how to act in this moment.

"Ben..." I say, leaving it at that.

He turns me, facing him. I look up. Our bodies are only inches apart. I feel the butterflies coming back to life deep within my belly. My breath catches as he peers down at me. His eyes tell me more than his silence does. The intensity of his gaze is like a magnet to my soul.

I hear something move beside me on the counter, and I look over to see Bob sniffing the breadsticks. "Bob, no! Get down!" I place him on the floor. "Bad, Bob!"

I lean against the counter and look sheepishly at Ben. I can feel my cheeks flush as I try to think of what to say. I open my mouth to speak, but nothing comes out.

My own cat just cockblocked me.

Bob stares at me from the floor, and I squint at him.

"Sorry about that." I take the leftover pizza and breadsticks and place them in the fridge along with the salad, avoiding his gaze. I'm not sure what else to say or how to act, so I walk around Ben and make my way back to the living room. He follows me. "Do you want to watch a movie?" I ask as he sits back down beside me on the couch.

He nods.

I think the moment has passed, and it's clear that neither of us is going to be addressing it. I feel awkward as hell. I remind myself that we're just friends. And I repeat this over and over in my head as I scroll through movies.

"See anything you like?"

We settle on a new release, and I bring my legs on the couch, trying to get comfy. Ben grabs my feet and places them across his lap. "This, okay?"

I nod and focus my attention on how it feels to have his

hands on me. I suddenly wish my mouth was also on him. The more I try to convince myself that we are just friends, the more the friendship lines blur and become indistinguishable.

We watch the movie, and about halfway through I can feel my eyes growing heavy.

I hear the credits rolling when I feel Ben move underneath me. He lifts my legs and stands, setting my feet back down gently on the couch.

I'm only mildly awake as I feel his lips brush my forehead softly. I murmur as he says goodnight. I turn over on the couch as I hear the door click close behind him.

CHAPTER THIRTY-FOUR

Miriam runs her hand through her thick, dark auburn curls. She's sitting, her back straight like a board, tall in her expensive leather chair, watching me. She reminds me a bit of Briar.

She's just asked me to join her team as a junior editorial correspondent, and I'm stunned. "I had no idea there were even any openings," I say, fidgeting with the fringe on my bag.

"There wasn't." She smiles. "You're great to work with, and the people love reading your articles. It's a win-win for me. I'll make room for you. There is one condition, though." She purses her lips.

I feel nerves run through my body and eye her, waiting for her to continue.

"You have to write one more article on your dating segment."

"But I've finished all the articles, I don't have any more dates, and I've deleted the App."

I hear her laptop ping with a new email, and she ignores it, her gaze not faltering.

"Your readers want to know who this guy is that you mentioned in your last article. You've left them all wanting more." She leans onto her desk, coming in closer to me as if she's about to tell me a secret. "Who is he?"

"Oh." I look down at my hands. "He's just a friend, actually."

"Is he, Sofia? Tell me about him," she says.

I brief her on our relationship. The kiss, the stolen moments between us. "But nothing will happen between us," I claim.

"Why won't it?" she asks. "You know, Sofia, you have to go after what you want. And you clearly want Ben." She winks at me. "I want you to go after him, get your guy, and when you do, I want the article." She straightens her back again.

"What if I don't get him? Is the job still mine?" I say, unsure about going after Ben. "I mean, I need to think about it - the article."

"You'll get him, and you'll write the article," she says confidently.

My heart begins to race. "I'm not so sure."

"I think you know that he wants to be with you, and you clearly want to be with him. Take this as your push. And you start in three weeks. Is that enough time to notify your current employer?"

She's turned back into business boss mode.

I look right at her, fear mixing with nerves now. I'm excited, I'm going to be working full time for Lace & Dots magazine, and I'm thrilled. "I really was not expecting this," I say. "Yes, three weeks is enough time to notify Jeffrey and find a replacement. About the article though, and Ben…"

"Have it sent to my email in two weeks," she says.

"And if I don't?" I'm nervous as hell. What if Ben doesn't want me?

CHAPTER THIRTY-FOUR

"You will." She speaks as if she knows something that I don't. As if she's looking into a crystal ball and can see my future.

We go over all the details of the new job, salary, and expectations. I can't believe this is happening. I'm going to miss working at the bookstore with Emily and the local authors…and with Ben. I can't believe I'm going to do this. Am I really going to chance things with Ben? I think back to a few nights ago when I woke up on my couch, and he was gone. I was covered with a blanket and sleeping so peacefully, dreaming of his lips on mine, when I remembered the brush of his lips so softly on my forehead. I texted him that morning, apologizing for falling asleep.

I stand and shake her hand. "Thank you so much for this opportunity."

I decide to accept her offer, and I'll write the piece whether Ben rejects me or not. "I'm super excited and can't wait to get started."

"Welcome aboard, Sofia. I'll send you all the details we've gone over in writing, and if you have any questions, don't hesitate to ask."

I thank her again. Miriam is great, and I can't believe she actually offered me a job. I can't wait to tell Lucy, Briar, and Ben. But I can't exactly tell Ben about the article, can I?

I walk out of the large glass building and turn to look up. I can't believe I'm going to be working for Lace & Dots!

* * *

I text Lucy and Briar as soon as I get home. They're thrilled. We're all excited to celebrate my new job and Lucy's promotion at her big event on Friday. It's confirmed that Briar, Alex,

Ben, and I are all going together. I'm so excited to get all glammed up.

These events are glamorous. I have a couple of dresses from past events that I kept and will try on later, but I might take a stroll to the cute little vintage shop near Plants, Pottery & Books and see if they have anything that stands out. They always have dresses in the window.

And I have to talk to Ben.

I don't know how I'm going to tell Ben that I won't be seeing him every day anymore.

I'm kind of sad about it. But I'm also really nervous. I want Ben. I just don't know how to tell him that. I feel like a character in a romance novel. Like I lost the girl, and now I need to do some big grand gesture. Although in my case, the tables are turned, and I lost a great guy.

I work the afternoon shift today, and I have another couple of hours.

I feed Bob and myself lunch, change out of my professional clothes, and swap them for jeans and a t-shirt. The fear of rejection sets in as I apply a fresh coat of lip gloss.

I drive to work, leave my car at the store, and walk around the shops on Main Street. I step in front of Indian Summer, the vintage dress shop, and in the window is an amazing black sequin dress. Excited, I open the door and walk in, setting off the jingling bells hanging above me. The shop owner, Jane, greets me while she rings up a customer.

I roam the selection, touching everything. There are beaded dresses, sequin dresses, thick cotton, silky satin, and lacy dresses. I'm looking at a rack of cocktail dresses when Jane comes over.

"What can I help you find today?" she asks.

CHAPTER THIRTY-FOUR

"I'm going to an event tomorrow, kinda last minute," I reveal.

"Well then, let's find you something. What are you leaning towards?" she asks, ruffling through the rack I just looked at.

I pull out a black lace, knee-length dress and smile. "I love this one."

"Good choice."

"Yeah, I think so."

"I have a few others I think you might like too. Let me get you started in a change room, and I will pull them while you try this on."

I follow her to a dressing room at the back of the store. She hangs up the dress and closes the curtain behind her.

I manage to pull the dress over my head and down my body as she returns.

"How are you doing in there?"

I pull open the curtain. "Can you zip me?"

She zips me up, and I look at my reflection in the large antique mirror on the wall. "Oh, wow! I love this."

She clasps her hands. "You look amazing."

I look across at my reflection and see how the hem lands straight above my knee. The thin lace stretches smoothly over my curves. The neckline is in a low scoop, half off each shoulder, revealing my neck and short hairstyle.

"I brought these for you." She gestures to more dresses. "But honestly, I think the one you have on is it."

I run my hands down the front of my body and turn to catch my butt in the mirror.

She laughs. "Your ass looks great, don't worry about that." I laugh as I see how I look in the mirror, twisting and turning, trying to get a glimpse.

"I think you're right. This is it."

I'm beaming. I can't wait for tomorrow night. I go back into the changing room and stare at myself in the mirror for a few seconds before changing into my jeans.

* * *

I walk into the front door of Plants, Pottery & Books with my dress bag in hand. I haven't been able to stop smiling since this morning. First, the job, and now I find the perfect dress on the first try. My smile fades, though, when I see Ben look up at me. I have to tell him. Now. My heart sinks. How am I going to go to work every day without him there? The weight of leaving is finally sinking in.

He approaches me. "What did you buy?"

"I got a new dress for tomorrow night."

"Didn't you just get rid of a ton of clothes?"

"Yeah, to make room for new ones," I say, laughing. "Kidding, tomorrow is kind of a special night."

"Yeah, it'll be fun. I hope Lucy gets that promotion."

"Yeah, she will. I know she will." I take my dress and set it down on the edge of a table. "There's also something else to celebrate tomorrow..."

His eyebrows raise. "Oh, yeah? What are we celebrating?"

"I, uh, I saw Miriam this morning."

"And how did that go?"

I pull at the fringe of my purse again, urging myself to go on. I need to just let it out. The longer I keep it to myself, the more it will cause me stress. Ben sees the discomfort on my face and takes a step closer to me, grabbing my hands. It sends a shock through me. I glance into his beautiful eyes and smile. Shit, I'm nervous as hell.

CHAPTER THIRTY-FOUR

"Miriam offered me a job, full time."

I watch his reaction, waiting for him to take it in.

He lets go of my hand. "That's great, Sof." He pulls me into a tight hug. "I'm so happy for you." I smell his body wash, the scent sending tingles through me. His tight embrace wakes the butterflies that have been dormant since the other night, waiting to fly. He pulls back and faces me. "I'm sure as hell going to miss you here, though."

"I know, me too." I let go of his hands and pick up my dress to put some distance between us. Now is not the time to tell him how I feel. I'll tell him tomorrow, at the event. "It will be weird, for sure, not coming in here. I'm going to miss this place."

I look around at the plants. I will miss it here. This has been my home for two years.

"It's time for you to begin your next adventure," he says, returning behind his counter and moving some empty pots around, busying himself.

This is weird. This feels so weird. I'm not sure what to do. I look up at the clock.

I start backing up. "I better get to the bookstore so Emily can go."

CHAPTER THIRTY-FIVE

I step my red heels into the passenger side of Briar's car and wiggle into the seat beside her.

We're running a bit late, sort of my fault, I couldn't zip up my dress and had to get Briar to come up and help me. But this dress is amazing, and I feel like a warrior Goddess in it. Alex texted, saying that he and Ben were already there and that they scored us seats at a table in the corner of the room where we might seem the least conspicuous.

I smile like a kid in a candy store and turn to look at Briar. Her hair is pinned up on one side, revealing a new shave underneath, and she is rocking a turquoise sequined number. She looks hot.

We make the drive to the convention center where the event is being held, and it takes us about twenty minutes with traffic. There's even a valet. Lucy's company goes all out for these big client deals. They make them millions, so I guess their motto is you have to spend money to make money.

We climb out of the car, and a young guy takes the keys to

CHAPTER THIRTY-FIVE

her Malibu from her fingers.

We're walking slowly, I might add, as we are both in four-inch stiletto heels.

I'm nervous.

I haven't seen Ben since I told him about my job offer. It's been busy. I handed in my resignation, and I feel like I have been running around at the shop since. It all kind of worked out, though. The day I handed in my letter, Avery visited the shop and said she would love to work in a bookshop while she drafts her next novel. Emily was immediately excited, so I called Jeffrey in, and we introduced her. She was hired on the spot.

I think Jeffrey was just thrilled he didn't have to post and interview anyone. Emily and I vouched for her, and he took our word on it. So, I have been training her every shift. I'm taking a week off between jobs, so technically, my last day is next week. I've been working on my character design and plot since the picnic with the girls, and I am so excited to get started on my own novel. Plus, I need to go shopping for some new work clothes. Lots to do. And the article. I need to somehow manage to tell Ben my feelings and write an article to declare my feelings for all to see. Including all my new coworkers. Talk about being vulnerable.

We make our way into the large room that is filled with fairy lights and white drapes. It's fancy as hell.

We see Lucy as she grabs a glass of champagne, and we make our way through to her. We're only with her for a minute when her boss takes her by the arm to lure her away to greet potential clients.

"Enjoy the free drinks. I'll catch up with you later," she whispers.

The Dating Debacle

We do a round, getting ourselves some champagne while we're at it.

We're just making our way towards the table when we see Alex. He's alone, and I wonder where Ben could be. My heart stops in anticipation. I feel someone grab my hand from behind, and I let out a yelp. I turn to see who's caught me when his voice catches me off guard.

It's James, the realtor-dicpic douche. "Sofia, you look fantastic. How are you?"

Briar looks towards me questioningly, and I introduce her.

"James, what are you doing here?" I ask, eyeing him.

I try to take my hand back, but he has a good grasp on me. I don't want to make a scene, so I let it be for now, waiting for his response.

"I have some clients here tonight, found out about this little shenanigan, and thought there may be more opportunities, business opportunities to claim. Or, you know…" he winks at me…"Some opportunities to meet some fine, looking ladies."

He eyes me up and down as he says this, and a shiver runs through me. Not the good kind, the heeby-jeeby kind. The Tom kind.

Out of nowhere, he spins me. I lose my balance, teetering on my four inches of shoes, and I fall into his chest.

"Oh, baby, I thought I was going to have to get you drunk first, and look, you're making the first move." His gaze narrows. "must have been the picture I sent you, eh?"

I try to straighten myself, pushing the thought of my first unwanted dicpic out of my mind as I shake out of his grip.

Briar cries out, "Ben, no! Sofia…"

I feel her take hold of me and help me escape the firm grip of James' fingers. I see anger flash over Ben's face as he turns

CHAPTER THIRTY-FIVE

to leave.

"Ben…" I call out, trying to steady myself enough to go after him, but he's too quick.

I follow him all the way to the entrance, but he's in a car and off before I can open the large glass door in front of me.

Briar and Alex are behind me.

I turn to them and feel the tears coming. They both embrace me and lead me back to a table in a dark corner, where we're hidden from James and the fancy clients Lucy is entertaining.

When I've managed to stop shivering, Briar places a hand on mine. "Who was that?" she asks.

"That was my first date from the App, James, the realtor, the dicpic - the guy that was rude to the server."

"Oh…" Briar exchanges a look with Alex that I was probably not meant to see.

"This is bad, isn't it?" I ask them. "Ben thinks I'm hooking up with that guy."

My heart sinks. Until the moment James appeared, I couldn't wait to see Ben. To have a chance, maybe even a dance with him. To tell him all the things I have been holding inside of me. I planned the whole thing in my mind.

Instantly, our eyes would connect. I'd feel my heart flutter and my breath quicken. I would feel the spark between us, and I would want nothing more than to grab his hand and make a run for it. Find a corner somewhere and wrap my arms around his neck, letting his mouth take over mine with urgency.

And it's ruined. James ruined the night. My chance with Ben is gone.

"I was going to tell Ben tonight," I admit.

I'm upset that Ben might be hurt right now. I don't want

him thinking that we're going back on this rollercoaster ride. He's it for me. I'm so caught up in my emotions right now, I can't think straight. I don't know how to make this right. I just want to wrap my arms around Ben, look him in the eyes and tell him what a goof I have been, and how much he means to me.

Alex places a hand on my shoulder.

"This isn't the end," he says. "That guy is crazy about you. He has done nothing but talk about you since I picked him up."

"Really?"

"Yeah."

"Sofia." Briar touches my hand. "You know Ben has liked you for so long. This isn't going to change anything. He just saw something that set his ego off, and he will cool down. You need to talk to him. You need to explain things and be vulnerable."

"Ugh," I clasp my hand on my forehead and lean my elbows on the table. "What a mess. How am I going to convince him I'm not with James?"

They both look at me, unsure.

"Why don't you try calling him," Alex suggests.

I pull out my phone and open my text history, hitting the call button from our last message. My heart sinks when it goes straight to voicemail.

"His phone must be off," I say, placing my phone back into my tiny clutch.

Briar squeezes my hand. "Listen, he's going to cool down and come to his senses. Why don't we focus on Lucy? It's her night, and let's celebrate your new job with free champagne." She nods excitedly. "This will all blow over. Come on. Let's

CHAPTER THIRTY-FIVE

grab another drink and hit the dance floor."

"She's right," Alex says, "Congratulations on the job, by the way."

We all stand, and he takes my hand and pulls me into a hug. I feel Briar join in from behind, and I start laughing.

"Guys, you're squishing me."

Briar giggles and releases me. We make our way to the bar and order drinks. I don't know how I can have fun with the weight of how Ben must feel in this moment. I tell myself I will try calling him again in a little bit. I focus my attention on Alex.

"You look great, Alex," I say, and he blushes.

Briar chimes in, "You really do. You look great in navy."

I watch as Alex's cheeks darken another shade.

I grab both his hands. "Come on, you dance, don't you?"

"Uh, not really," he stammers.

"You do now," I say.

The three of us make our way to the dance floor and I spend the next hour trying to enjoy the music and the free flow of drinks. My mind keeps taking me back to Ben, and I can't help but worry that I once again have lost my chance with him. By the time Lucy's boss makes her way to the podium, the room is spinning slightly, and I feel the lace of my dress sticking to me.

There's a nice speech praising Lucy that ends with the reveal of her promotion. Everyone cheers.

I take my phone out and turn on the screen.

Ben: We need to talk. I'm waiting outside your apartment. Take your time.

I show the text to Briar and Alex.

"Catch an Uber and get your man," Briar says. I smile at

them.

"I'm going to."

By the time I weave through the crowd and find Lucy, an uncomfortable amount of time has passed. We hug, and I congratulate her, then we make plans to meet and celebrate more. She wishes me luck with Ben.

I'm in the backseat of the Uber when I come up with a plan. I need donuts if I am going to make this work. Now is the time to win Ben back. We roll up to the donut shop near Plants, Pottery & Books, and I'm so grateful to see they're still open this late. I make my way into the shop while the Uber waits for me at the curb. Garrett is behind the counter and stands when he sees me.

"Hey!" I say feeling a little breathless from all the commotion. He smiles and asks what I'd like tonight. I ask him if he has a colorful marker before putting my request in for donuts. His expression is one of curiosity, but he doesn't say anything when he opens the drawer under the cash register and produces three markers. I smile at him and ask him for one of their boxes. Without question he takes out a pre-built yellow box and hands it over.

I eagerly snatch up the markers and box, making my way to one of the small tables. When I finish, I walk back up to the counter and request Ben's favorites, handing the box back to Garrett. After reading what I've written inside, he looks at me and chuckles softly.

He smiles, his tired eyes and the lines around his mouth revealing a long day of serving customers. "This will win him over."

"I hope so." I reply, hoping it's not too late.

I make my way back to the waiting car, and we head towards

CHAPTER THIRTY-FIVE

my place. My palms are sweating, and I feel a rush overcome me as I sit waiting, staring out the window.

When I spot Ben on the front steps of my building my heart skips a beat. His suit coat is off and hung on the railing. A few buttons are undone at the neck, and he's rolled up his sleeves, showing his bronzed forearms under the glow of the fluorescent streetlight.

I step out of the car, a little shaky, as Ben stands.

I'm standing on the sidewalk facing him, not moving, yellow box in hand. I can feel the nerves running through my body. I'm swaying slightly in the cool night breeze, and I shiver.

I start walking towards Ben as he starts walking down the steps.

It's as if we're walking in slow motion. My head is buzzing from a little too much champagne. I blink a few times, trying to focus on Ben.

In a sudden state of recollection, I remember the box in my hands and take a small step back. With anticipation, I open the box to reveal the message hidden within. I wait for his response as I watch his eyes light up. A sense of calm washing over me.

"I donut know what I'd do without you," he reads. I watch as his expression turns from one of turmoil to one of relief.

CHAPTER THIRTY-SIX

We stare into each other's eyes. We're communicating without words. Our eyes say everything we've needed to say for months.

I close the box and take one last step until I am as close as I can get.

This is it. This is my guy and I need to tell him.

"Ben, I am so sorry for the past few months." I stop, trying to gather my thoughts and put them in chronological order without success. "I'll start by first saying that I had no idea James would be at the event tonight."

"I know, Alex messaged me."

"What? He did?" I asked, confused. He must have done that when he went to grab us more drinks. I'll have to thank him tomorrow. "Anyways, where was I?" I shiver again with the cool night air circling around us.

"Let's get you inside, and warm up."

He takes the box of donuts from me, and curls his fingers in between mine, leading us to the second floor, and into my

CHAPTER THIRTY-SIX

apartment. Once we have settled inside, and the box of donuts has been placed out of Bob's reach, I make my way to Ben.

I pull his face down to meet mine, and I kiss him.

After a few minutes we pull apart, "You look amazing," he says, smiling.

I smile back. Now drunk on love as well as champagne. "You look pretty good yourself," I respond.

I wonder if we're going to talk or just kiss for the rest of the night.

"I'm sorry," Ben says as if reading my mind, "I'm sorry I took off."

"It's you," I reveal.

His hand settles on my waist, pulling me closer to him.

"It's you," he repeats my words to me.

He leans down and kisses me softly. I pull away to catch my breath for a second, and I take his hand and pull him towards my bedroom.

He follows, not uttering a single word.

We walk in, and I face him when I reach my bed. I unbutton the rest of his shirt and slide it down his shoulders. He leans down and kisses me. Harder than before.

A necessity is building within me. I need to feel more of him. I want him to feel more of me. His lips trail down my neck, my wide scoop neck revealing just enough skin to allow him to tease me.

He stops and spins me around. I'm facing my bed when I feel his fingers grab the clasp of my dress. He slowly starts to unzip it until it falls loosely at my feet, leaving me in nothing but a matching black lace thong. I turn to him and see him take in every inch of me. His eyes glow with desire.

I place my hands on his waist, kissing his mouth like we did the first night he was here. Our breaths grow more frantic, his hands taking more of me. I reach for his belt and unbutton his pants. He steps away from me, his eyes never leaving mine as he takes his pants off, leaving no clothing behind.

He places a single hand on my cheek, running his fingers down to my chin. I feel his other hand grab the back of my neck, his fingers twirling between short pieces of my hair. His lips press against mine, a deep and comforting sensation that fills me with warmth. His arms wrap around me, pulling me closer. His touch is like fire, sending pleasure through my body.

He lays me down on top of my soft duvet and comes down on top of me. I feel him press into the soft fabric that's still covering me. I watch him as his expression changes to one of bliss as he runs his fingertips down the side of my face, taking me in. He rolls onto his side, and I shift to face him, gazing at the guy in front of me. A light sound escapes my mouth when his hand takes hold of my hip.

We kiss again, our hands exploring each other. I feel his fingers move and take hold of the elastic around my waist, tugging.

I feel a rush of pleasure, and a sound escapes him as my fingers brush against his skin. He reaches out for me, our bodies pressing together, and I can feel his breath against me. I take a deep breath, appreciating the moment, and I allow myself to let go and feel every touch and kiss he settles on me.

**

I wake up to the smell of bacon, and roll onto my back, staring at the ceiling. I know Ben isn't with me in bed, I can feel the

CHAPTER THIRTY-SIX

lack of his presence, but I can hear him in my kitchen.

I replay last night's events, and my heart is flooding with joy.

We had a long talk before falling asleep in each other's arms. I told him about the seething jealousy I felt when he got back together with Mel, and he revealed how worried he was about me online dating. We talked, staying up for hours with our box of donuts in bed with us, nothing but sheets between us.

Ben makes me laugh, and I don't think I have ever felt this comfortable around anyone besides Lucy and Briar. I can feel a genuine connection starting to form between us.

I hear Ben clear his throat, and my thoughts dissipate. Smiling, I sit up, "Good morning."

"Good morning. I made you breakfast in bed," he says, walking towards me with a tray in hand.

"Where did you get all this stuff, my fridge is mostly empty." I admit, glancing at everything on the tray, my stomach grumbling in appreciation.

He sits down beside me, and I notice a plate for him as well. We adjust ourselves so we can both eat off the tray without making a mess. "I couldn't sleep, so I went to the market down the street."

"This is so good, thank you." We eat in a comfortable silence.

When we've both finished, I take the tray back to the kitchen and set it on the counter to wash. Before I can move, I feel Ben press up against me from behind, and I find myself gasping in surprise.

I turn to him, my mouth meeting his instantly.

"How about we get in the shower?" I ask, my eyes gleaming with mischievousness. I feel his answer before he can utter a word.

The Dating Debacle

We make our way to the bathroom, the sound of running water and warm steam quickly fills the air. We both climb in, and I immediately feel the comforting sensation of the warmth cascading over me, washing away all the troubles that have weighed me down for the past few months. As Ben takes me in his arms, I let myself enjoy his embrace and the softness of his lips as they meet mine. I feel a sense of pleasure wash over me as his hands make their way down my body.

The next two days are a blur of bliss and uncontrollable laughter.

* * *

So, I decided to date online...
  by: Sofia Daria

So, I decided to date online...and he was right in front of me the whole time.

It seems that in my last article on my adventures in dating online, I may have led you to believe that I had found my match, my person. Well, let me just say this: you're not wrong.
  I did!
  Let's call him Ben because, well, that is his name.
  I've known Ben for a little more than two years now. I worked with him. I saw him almost every day, and he became one of my best friends.
  When I met Ben, I was in a relationship, and the thought of ever being with him never crossed my mind. Sorry, Ben, if you're reading this! But I was in a relationship, and I guess Ben and I

CHAPTER THIRTY-SIX

were not meant to be together at that time.

I've changed a lot in my two years following college. Don't we all?

We're thrown into this world where we have to learn to become individuals, learn to survive on our own, and start a career that we're supposed to love immediately. We don't yet have experience in the workplace, but all our dream jobs require experience. It's hard, let's leave it at that.

So, I've changed.

I've grown.

I know I'm not done growing, and I am only just starting my dream job, but now I get to share it with someone I truly care about...myself.

Kidding! I get to share it with my best friend, Ben.

Let me start at the beginning.

So here I was, a young girl out of college, wanting to be a writer.

I wanted to work for an amazing magazine or a publishing house. I also wanted to write a novel.

What I found was the cutest little bookstore and a friend.

Check out Plants, Pottery & Books, if you have yet to - you'll get to shop for some beautiful plants and check out a cute little bookstore with loads to choose from.

This place became my second home.

I have always loved books of all kinds. But especially romance.

I wanted to live these romances that I so often read about.

I was also lucky enough to live with two parents who shared such a romance.

And so my dream of writing about it came alive.

When my relationship ended abruptly, it put things into perspective. I think I got lost along the way, and I just kept going with the familiarity. Online dating changed that.

The Dating Debacle

I was taken out of my comfort zone, forced to socialize with strangers, and put myself in awkward positions that I didn't quite know how to navigate.

But without doing so, I never would have realized my worth or the love I have around me. I realized that I don't need to wait to write about romance. I can write about love now. Love with friends and love with life.

I can't say I am in love with Ben yet. I mean, I love him as a friend, but we're just getting started. I'm excited for what's to come, in friendships and in love.

So, if you're looking for that love, maybe start by looking within. Make sure you're living the life you want to. One that you could be proud of. Fall in love with yourself first, and maybe don't try so hard. He, She, or They could be right in front of you.

CHAPTER THIRTY-SEVEN

Our hands are interlaced under the table as Ben leans over and kisses me. I'm beaming. I know I am, and everyone can see it. And I don't care.

"Quit staring at Ben and pass me the toast," Lucy exclaims, smiling at me.

I pick up the basket of toast and hand it to her. "I'm not staring," I say, looking at Ben, who is now staring at me. I feel the tingles all through my body.

"Uh, yeah, you are," says Alex.

"Whatever," I say and roll my eyes, laughing. I take a piece of bacon and bite into it.

Briar lifts her mimosa. "Now that we're all here together, I think we should toast," she says, starting with Lucy. "Congratulations, Lucy, on your promotion." She turns to me. "And congratulations, Sofia, on your new job."

We all clink glasses.

"Thank you," Lucy and I say in unison and laugh again.

I raise my glass. "And good luck to you, Briar, on the

The Dating Debacle

amazing retreat you are about to go on. I wish you safe travels, and may you not run into any gigantic spiders on your journey!"

We clink again, Briar smiling widely.

"Thank you," she says. I see her look around at us. She takes a deep breath.

We finish breakfast, and we each pay our portion of the bill. We walk outside to say our goodbyes so we can make room for others waiting for Sunday brunch.

I hug Lucy, Briar, and Alex. We'll see Briar before she goes. We're going to have our sleepover next weekend.

Ben takes his hand in mine. Thankfully, neither of us works today, and we can spend the day together. I can't seem to get enough of him.

He takes me back to his place, and I sink into the soft brown leather of his couch.

"I have something for you," he says.

My face lights up. "You do?"

I've only ever been to his place once before, and I notice how clean he is for a guy living on his own. I see he has a few books on his TV stand. He has a picture of him and his parents on the wall and another one with Jeffrey. Soon, Ben returns with a gift bag in hand. I see bright yellow tissue paper popping out, and I clap my hands together. I love presents.

"What is it?" I ask excitedly.

He hands it to me as he sits beside me. "It's for your new job," he says and plants a kiss on my cheek.

"Thank you."

After tossing aside the tissue paper, I pull out the most beautiful laptop bag I've ever seen. A beautiful pink and cream bag. Lifting the handles, I run my hands over the soft leather.

CHAPTER THIRTY-SEVEN

Appreciating it. I've never owned something like this before. I place it on the coffee table in front of me and turn to Ben. "I guess you noticed I was using a tote bag to carry my stuff?" I say sheepishly, shrugging my shoulders.

"Yes, and you need something better than that if you're going to be working for Lace & Dots magazine." He winks at me.

"Thank you, thank you, thank you! I love it, Ben!" I throw myself onto his lap and wrap my arms around him. He kisses me, and I feel myself melting into him.

All the butterflies have been set free.

Epilogue

Two years later.

My stomach is swirling. I wrote a freaking book. I still can't believe it, honestly. Uncrossing my legs under the low table that Emily set up for me, I bump my knee.

"Shit," I mutter, but my smile doesn't fade.

I'm ecstatic.

As I scan the room, I notice a mix of familiar faces, their warm smiles providing a sense of comfort, and a few unfamiliar ones that I have yet to meet. I place the cap back on the tip of my pink sparkly gel pen, and I stand. I glance at my watch and wonder where Ben is.

I moved into Ben's two-bedroom apartment last year. We've been inseparable since the night of Lucy's gala. Between Ben, the book, and my job at Lace & Dots, I feel like I really am living my best life. I'm incredibly relieved that I took risks and listened to that fortune cookie, ultimately finding my fate.

There's a stir at the door, and I swiftly spin to my left to see what the commotion is all about.

Epilogue

There he is.

My guy.

Ben.

And there it is. The famous yellow box that brought us together. Seriously, without those donuts, who knows what would have happened. Ben is carrying a small yellow box.

He's so sweet, always thinking about me. My eyes drift from the box in his hands up towards the wide smile that spreads across his face. His gaze is intense, focused on me as he walks towards me.

I watch him for what feels like forever. My heart beating fast. Those butterflies still find their way into my chest when our eyes meet.

"Ben, I thought you would have been here by now." I walk around the table, ready for the bear hug that I've grown accustomed to. That, and a sweet peck from those soft lips I love so much.

His smile reaches his eyes and his forehead crinkles. "You know I wouldn't miss this for the world, Sof." His hug is brief, and it leaves me wanting more.

I back up and my eyes trail down to that bright yellow box.

"I'm sorry I'm a bit late," he continues. "I had to pick up a little something." He nods at the box in his hands.

I back up towards the table where I have been signing books for the last hour, and rest my hip on the edge.

"That's okay, Ben. I'm glad you're here now."

"I'm so proud of you, Sof. You are such an amazing woman. The last two years have been a dream, and I'm so happy you're mine." I watch as he takes a step back. I can tell he's not finished his thought. He's looking up towards the ceiling as if trying to de-clutter the words in his head. He always does

The Dating Debacle

this when it's something important.

I wait patiently, my heart skipping a beat as Ben slowly gets down on one knee.

What in the cheese and crackers?

My hands spring to my cheeks, where I can feel heat pooling at the surface of my skin. Ben is on one knee, and I can't believe what's about to happen. Remaining silent, I smile, and wait for him to unscramble his thoughts.

I watch as he lifts the top of the small yellow box, and I gasp.

"Sofia, being with you makes me happier than I have ever been. I love waking up to you every morning, and I love the way you nestle into my neck when we cuddle and watch TV at night. I am so proud of everything you have accomplished on your own, letting me be here by your side, rooting for you every step of the way. I will always support all your dreams. But right now, I'd love for you to make one of my dreams come true." He looks down at the box he's holding and removes the rest of the lid until I can see inside. In bright pink marker, written on the inside of the box is, "I donut want anyone else but you. Will you marry me?"

"Yes! Yes! Yes!" I exclaim loudly, forgetting where I am.

Ben is back up on his feet, closing the distance between us. I see it then, sparkling in the light. A small oval diamond glistening on top of a yellow gold band propped up on top of a raspberry sprinkled donut.

Ben takes the ring off of the donut after sitting the box on the table beside us. I hold up my left hand, waiting for the ring to meet my finger, and watch in awe as it slides on so elegantly.

I wrap my arms around his neck, and we kiss as if no one is there. I hear Lucy yelp behind me, and suddenly voices and

Epilogue

clapping fill the air, and I'm brought back down to earth.

I pull away from Ben and look him in the eye.

"I love you, Ben."

"I love you too, Sof."

READERS GUIDE

DISCUSSION QUESTIONS

1. How did you feel about the character Sofia? Could you relate to her, and if yes, how?
2. What did you think of Jake's public proposal? Do you believe proposals should be private between two people or shared with family and friends—or strangers in Sofia's case?
3. Which was your favorite date idea?
4. How did Briar and Lucy impact or influence Sofia or the story?
5. What would you say to your date if they kept getting calls or texts throughout? Would you have reacted differently than how Sofia did with Callum and the calls from his mom?
6. Do you think it was wrong for Ben to kiss Sofia knowing she was dating others for her career?
7. How did Sofia grow throughout the story?
8. What is your worst dating experience?

9. How did the book make you feel overall? Did it conjure any emotions? Make you laugh or cringe?
10. Who would you cast as Sofia and Ben if this were to become a movie?

Manufactured by Amazon.ca
Bolton, ON